A Novel

Snatched

A Novel

DAVID SAPERSTEIN

INFINITE WORDS

NEW YORK LONDON TORONTO SYDNEY

INFINITE WORDS
P.O. Box 6505
Largo, MD 20792
www.simonandschuster.com

© 2015 by David Saperstein

ISBN 978-1-59309-646-5
ISBN 978-1-4767-9363-4 (ebook)
LCCN 2014943298

First Infinite Words trade paperback edition May 2015

Cover design: Keith Saunders / Marion Designs
Book design: Red Herring Design, Inc.

10 9 8 7 6 5 4 3 2 1

Manufactured in the United States of America

For information regarding special discounts for bulk purchases, please contact Simon & Schuster Special Sales at 1-866-506-1949 or business@simonandschuster.com

The Simon & Schuster Speakers Bureau can bring authors to your live event. For more information or to book an event, contact the Simon & Schuster Speakers Bureau at 1-866-248-3049 or visit our website at www.simonspeakers.com

For my first six "older" women

Celia Saperstein
Lillian Eisen
Belle Keller
Henrietta Luchan
Stella Zimmerman
Cherie Bernard

ACKNOWLEDGMENTS

The author gratefully acknowledges the help and inspiration provided by the following: Ellen Saperstein, Sara Camilli, Carl Sagan, Susan Schulman, Myron "Micky" Hyman, and Ivan Saperstein, Esq.

And to all Earth-humans who look beyond our home planet, this tiny, third rock from the sun, and dream of Universes that await us, filled with life and love.

TABLE OF CONTENTS

CHAPTER ONE *Rosie* 1

CHAPTER TWO *Julie* 5

CHAPTER THREE *Freida* 9

CHAPTER FOUR *Six Friends For Breakfast* 11

CHAPTER FIVE *The Museum* 17

CHAPTER SIX *Lunch On Cape Fear River* 25

CHAPTER SEVEN *Gifts At Lunch* 33

CHAPTER EIGHT *Candy-Stripers* 39

CHAPTER NINE *Confession* 43

CHAPTER TEN *Turnaround* 49

CHAPTER ELEVEN *Something Happened On The Way Home* 53

CHAPTER TWELVE *Missing, Then Gone* 57

CHAPTER THIRTEEN *Three Years Later* 61

CHAPTER FOURTEEN *A Knock On The Door* 65

CHAPTER FIFTEEN *To Boldly Go* 71

CHAPTER SIXTEEN *On Land And Sea* 79

CHAPTER SEVENTEEN *Q & A* 85

CHAPTER EIGHTEEN *Where Do We Go From Here?* 95

CHAPTER NINETEEN *Bishop Draper* 99

CHAPTER TWENTY *A Question Pondered* 105

CHAPTER TWENTY-ONE *A Doctor In The House* 109

CHAPTER TWENTY-TWO *A Messenger To Cambridge* 115

CHAPTER TWENTY-THREE *Church Politics* 121

CHAPTER TWENTY-FOUR *Into The Wing* 125

CHAPTER TWENTY-FIVE *Reunion* 133

CHAPTER TWENTY-SIX *Gather Round* 137

CHAPTER TWENTY-SEVEN *Marlino* 141

CHAPTER TWENTY-EIGHT *Gimm* 149

CHAPTER TWENTY-NINE *Roonio* 9 155

CHAPTER THIRTY *Nicole* 163

CHAPTER THIRTY-ONE *All We Can Say* 165

CHAPTER THIRTY-TWO *The Doctor's Dilemma* 169

CHAPTER THIRTY-THREE *A Dive, A Kick, And A Blip* 173

CHAPTER THIRTY-FOUR *A Question Of Genetics* 181

CHAPTER THIRTY-FIVE *Secrets On The Beach* 185

CHAPTER THIRTY-SIX *Three Meetings* 191

CHAPTER THIRTY-SEVEN *Outward And Inward Pressure* 201

CHAPTER THIRTY-EIGHT *Two More On Board* 211

CHAPTER THIRTY-NINE *Unexpected Movement* 215

CHAPTER FORTY *Settling In* 223

CHAPTER FORTY-ONE *Up From The Deep* 227

CHAPTER FORTY-TWO *Rooms* 235

CHAPTER FORTY-THREE *Exams And Plans* 241

CHAPTER-FORTY-FOUR *Snoops* 247

CHAPTER FORTY-FIVE *Family Matters* 255

CHAPTER FORTY-SIX *Jocyan* 261

CHAPTER FORTY-SEVEN *A Convenient Distraction* 267

CHAPTER FORTY-EIGHT *The Gang's All Here* 273

CHAPTER FORTY-NINE *A Time To Move* 283

CHAPTER FIFTY *Last One Out Turn Off The Lights* 293

CHAPTER FIFTY-ONE *All's Right – Or Is It?* 299

CHAPTER FIFTY-TWO *Into The Night* 305

EPILOGUE 313

Who are we? We find that we live on an insignificant planet of a humdrum star lost in a galaxy tucked away in some forgotten corner of a Universe in which there are far more galaxies than people.

For me, it is far better to grasp the Universe as it really is than to persist in delusion, however satisfying and reassuring.

Somewhere, something incredible is waiting to be known.

—CARL SAGAN

CHAPTER ONE
Rosie

When she awoke, it was a little before six a.m. The view, framed by the window near her bed, set her mood for the day. The rising sun was slightly above the flat horizon. Its orange rays backlit a few puffy, non-threatening clouds. The Atlantic Ocean was calm as it caressed and defined the North Carolina shoreline this June morning.

Roseanne Conlon, who preferred being called Rosie, smiled at the sunrise. She lifted her head from her allergy barrier pillow, shed the lightweight blue comforter, rolled to her left and swung her feet out of bed onto the carpeted floor. Before standing, she inhaled deeply through her nose, held her breath and counted silently to ten. Then she breathed out slowly through her mouth to another silent ten-count. A calm that matched the tranquil sea inhabited her seventy-three-year-old body. Rosie stood, stretched out her arms, palms up, then up above her head and finally forward and back ten times. These were the movements that began her every day. Every day.

Next were a few steps into the bathroom where she shed her nightgown and stepped into a warm shower. Rosie took one in the morning and one at night; a routine with purpose. The morning shower warmed her muscles, tendons, ligaments and bones, warning arthritis to stay away. She stretched up on her toes, arms up and to the side, pushups against the tile wall, pulled her knees up to her chest one at a time, grasped her feet, one at a time, and pulled them up behind her to stretch her thigh and hamstring muscles. Finally, she bent over and reached for her toes as far as she could. She came up short by about ten inches.

There was a time, she mused, when I could bend over and touch my palms to the floor. But don't complain, Rosie, old girl; ten inches short isn't bad for seventy-three years and arthritis.

Her last in-shower exercise was squatting under the warm water and flexing her thigh and gluteus maximus muscles as tight as she dared. All of these movements were repeated ten times.

The purpose of her evening shower was to wash her body and hair, and relax her mind for sleep.

Rosie had followed her morning routine every day for the nearly five years that she had lived at the Wilmington Parish Retirement Home for Ladies. For those who lived and worked there, it was just called the Residence. The facility was run by the Diocese of North Carolina, headquartered in Raleigh at the Sacred Heart Cathedral.

Locally, the Residence was referred to as the Catholic Ladies' Home, although many of its forty-seven residents were not Catholic. The simple reason for that situation was money. For the home to be self-sustaining, its fifty rooms had to be at least seventy-five percent occupied.

After drying herself, Rosie brushed her teeth. Her cropped salt-and-pepper hair required little attention. When she wiped away the condensation on the bathroom mirror, the face that looked back at her was familiar, to be sure. She moved closer. Beneath its lines, wrinkles and emerging age spots, she sought to find that vital, pretty, young woman who used to stare back at her those many years ago. She smiled, remembering her. She felt a tinge of melancholy for days long gone.

Gazing down at her breasts in the mirror, she let flow a few sweet memories of how her husband, Jimmy, would at times come up behind her after a shower. He'd kiss her moist neck and caress her breasts with his large hands, calloused from his work as a carpenter. He would whisper how beautiful she was and how much he loved her. Sometimes, she remembered, smiling, that would lead to what they called their "SBB"—sex before breakfast.

They were married for fifty years. He was gone now for nearly seven. Lung cancer. He smoked unfiltered Camels and quit when it was too late.

Their daughter, Kate, lived in Cambridge, Massachusetts, where she worked for the Deputy Chancellor of Public Schools. Kate Conlon, formerly Kate Conlon Legum, was forty-eight and divorced. After Kate's children, two boys one year apart, finished college, they both moved away—Herbie, twenty-eight, to Los Angeles; Alex, twenty-seven, to Hawaii. Once a year, since Jimmy died, Kate sent Rosie a plane ticket to visit her at Christmastime. When they were able, the boys would also come to Boston for the holidays. Neither was married.

But this past Christmas, Kate had a new boyfriend. Arthur was an Adjunct Professor of New Media Law at Harvard. Kate had had several affairs since her divorce, but this relationship was serious. As a surprise, he booked the Christmas break at the Atlantis Resort in the Bahamas. The boys in L.A. and Hawaii were not coming East either. So, without family, Rosie spent the holidays with a few of her friends at the Residence who had no family nearby, or at all.

Rosie dressed and went into her small living room. She turned on the local TV news. She then settled into her favorite wing chair. It was one of the few furniture items that she had brought with her from their rental apartment on nearby Wrightsville Beach where they had retired. Jimmy's cancer showed up a year and three months after they had settled in there. It took him from her quickly. She had made no friends in the area, and was quickly depressed living alone. Kate had made what seemed like a half-hearted offer for her to come to Boston. Rosie knew that would never work. Finding the Residence was a Godsend. She adapted to this new life, and was happy here. It was previously a resort hotel, was built back in the 1930s. The Raleigh Diocese took it over in 1985, after it was nearly destroyed by Hurricane Diana that made landfall at Cape Fear on September 13, 1984.

The dining room opened at seven-thirty for breakfast. Most of her friends at the Residence got up later. Rosie had nearly an hour to kill. She chose a magazine from the pile on the table next to her and flipped through the pages. It was a Victoria's Secret Spring Catalogue that she had brought up to her room from the lounge. Something caught her eye. It was a centerfold display of a new line of lace slips, garters, teddies and bustiers. A thought brought a sly smile and mischievous twinkle to her eyes. She stopped for a moment to consider it.

"Yes!" Rosie said aloud. "Oh, yes! This is a must!" She stood up, grabbed the remote, and turned off the TV. Then she took the magazine to a small desk where she sat down and proceeded to tear out the order form from the catalogue. Giggling, Rosie picked up a pen and began to carefully write out an order for several items.

CHAPTER TWO

Rosie's oldest friend at the Residence, Juliette Lobato, was two years younger. Everyone called her Julie. Juliette and Roseanne—Julie and Rosie. They were a mismatched pair who, when finding themselves alone for very different reasons, found each other. And like their small group of friends at the Residence, they were poster women for, "The new seventy is fifty," syndrome.

Julie's morning rituals were very different than Rosie's. She needed an alarm clock on the night table next to her bed. She needed a second alarm clock across the bedroom on her four-drawer dresser. It was set to ring ten minutes later than the first because her response to the first alarm was to reach over, shut it off, and go back to sleep. The habit was a throwback to the days when she played semi-professional poker well into the wee hours of the morning, sometimes to dawn, while sipping Bourbon neat with a side of branch water.

Julie slept naked. It was seven a.m. when the second alarm announced itself. She threw her white cotton blanket aside, and slipping out of bed, staggered across the room to silence it. The air in the darkened room was chilly, so she grabbed her terry robe, and while putting it on, walked to her bedroom window. She opened the drapes, then opened her robe and let the warm rays of the morning sun soak into her body. It felt very sensual. Memories of a few times, after her divorce, when she shared a similar scene with different men standing naked beside her, brought a wry smile. Julie took a deep breath and sighed. The memories quickly faded, but her body shuddered slightly.

Face washed, teeth brushed, removable bridge in, long dyed black hair combed, panties, bra, slacks, blouse and low-heel shoes on; all in fifteen minutes. Julie was ready for the day.

Her first item of business was to turn on her laptop, a Dell that her ex-husband had given her for her sixty-fifth birthday. He spent four hours teaching her how to operate it and the programs he'd had installed.

Three days after that, he announced that he had met "someone" and wanted a divorce from their ten-year marriage. Julie was South Side Chicago tough. Not an easy person to live with. It was his second and her third marriage. Neither the new woman, nor Julie, had children.

She was delighted to grant him an uncontested divorce for two reasons. The first was that he had money, which she knew she could get in place of the house because he wanted to keep it. It was his house that he had built for his first wife. Julie's goal, which she accomplished, was to extract enough cash to give her, along with her social security and modest bank account, a decent nest egg and income for the rest of her life.

"No point in giving it away to lawyers," she had told him. "Call it cash for freedom." He quickly agreed.

The second reason was that she no longer had any interest in sex, while he, being four years younger than she, had become a Viagra junkie. He was desperately trying to hold on to what he called his manhood, which he defined as being able to have an erection that lasted more than five minutes.

At the time, he was sixty-one and owned a Toyota dealership in Charlotte. The "someone" he had found was forty-six. She worked for him in his service department. Julie knew they had been having an affair for at least three years. So she negotiated a large cash settlement and wished him good luck. Her parting words to him were that he was the lousiest lay she had ever had—with or without Viagra.

It took a few minutes for Julie's computer to boot up and another few to show her that she had two winners at the Tampa Bay Downs racetrack through on-line betting. No such luck with her four Mega Millions lottery tickets. The grand prize was now up to four-hundred-fifty million dollars. So her gambling results for yesterday were up $41.75 at the track and down $20 on the lottery. She decided she would put her winnings into $40 worth of lottery tickets and lay off the ponies for a day or two.

With those morning chores done, it was seven forty-five and she was ready to meet her friends for breakfast.

It was seven twenty-five when Freida Riggs took up her violin and began her morning practice session. This month, the piece she chose was Mozart's *Violin Concerto No. 5 in A Major.* She tuned the G, D, A, and E strings, in order, by ear, and settled the instrument comfortably beneath her jaw and shoulder, resting it lightly against her neck. She reached for the play button on her SONY combination VCR, DVD and VHS player and pressed it. She then played along with a DVD of master violinist Itzhak Perlman, and the New York Philharmonic Orchestra. Freida started and finished on time with them, but was upset because she missed several notes, and her bowing was off a bit.

After putting away the violin, she ran her hands under warm water for a few minutes. Then she took two blue Aleve tablets and stared unhappily at her increasingly arthritic seventy-five-year-old hands. The aging of her body was becoming an enemy to her greatest pleasure. While finishing dressing, she wondered how she could possibly keep up with her next selection, a duet with Yo-Yo Ma playing the prelude to Bach's *Cello Suite #1.*

Freida had reached the peak of her career as second violin in the North Carolina Symphony, headquartered in Raleigh, eleven years ago. She had been with the well-established orchestra for twenty-three years. She never had ambitions to make the first violin chair, or to perform as a professional soloist. However, she had appeared many times at various synagogues in the Carolinas and Georgia, with her flautist friend, Ruth Sterner. They were in demand, playing the musical accompaniment to Kol Nidre, the haunting liturgy that traditionally began the evening service for Yom Kippur, the Jewish Day of Atonement.

Her husband, George, a career officer in the Marines, commanded a search and rescue helicopter unit aboard the Essex-class aircraft carrier, USS Hancock. After Vietnam, they tried to have children, but without success. Testing showed George was sterile. His potentially long deployments aboard ship made them poor candidates for adoption.

George and Freida found prejudice alive and flourishing in North Carolina when he was stationed in Camp Lejeune, North Carolina. As a Marine, he could not become overtly involved in the Civil Rights Movement. But Freida could, and did, after she saw the treatment of black veterans returning from the war.

George died of pancreatic cancer when he was only forty-nine. Years later, the Veteran's Administration admitted that the cancer, and his sterility, might have been the result of the heavy doses of Agent Orange that he was exposed to during extensive operations in Vietnam along the Ho Chi Minh Trail.

After George's death, Freida devoted herself to her music. Though born into the Pentecostal Church, she eventually found comfort in Reform Judaism and converted.

Freida Riggs dressed and said her morning prayers with a special side remark to God, asking that He please cut back on her advancing arthritis and diminishing concentration. Then she went downstairs to the Residence dining room to join her close friends for breakfast.

CHAPTER FOUR
Six Friends For Breakfast

On her way into the dining room, Rosie had stopped at the front desk. It was just before seven-thirty. No one was on duty yet. She dropped a plain, stamped envelope, without a return address, into the out-going mailbox with a flourish.

"Go forth and do your thing," she told the envelope. It contained her Victoria's Secret order.

There were eight round tables in the dining room, each covered with white cloths and matching napkins. The plain white china was serviceable, as was the glassware. The durable, stainless steel utensils were set on top of the napkins that were placed above the entrée dish. Each table had a small vase with artificial, yellow and purple pansies. There were windows along the east and west walls, allowing for morning and dusk sunlight to warm and color the room. Rosie shared all her meals with her five best friends at a table next to the west window. In the summer, they all liked to eat dinner as late as possible, to enjoy the sunsets.

Sammy Kim, the staff dining room waiter, came toward the table as Rosie sat down. He was from South Korea. His given name was Sueng, but no one in the Residence could pronounce it correctly. So he told them to call him Sammy. He was a practical man, single, in his early fifties, with a quick wit and, at times, a sarcastic tongue. He flirted with some of the residents, being very astute at figuring out which of them would enjoy it.

"Good morning, Miss Rosie," he greeted cheerily, with a carafe of hot coffee in hand. "Coffee?"

"Pour away, Sammy," she said. He leaned over her left shoulder, gently brushing against it, and filled her cup.

"You looking really nice this morning, Miss Rosie," he half-whispered in her ear. "Is that a new dress?"

"This old thing? No. I'm sure you've seen it before."

"Well, it suits you. And it's not even a suit." He laughed at his own little joke. So did she. "Brings out the blue in your eyes." He smiled and winked at her as two more of Rosie's group, Gina Ferrari and Bonita (Bonnie) Apollo, arrived.

"Are we interrupting anything?" Gina asked.

"Nothing we can't continue later," Rosie said, winking back at Sammy.

"Go for it, girl," Gina said, sitting down.

"Good morning, Rosie," Bonnie said as she sat down, leaving an empty chair between herself and Gina.

They were two of the six friends who sat together. In fact, the six did mostly everything together. These were women who had been basically left alone in the world and had found pleasure in each other's company as long as they were flexible and tolerant of one another's quirks, likes and dislikes.

"You ladies special. So pretty all the time," Sammy told them. "Coffee?"

"Oh yes, Sammy. I need a quick transfusion this morning," Gina joked, lifting her cup for him to fill.

"And tea for you, Miss Bonita?" he asked after pouring.

"What have you got?" she asked.

"I have new Celestial Seasonings. Name Morning Thunder."

"Sounds strong. Anything lighter?"

"Green tea. Dragon Fruit Melon. Has vitamin C."

"I hope you don't think I look like a dragon this morning, Sammy."

"Oh, no, Miss Bonita. You very lovely."

"Okay," she said, smiling. "Let's give the dragon fruit whatever a try."

"Good choice. You wait for your friends before ordering?"

"Don't we always?"

"Yes. But sometimes not always. I be back with Miss Bonita's tea." He left.

"He's always so pleasant in the morning," Rosie said. "Oh, here come Julie and Eva."

At seventy-seven, Eva Kobva was the oldest of the group. She had come to America at the tender age of eighteen—a refugee after World War II. But there was nothing tender about her. Her mother was Jewish, as were most of the people in her village, including her two best friends. The three girls, barely fourteen then, ran into the woods a day before the Germans arrived. Eventually, they joined up with a band of Hungarian partisans. She became a war-hardened fighter who had a personal vendetta against the Nazis. After the war, she had no love for the Soviets who moved in and took over her country. Back in her village, her parents felt differently.

Eva left, on her own, and found her way to the American Army in occupied Germany. The U.S. command in Berlin had the record of her Partisan service and facilitated her emigration. Through the New York City Catholic Diocese, she found support and work, learned English, went to night school at City College, and eventually became a grade school teacher. She was widowed at sixty-two, when her husband, an electrical engineer and power plant supervisor with Con Edison, suffered a massive coronary on the job.

Eva was an introspective person. She rarely spoke of her life in the forests of Eastern Europe, fighting the Nazis, and then, only in passing if pressed. Her parents died under communist rule. She had a few relatives in Hungary, but never made any meaningful contact with them.

Twelve years ago, she retired to Asheville, North Carolina. Four years

*ago, after a successful three-year battle with breast cancer, she moved
to the Residence where she found sincere friendship and good company.*

Julie sat down next to Rosie. Eva sat in the chair left empty between
Gina and Bonnie.

"Good morning, one and all," Julie said.

"Yes. Good morning," Eva echoed. "I see Sammy has been here," she
continued, gesturing to Rosie's and Gina's half-empty cups of black
coffee.

"He'll be back soon. He's getting me some dragon tea," Bonnie told
her. Rosie saw Sammy come out of the kitchen with a teapot in one
hand and a carafe of fresh coffee in the other.

"Heeere's Sammy," Rosie said, mimicking the "Heeere's Johnny"
that Ed McMahon was famous for saying when introducing Johnny
Carson on *The Tonight Show.*

Sammy poured the tea for Bonnie and then coffee for Eva. He filled
Julie's cup, and then freshened the other ladies' coffee cups as Freida,
the last to arrive, joined the group.

"Good morning, everyone," Freida said. "Good to see we all lived
through the night."

"Now there's a cheery thought," Eva remarked.

"But a fact," Freida responded.

"I guess it's also a fact that no one at the table is pregnant," Gina
said sarcastically.

"Speak for yourself," Rosie told Gina, smiling slyly at Sammy who
had no idea why.

"That's right," Bonnie said. "When we got here, Rosie was having a
moment with Sammy."

"What is moment?" Sammy asked.

"Yes. That's true," Julie said. "Maybe those two had a little tryst last
night." Everyone looked at Sammy.

"What is tryst?" Sammy asked.

"Something these girls all had in their dreams last night," Rosie told him. Sammy, used to being teased, played along. He smiled.

"Nice pleasure to be in your dreams. This morning, in honor of the tryst, new chef is making special omelets to order. We have ham, pepper, onion, turkey bacon, cheddar cheese, Swiss cheese and egg whites only, if you want."

The women oh'd and ah'd and ordered. Sammy left.

Sister Mary Francis, the assistant administrator of the Residence, came by the table. She was a Carmelite, who long ago had set aside wearing her nun's habit. She felt it had been a deterrent for people, especially women, to be open with her. Many seemed to think of the habit as intimidating. This was especially true in a senior female Residence, such as this, where several of the residents were not Catholic.

"A lovely June morning, ladies," Sister Mary greeted. "And how is everyone today?" They all answered with nods, smiles and "goods." "I see by the schedule that you are all together on an outing today."

"The museum," Rosie offered. "Who's driving?"

"Nicole will take you in the van," Sister Mary told them.

"She passed her driver's test, then?" Gina asked.

"Yes. Got her license yesterday."

"You know," Bonnie said, "one really doesn't learn to drive until they get their license and get some real-life road experience."

"Then I guess we're destined to be new-driver Guinea pigs," Gina commented.

"Now, now. Nicole is an excellent driver," Sister Mary chided them. "She's been driving with Father Bernard for two months now. He taught her himself, and he says she's ready."

"Like the last two chefs he hired were 'ready'?" Freida asked, using her fingers as quotation marks. That got three snickers, two nods and an "uh-huh."

"Well, ladies, I look at it this way," Sister Mary told them. "Driving is quite different from cooking."

"The question is, Sister Mary Francis, which is more dangerous?" Rosie asked.

Everyone at the table waited for what they knew would be the inevitable answer. Sister Mary Francis always enjoyed sparring with this group of residents. But she was, in the end, a woman of faith.

"Neither, or either," the good Sister answered. "In the case of the chefs, Father Bernard might have avoided all of us being poisoned. Let us hope, unlike in baseball, there are more than three strikes before we're out. And as far as our dear novice Nicole's driving is concerned...well, I suggest you trust in the Lord, and the wisdom of the Department of Motor Vehicles of the great state of North Carolina. Enjoy your breakfast and the museum, ladies. I look forward to a thorough report from you at dinner."

CHAPTER FIVE

The Museum

Nicole Mallory, the novice in her sixth month of her novitiate at the Residence, had the Dioceses' 2003 Chevy Venture, eight-passenger van, parked in front of the main entrance of the Residence. The motor was running—perhaps chugging was a better description. The windows were open. She sat behind the wheel, anxiously watching the front door for her passengers. None were in sight. She looked at her wristwatch and tapped the horn indicator on the steering wheel lightly. Nothing happened. She pressed it harder and a blaring HONK emerged.

Nicole Mallory had grown up in Elkhorn, a suburb of Omaha. Her family roots were those of Irish Catholic settlers—pioneers, who came west in the land rush of 1873, by train, when one hundred-sixty acres of land could be had for ten dollars, and the promise to live on the land for five years. They had long since abandoned farming. An only child, her mother was a high school biology teacher; her father a chemical engineer for Monsanto.

The decision to be a nun came to Nicole when her freshman high school class spent a day sorting and wrapping Christmas presents for homeless children in Omaha, Nebraska. After graduation, Nicole joined the Order of Servants of Mary through their motherhouse, the Lady of Sorrows Convent in Omaha. In keeping with their mission of community service, Nicole was assigned to the Residence in Wilmington. The decision to take her final vows was still several months away.

Five of the six ladies were waiting in the lobby for Freida. They heard Nicole's horn blast.

"Our driver seems to be impatient," Rosie said. She was cheery, as usual. It was her idea to go to the museum today. They had a new exhibit of early Native American life.

Eva, on the other hand, was distressed. "Let's hope she's not as impatient on the road," she muttered.

"Feeling any better now, dear?" Bonnie asked her. Eva had bitten hard into a toasted bagel at breakfast and a filling came out of one of her molars. Sister Mary Francis had called and made an appointment for her at the dentist who serviced the Residence.

"Not at all. It hurts. And I'm going to miss the museum, assuming our freshman driver gets us to town alive." Eva pouted. "It's always something."

"That's what Roseanna, Roseanna Danna said," Julie told Eva, hoping to cheer her up.

"What? What are you talking about?" Eva asked.

"Gilda Radner. You never watched *Saturday Night Live*, Ava?" Julie always called Eva, Ava. She said it was how they pronounced it in Europe, and since Eva was originally from Hungary, she thought that was the polite and correct thing to do. On the other hand, Eva put everything Hungarian in her life behind her. They usually had a fun argument about it, but this morning, Eva was in no mood.

"No," she told Julie curtly. "I never watched such foolish things."

"Well, you would have liked her. She was Jewish, like you. And funny. She used to say, 'It's always something...' when there was something going wrong in her life."

"My bad tooth is not just something. It hurts and it's not funny."

Julie shrugged. "Sorry, dear. The dentist will make it better. Sadly, she died young."

"The dentist died?" Eva was confused.

"No. Gilda Radner. Ovarian cancer. She was only forty-two."

"That's too bad. Really. Now please, where is Freida?" Eva asked.

"She looked a little off this morning," Rosie commented.

"Yes. A little sad, I thought," Gina added.

"It's the arthritis," Julie told the others. "I heard her playing this morning. She stopped a few times. Lost her place. I don't think her fingers move the way they used to."

"Just her fingers? She's lucky. Nothing on me moves the way it used to anymore," Bonnie offered, smiling.

"Ain't that the truth?" Rosie said. She looked down the hall and saw Freida coming down the stairs. "Okay, girls. Here she comes. Game on." Rosie started to applaud.

All, except Eva, joined in. Freida arrived, stopped in front of them, and took a theatrical bow.

"Thank you, my public. Thank you, one and all from the bottom of my heart. I accept this award..."

"Speaking of bottoms," Gina interrupted as she headed for the door, "how about we all get ours into the van so Nicole can show us how quickly she can wreck it." They all followed her, laughing, except Eva. She rubbed her jaw and grimaced in pain.

The Cape Fear Museum, founded by the United Daughters of the Confederacy, has been around for nearly one hundred twenty years. It is situated in downtown Wilmington, just eight blocks from the Cape Fear River waterfront. The ride from the Residence at the south end of Shell Island, to the Museum, was a little over fifteen miles.

When the six ladies were on board with seat belts fastened, Nicole pulled away from the front entrance and out onto Waynick Boulevard. She turned left and headed north to the bridge that connected the island to the mainland. The ride was smooth; her turns were efficient and controlled.

"That's very nice, Nicole darling," Rosie complimented her. "Very professional."

"Thank you, Miss Rosie. Father Bernard is a good teacher."

"Father Bernard taught you?" Julie asked, acting surprised.

"Yes, he did."

"I wonder if he has a license to do that," Julie mused aloud. "Maybe we should report him?" she teased.

"Oh, leave Father alone, Julie," Gina told her.

"License? He don't need no stinkin' license," Bonnie chimed in with a decent imitation of the famous line from the classic movie, *Treasure of Sierra Madre*, uttered by the Mexican bandit to Humphrey Bogart—"Badges? We don't need no stinkin' badges!" Everyone, except Nicole, laughed heartily, not only at the sixty-five-year-old movie reference, but at how it was enhanced by Bonnie's normal Hispanic accent. Even Eva, with her sore mouth, had to smile.

They made one stop when they arrived downtown to let Gina Ferrari out. She didn't want to go to the museum. Her favorite thing to do in Wilmington was shop. There were several nice apparel and jewelry stores along the Cape Fear River waterfront. Eva's dentist appointment was in an hour. She also chose to get out and join Gina for a while before walking to the dentist's office, which was only six blocks away.

"This is the exhibit I wanted to see!" Rosie exclaimed as they entered the hall of the Cape Fear Museum dedicated to exhibits that were on temporary loan from other, larger museums.

The others, Julie, Freida, Bonnie and Nicole, followed behind her.

A large sign across the rear of the hall announced: 'This exhibit, Early Native American Life, is graciously on loan from the New York Museum of Natural History."

There were five sections to the exhibit covering pre-Columbian tribal lives of the Plains, Northwest, Eastern, Southern and Eskimo peoples. The most interesting part was a section of life-size dioramas depicting scenes of hunting, ceremonies, dress and family life of each tribal area.

The women worked their way through the hall slowly, commenting on how lifelike and detailed each diorama was. They found the presentations of family life the most interesting. Some scenes, especially those that showed wives, husbands and children, brought a melancholy feeling to the four older women, while Nicole kept saying how lovely and warm the scenes were.

Bonnie, the oldest, noticed the silent, knowing glances between the usually effusive Rosie, and Freida.

The last exhibit in the hall was a large diorama depicting Eskimo family life inside their igloo. The father sat near the fire, sharpening a whalebone tool. Two children played with a husky puppy. The mother prepared food while nursing an infant at her breast. In the corner, a very old Eskimo woman sat chewing on a piece of sealskin. Her face was lined and weathered. Her facial expression was a contented smile as she watched the children play.

"That's a lovely scene, isn't it?" Bonnie said.

"Even the old lady looks happy," Rosie responded. "See how she watches her grandchildren."

"That's so nice," Nicole added.

"Nice, huh?" Julie said. She was standing behind them. "Did you know Eskimos leave their old folks out on the ice to die when they're sick, or if there's not enough food?"

"Not anymore," Rosie corrected her.

"Right. Now they just dump them into nursing homes," Julie retorted angrily. "Or on the street if they're lucky. I saw this TV documentary special about those... What are they called?"

"Bag ladies," Freida said softly. "It's very sad."

There was a long, quiet pause as the four older women gazed at the diorama. Nicole watched them. Their expressions seemed suddenly distant and emotional—something that she did not understand. But the women did. They saw themselves as that Eskimo grandmother. Not that they had been discarded, but rather that life had dealt them each a journey that had brought them to loneliness, and now to live out their days with each other in the Residence. Not an ice floe, but a separation from family and the productive, active lives they once knew.

"Anyone hungry?" Nicole asked, breaking through the emotionally heavy atmosphere in front of the diorama. Bonnie looked at her watch.

"Why do you do that when someone mentions eating?" Julie asked Bonnie. "You always do that."

"It's just a habit," the retired schoolteacher answered. "We only had thirty minutes for lunch at school so we... Oh, forget it. I don't have to explain myself to you."

"Okay, girls," Rosie interjected. "You can put on the boxing gloves when we get home. Meanwhile, let's cruise around for a while through the rest of the museum. Then I suggest we pick up Gina and Eva and have some lunch at that Riverboat Landing restaurant on Water Street."

"Is that the one where you can sit out on those little balconies?" Freida asked.

"Yes. But they're only for two people. If we all tried to fit on one, we'd immediately be eating in the street below."

They all laughed at Rosie's joke, breaking the tension between Julia and Bonnie.

"How about the exhibit that has all those great Cape Fear stories and history?" Bonnie suggested. "I hear there are a few new ones."

"Sounds good to me," Rosie agreed. "Lead on, Senorita."

Bonnie turned away from the Eskimo diorama to get her bearings. "This way, I think," she said, pointing to the right.

She walked in that direction. The women followed.

Freida paused and looked back at the diorama. She imagined, for a brief moment, that the Eskimo grandmother was now smiling at her.

"There!" Rosie shouted. "There she is."

Gina Ferrari was standing in the shade of a tall tree in front of The Basics, a modestly priced restaurant. It was next to the entrance to the Cotton Exchange, a mini mall that had shops, galleries and a few nice restaurants. Nicole pulled the van over to the curb. Seeing it, Gina bent down and picked up three packages that she had placed on the sidewalk next to the large sculpted urn at the Cotton Exchange entrance.

"Jesus H! She's been at it again," Julia announced, noticing the packages.

"I wonder what she bought this time," Bonnie ruminated aloud.

"I'm betting shoes," Julia said. "She loves shoes."

"Maybe a bathing suit," Freida suggested.

Nicole got out and went to the rear of the van to open the door to the van's storage area. Gina, who was walking with a slight limp, met her there. She put the three packages in and then limped around to the street side door that Rosie had slid open. Gina got in and cautiously moved past Rosie to the third row of seats.

"So, Gina, how'd you do?" Rosie asked.

"Don't ask," Gina answered curtly. Her tone of voice inferred that she was annoyed.

"What happened?" Rosie asked, as Nicole, who had shut and locked the rear door, got into the van. "And why are you limping?" Nicole called Eva on her cell phone to tell her they were on their way.

"I had a moron of a clerk in the shoe store," Gina answered. She folded her arms.

"What did he do?" Bonnie asked.

"First of all, *he* was a she. Second of all, she brought out the wrong size of a boot that I wanted to try on. I wear a ten wide. She had an eight narrow. But I didn't realize that until she insisted on pushing my foot into it. She damned near tore off the bunion on my right big toe."

"Oh, my," Freida said. "I feel your pain, darling. I have one there myself."

"So what did you do?" Rosie asked.

"You mean after I howled like a banshee?"

"Missus Kobva is already at the restaurant," Nicole said, interrupting Gina's story. "We'd better get going." She gunned the motor and swung the van out into the Market Street traffic. The sudden move silenced everyone in the van. Bonnie crossed herself. But Nicole was up to it. She slid the big van into the flow of traffic like a pro. There was a collective sigh of relief.

"Like a banshee, you were saying?" Rosie asked Gina.

"I thought she tore the damned thing off. I guess I kicked her with my other foot."

"You guess?" Julie asked.

"I kicked her onto the floor. It was a reflex."

"And?" Freida asked.

"And what? I told her to get me the right size." There was silence in the van. No one was surprised.

Gina Ferrari was seventy-four. In her previous life, she had been a dancer. Well, actually a showgirl at Caesar's Palace in Las Vegas. Before that, she had worked in the chorus on several Broadway shows, and before that, she was a Rockette at Radio City Music Hall.

Gina grew up during the 1940s and 1950s in a heavily Italian section of Brooklyn called Bensonhurst. She loved dancing. After high school, in 1960, she took several dance classes in Manhattan while working for her father in his Brooklyn restaurant. One of her father's best customers, and friend, was Joseph Profaci, the head of what was called a Mafia family. At that time, Profaci was sick with cancer. It took his life in 1962.

When the crime boss heard that Gina wanted to be a professional dancer, he made a few calls to some "friends" on Broadway. She got an agent and auditions. The reason Gina got those auditions was not lost on the choreographers. They were nervous, but when, to their relief, they saw what a raw talent she was, they were relieved and happy to hire her.

Gina dated several members of the Lucchese and Gambino families, but never married. Eventually, one of her guys set her up as a dancer at Caesar's Palace in Las Vegas. After many years, she quit being onstage and worked as the assistant choreographer and all-around den-mother to the showgirls. She went to church every Sunday and to confession once a month; less and less as she grew older.

The move to South Carolina was to take a nice, easy job as a hostess at the Sunrise Inn, in Georgetown. She kept in shape and had some cosmetic surgery done the week after she signed up for Medicare. On her seventieth birthday, she officially retired from the business and moved one hundred miles north to The Catholic Women's Residence in Wilmington. Gina was an experienced woman for whom the title "spinster" was hardly appropriate. She was financially comfortable, but found, after a very social life, that living alone was stressful. The five friends, her own age, that she'd made at the Residence might not be as worldly as she was, but they were solid, loyal, and for the most part, fun.

"And how was doctor bloody gums?" Rosie asked Eva after the group had settled at a round table that the maître d' of the Riverboat Landing had reserved for them. Eva was already there. A half-empty Grey Goose vodka martini, straight up, was in front of her.

"As usual...a torture chamber!" Eva answered. "The man won't give anyone over sixty gas." She sipped her drink. Some of it ran down her chin because her lip was still numb from Novocain.

"I used to just love that nitrous oxide," Bonnie said, smiling.

"Me too," Freida concurred. "A wonderful nap."

"The thing to remember is that dentists are not doctors," Julie chimed in.

"Whadda ya talkin'?" Gina said. "Of course they are."

"No," Julie insisted. "Dentists are like engineers. They like to build and fix things. When they were babies, they played with erector sets and Lincoln logs."

"He's still a baby," Bonnie said. "I don't think he even shaves yet."

"A baby with a heavy hand," Eva said, rubbing her jaw, and then wiping her chin. The Novocaine was wearing off.

"Maybe if you took better care...you know, floss and have regular cleaning," Freida suggested, "you might prevent what happened."

"What happened was that our new Polish chef makes toast like rock candy. You'd need a hammer, not floss, to get any of that out."

"So did he?" Freida asked.

"Did he what?"

"Use a hammer?"

Gina forgot her aching toe and laughed. So did Julia and Rosie.

"That's not funny, Freida," Eva said seriously. "Maybe I'll use a hammer on you."

Freida acted startled at the response. Always one to get in the last word, she smiled at Eva. "But I didn't have any."

"Any what?" Eva asked, frustrated.

"Polish toast," Freida said innocently. "I grew up eating grits." Then she smiled. Eva rolled her eyes and smiled too.

There was more laughter now from everyone, including Nicole. She always enjoyed the way this group of women sparred and taunted one another. Deep down, she knew how much they cared for one another. For most of the ladies at the Residence, their friends there were all the family they had.

The waiter, a local college student, arrived at the table of laughing women. Eva's sore jaw and Gina's sore foot were forgotten.

"Well, that must be quite a funny joke," he said, trying to be friendly. But it came out sounding patronizing. The laughter stopped abruptly. The ladies all stared silently at the waiter. A long moment passed.

"My friend here," Gina said, pointing to Rosie, "was telling us an amusing story of how she had sex with a priest last night. Would you like to hear about it?"

The waiter's mouth opened and then closed and then opened again, as if he was trying to answer, but his brain supplied no words. Finally, he cleared his throat. "Would you like to order now, ladies?" His voice quavered slightly.

"I'll have another one of these," Eva said immediately, pointing to her martini.

"And separate checks," Freida said, "except hers." She pointed at Nicole. "Spread hers evenly among the six of us." The waiter wrote furiously on his pad.

"Any other drinks, ladies?" he asked.

"Of course. But not her," Gina said, also pointing at Nicole. "She's not old enough. Bring her a Mountain Dew."

"Diet Pepsi, please," Nicole told him. "And actually, I am old enough. But I'm the designated driver today."

"Good point," Rosie said. "I'll have a gin and tonic."

"Make that two," Julie said.

"Three," Freida added.

"I want a Brandy Alexander," Gina announced.

"That's mucho calories, girl," Rosie offered.

"I don't have to worry about that, like some people I know," Gina said, smiling at Rosie who was, as she liked to say when the subject of weight came up, pleasingly plump. That brought a moment of silence.

"Well," Bonnie finally said, "I guess I'm last." Everyone looked at her. They knew that something exotic and complex was coming.

"Do you have any papayas?" Bonnie asked.

"Yes, Ma'am, we actually do."

"Wonderful. Skin and cut one up. Put it in the blender with a jigger of vodka, a jigger of dark rum and three ice cubes. Whip it up good and frothy. Top it with a maraschino cherry and a straw." The young man wrote furiously.

"What about an umbrella for your Shirley Temple?" Gina asked.

"That's not a Shirley Temple, Gina dear," Bonnie answered. "A Shirley Temple has no alcohol." She looked back at the waiter. "But an umbrella sounds divine, if you have one."

"We do, Ma'am. Thank you, ladies. Do you want me to get these first or are you ready to order now?"

"Drinks first, please, young man," Rosie said politely. "We've just come from our AA meeting and we're thirsty as all get-out."

"Oh. Well then, uh, then I'll get these in the works and come back for your lunch order." He left in a hurry.

"Nice touch, Rosie," Julie said. "I'll bet he'll have a good story back at the dorm tonight."

"She's dead," Eva said, and drained her martini.

"Who's dead?" Nicole asked.

"Shirley Temple."

"Who was she?" the young Novice wondered.

"A little girl who sang and danced in movies long before any of us were born."

"Wow," Nicole said. "She must have been real old."

"Ancient. Eighty-six, I think," Freida guessed. Silence at the table. It happened often these days when someone brought up the subjects of sickness, death or age.

"I'm going for the flatbread pizza," Julie announced, breaking the moment of refection. "With roasted peppers and mozzarella. I'm not sure I can eat the whole thing. Anyone want to share?"

"How about pepperoni instead of the peppers?" Freida asked.

"No."

"Okay, then I'll have pepperoni and mozzarella," she said.

"I'm going to have the roasted vegetables, but no cheese," Mirabella announced. "Any takers?" Silence.

"I want the eggplant and lamb with feta, but no Mozzarella," Rosie said. "You like that, don't you, Eva?"

"No. I like it with mozzarella, no feta," Eva said. She sipped the last tiny drop from her empty martini glass and looked around for the waiter.

"I'll top mine with smoky sauce, brisket, caramelized onions, roasted peppers and mozzarella," Rosie said, reading from the menu.

"You must be on a diet, Rosie," Gina said sarcastically. But the remark didn't bother Rosie.

"You must have missed the news last night, Gina," Rosie told her. "There was a new study that said it's far healthier to keep your normal weight and not diet and starve yourself trying to be a skinny toothpick."

"Do we have to talk about teeth?" Eva interjected.

"Sorry," Gina said.

"So what are you having?" Rosie asked Gina.

"Well, since you told me about that study, I'll opt to keep my dancer's figure and have my pizza with summer vegetables, basil pesto, tomato and mozzarella. How about you, Nicole?"

They all looked at Nicole. This was her first luncheon outing with these ladies. Father Bernard had driven them before. She was studying the menu until she became aware of the silence at the table. She looked up and saw they were all staring, waiting for her to announce her choice. She looked down at the menu again, and following it with her finger, read off her choice slowly, one word at a time.

"Pan roasted shrimp and, uh, andouille sausage tossed with cremini mushrooms, uh, peppers and smoked bacon in parmesan cream sauce over soft cheese grits." She looked up. They were still all staring at her. "Sounds delicious, huh?" Nicole said.

"Someone hit the lottery?" Gina asked sarcastically. There was a momentary pause, but then all the women got it and burst out laughing. Nicole didn't understand.

At that moment, the waiter arrived with a tray, full of their drinks. Seeing them laughing again, he knew better than to say anything. He set it down on the stand next to the table and proceeded to hand out each drink carefully, without spilling a drop. When he was done, he asked to take their lunch orders.

It took two pages of his pad to write everything the ladies wanted. They ordered slowly and precisely. When, after the six flatbread pizzas, Nicole ordered her entrée, he was relieved. He looked up from his pad to see all of the women looking at him. He wondered what he had done wrong.

"Oh. Good choice," he told Nicole. They all smiled. "Would you ladies like me to read everything back to you?" he asked.

"That won't be necessary, young man," Freida said. "We won't forget what we ordered."

"Yes, but...I...Oh..." They were all staring at him again. "Right. Okay. Fine." He left.

"Priceless," Gina said.

"Yes, it was," Rosie agreed. "Brilliant, Freida."

"Although one of us was a bit more pricey that the rest," Bonnie noted, rolling her eyes toward Nicole. But Nicole still didn't get it.

"So, how was the museum?" Eva asked.

"Nice," Julie said.

"Interesting," Rosie added.

"I think the Eskimo Granny smiled at me," Freida said.

No one asked what she meant by that.

The next week, the six ladies, and twelve other women, were out on the west lawn of the Residence taking their Tai Chi class. As they followed their instructor, a forty-six-year-old mother of three teenagers who ran Tai Chi classes at the Wilmington YWCA, the women's various personalities were reflected in their energy, grace and movements.

Rosie was energetic. Julie was ambivalent, moving well, but not that interested. Freida's movements were deliberate and precise, as was her violin acumen. Gina, the ex-Vegas showgirl, still had the balance and grace of a dancer. Bonita, the oldest of the six friends, was slightly slower and less supple. Eva, who had kept her body lean, solid and athletic, formed that way from her days as a partisan fighter in the forests of Eastern Europe, exercised more as a martial artist than the others.

As the class came to a close, Rosie noticed the FedEx delivery truck come up the driveway and park at the Residence front door. While the others used the side door to get to their rooms to shower and dress for lunch, Rosie separated and went around to the front where she observed the FedEx driver go into the rear of the truck where he gathered six packages. She waited until he started toward the front door. At that point, she hurriedly walked toward him, timing it so that when she seemed to trip, they collided gently. Two of the packages slipped out of his arms and fell to the ground.

"Oh my," Rosie said, bending down to pick up one of the packages. "Clumsy me. I'm so very sorry."

"That's okay, Ma'am. No harm done." The driver picked up the other package. "Nothing fragile here." Rosie glanced at the label's return address. *Victoria's Secret, Columbus, Ohio.*

Unlike the way the residents staggered their arrival for breakfast, everyone showed up at the same time for lunch. Sammy Kim had a girl, a local student from nearby Brunswick Community College, help him serve. A different student worked during dinner. On special occasions, like Thanksgiving and Christmas, both girls pitched in setting tables, waiting, bussing and cleaning up.

This afternoon, ten days after their trip to the museum, Sammy was breaking in a new server, Linda Westbrook. She was a local nineteen-year-old Wilmington girl. Both of her parents worked at the EUE Screen Gems Studio in town in the special effects department. Linda was studying for an Associate Degree in Film. She excelled in photography and hoped to become a cinematographer or video-grapher.

Rosie, the last to come to the table, arrived just as Sammy was intro-ducing Linda to the group.

"Ah," he said to Linda, "and here is Miss Rosie. She is sometimes a very funny person. Make great fashion shows." He winked at Rosie, who winked back and sat down.

"Nice to meet you, Linda. Welcome to the Residence and our little table."

"Not so little," Sammy interjected. "These ladies like to eat. So, what do you like today?"

"What do you have, Sammy?" Gina asked.

"Pea soup. Green salad. Fish is flounder with mashed potatoes.

Meat is brisket with mashed potatoes. Vegetable is steamed carrots. Dessert is brownie. Linda will write your orders. I watch. You first, Miss Gina."

"Salad. Fish. No brownie. Coffee." Kate wrote carefully. Sammy watched over her shoulder.

"Miss Rosie?"

"Did you try any of these dishes, Sammy?"

"No."

"Why?"

"This new chef. We don't get along."

"Like the last two."

"Last two were terrible cooks. This one is good cook but crazy Polish man. I think maybe he put something in my food."

"Are you serious?"

Sammy looked around the table and moved closer to the ladies. Linda, tight at his side, moved with him. "Sister Francis said last two chefs were bad choice by Father Bernard. This one maybe good chef but in the kitchen he is crazy man. Always yelling and cursing. He don't like me."

"But the food is much better," Freida commented.

"That's for sure," Bonnie added. "It's actually palatable."

As Linda took the ladies' lunch order, Nicole, and Father Louis Bernard, the administrator of the Residence, came into the dining room. Each carried three of the six FedEx packages that were delivered a half-hour earlier. Rosie tingled with anticipation as the novice and the priest made their way toward her table.

"A good afternoon, ladies," Father Bernard said brightly. The six women looked at him and responded in near unison.

"Good afternoon, Father... Nicole."

"Well," the priest went on, "it seems you all got a package today. Federal Express, no less."

Father Louis Bernard was not a native South Carolinian. Far from it, he was born and raised in the Bronx, New York City. His parents were first generation Americans whose parents had happily emigrated from France to America seven months before Germany invaded in May of 1940. They were devout Catholics. As Louis grew up, they left little doubt that they dreamt of him becoming a priest. He attended Catholic grammar and high school, and was accepted to Iona College's Religious Studies Program in New Rochelle where he earned his degree, majoring in Psychology and Social Work. He then applied to Saint Joseph's Seminary and College in Yonkers, New York, where he was accepted.

Upon graduation, he received a six-month appointment as a deacon at Saint Nicholas of Tolentine Church, in the Bronx. This was part of the process of becoming a priest. It is a trial period where, although not yet ordained, Louis had to take the vows of celibacy and fidelity to God. When that was over, he received his call from the bishop to become a priest, and took his final vows. The New York Diocese, that usually places newly ordained priests locally, told the now Father Bernard that because of his excellent grades in Social Work and Psychology at Iona he was going to the Diocese of Raleigh, North Carolina, to fill a recently vacated position there in the bishop's office. Five years after that, having shown his talents, and commitment to his calling, he was moved to the Residence as the administrator.

Nicole and Father Bernard walked around the table, handing the packages to each as addressed. When the distribution was done, they all sat holding their FedEx boxes. The ladies noted the origin of the packages, but no one moved to open hers.

"Aren't you going to open them?" the priest asked. "It looks like everyone got a present." He had not noticed, or would he have understood, where they were from.

"Yes, ladies. Aren't you curious?" Nicole, who was very curious, asked.

"Well, I am," Gina finally announced, and proceeded to open hers.

Julie quickly followed. Then Rosie and Freida, and soon they were all tearing open the boxes. Gina lifted hers out first and held it aloft. "Well, girls, will ya look at this?!" she exclaimed, holding up a black Dream Angels Garter Slip.

"Oh, my God!" Bonnie squealed. She stood and held a blue pleated Baby Doll Teddy against her dress. She was a size ten. It was a flimsy, tiny, size one.

"And can you believe this?" Julie said as she and Freida got up simultaneously showing their "gifts"—matching white lace Dream Angels bustiers. "We're like twins."

The other residents were all now standing, amazed at the lingerie fashion show developing before their eyes.

Father Bernard's face had turned a bright red. He backed away from the table, slightly stunned. He was a modest man who had led a fairly sheltered life.

Nicole stood in her place with her mouth agape. She checked the label on Julie's box and understood where these garments came from.

"Holy moly!" Rosie shouted as she stood and showed everyone a blue silk and lace bra and panty set. She turned to the women at the other tables. "Whaddya think, girls?"

They were all smiling and nodding approval.

Last to stand up was Eva. Her "gift" was a skimpy, two-piece chartreuse bikini. The color was so dazzling that everyone stopped talking and stared at her.

"So, dollinks," she said calmly, with a thicker than normal Hungarian accent, "you want I should try it on here?"

Everyone burst into laughter. Sammy, who was standing near the table, and had observed it all, stepped forward.

"Hey, Father Louis. I think maybe it time this place go coed, huh?" The priest, now totally embarrassed by the display of the skimpy, sexy lingerie being modeled in front of him, was speechless.

Then slowly, one by one, five of the ladies turned toward Rosie. They were all of the same mind. They understood that only Rosie would pull a stunt like this. Many of the other residents watched and also understood. Father Bernard and Nicole did not have a clue.

"So, Rosie?" Julie asked, staring at her.

"So, what?" Rosie answered innocently.

"So this," Freida said, holding up her bustier.

"It's nice," Rosie told her. "Maybe a little, uh, revealing...but nice."

"They're all more than a little revealing, don't ya think?" Gina asked Rosie.

"Maybe. But besides Eva's bikini, they're all undergarments or sleepy-time stuff. Who's gonna see them?"

"Sleepy-time stuff? Really?" Bonnie asked. "And how could I possibly sleep in this. It won't even fit one of my legs." That broke everyone up. The room filled with laughter.

"So, I'm askin' again, Rosie?" Julie said when things had quieted down.

"So... well, uh, why don't you all consider these early Christmas presents!" Rosie answered proudly.

The entire dining room broke into applause and cheers. Even Father Bernard made believe he got the joke. He shook his head and smiled. Nicole, Sammy and Linda the server joined in the applause.

Most of the women who lived in the Residence had made the choice to live there, driven by similar circumstances. They were alone, aging, seeking company and safety. It wasn't that they were retired, or ill. Most were vital and active women who decided that communal living was an answer for their physical and emotional needs at this stage of their lives.

So, in the quiet, sometimes socially sterile life that these women chose, Rosie's creative antics had brought a breath of freshness and joy that made everyone's day much brighter.

Wilmington had several attractions that kept the ladies occupied. There were always concerts, shows and plays at the historic Thalian Hall. Every other Wednesday, they went to the movies. Two nights a month, they ate out at a restaurant on the island.

Father Bernard had made an arrangement with the New Hanover Regional Medical Center for those residents who wanted to volunteer. More than half of them did. The six ladies decided to do it together every other Tuesday. They took turns doing a variety of things — greeting patients who were checking in; answering the phone; taking messages; assisting with light clerical work; guiding patients to the various therapies — occupational, speech and physical; transporting discharged patients to the lobby and delivering flowers, gifts, newspapers, mail and e-mail to patient rooms.

One thing that happened too rarely, but that they all enjoyed the most, was being asked to hold crying babies in the nursery. Rosie was the only one of the six who had a child and grandchildren — her daughter in Boston and grandsons in L.A. and Hawaii. For the others, it was an experience they had some regrets about missing in their lives. But when they held and spoke softly to the infants, it was hard to tell who was comforted more — the babies or the ladies.

A fun volunteer assignment was in the children's play area. Two of the women were always there. Freida, who delighted in teaching the kids to play various musical instruments, and Bonita Apollo, the retired teacher, who read books to the younger children and discussed the stories with them in detail. She also brought age appropriate fiction books, and picked up schoolbooks, for the older kids. Her love of teaching had not faded with retirement. It gave her great pleasure to help these children keep up to date with the classes they were missing.

Three weeks after the Residence's Victoria's Secret luncheon fashion show, a name that Sister Mary Francis dubbed it, Nicole drove the six ladies to the Medical Center for their bimonthly day of volunteering. They arrived there right before nine a.m. As pre-arranged, she would be back to pick them up at six p.m.

This Tuesday, Freida had brought her violin to play for the children who were bed-ridden. Most of these were undergoing chemotherapy. She was assisted by three long-term hospitalized children, whom she had taught the basics of the snare drum, harmonica and guitar. The music was familiar songs from *Sesame Street*.

Bonnie went to the playroom with five new books she had ordered online. Three were from the Avalon: Web of Magic Series for tween-agers. The stories featured three teenage girls and their animal friends, with themes of friendship, love of nature, and triumph over adversity. The other two were for the younger patients, Doctor Seuss—*The Cat in the Hat*, and Laurie Hyman's *Sweet Tales*, Gina and Eva reported to physical therapy. Gina's job was to sign in the patients and guide them to their therapists. Eva assisted with setting up equipment and wiping down the massage tables with an antibacterial solution after each patient's session was over.

Julie answered the main phone line, giving directions and taking messages for the admitting office. Rosie was in the main lobby, greeting incoming ambulatory outpatients and helping them fill out the required forms before they were picked up and brought into the appropriate hospital system.

Since the six ladies were all on different floors, sections and schedules, and broke for lunch at different times, they rarely saw one another until Nicole met them at the main entrance to drive them back to the Residence. Although it was their home, they never referred to it that way. It was always the Residence.

This particular morning, Rosie had a flurry of check-ins between nine and eleven. Then things got slow. She asked one of the orderlies nearby to keep an eye on her desk while she went to the cafeteria to get a cup of coffee and her favorite, a jelly donut. When she returned to her desk, Rosie discovered there had been a delivery of new magazines to be distributed to the lobby's three waiting areas.

One of the magazines, *Women Pumping Iron*, intrigued her. The cover had a picture of a very pretty woman, around thirty, wearing a skimpy red bikini. She was holding a heavy barbell in her right hand and flexing a muscular arm. Her figure was solid, rippling with smooth, yet very well developed muscles. She looked very strong, but was also feminine, and from Rosie's point of view, kind of sexy. She tucked the magazine in the desk drawer and distributed the rest. They ranged from *Woman's World, Cooking Light* and *Good House-keeping* to *Time, Vogue, Sports Illustrated* and *National Geographic*. As she did so, she picked up the much older magazines and placed them in the paper recycle bin outside the cafeteria. Then things got busy—what Rosie called the afternoon rush—and didn't quiet down until a little after four p.m.

She went to get a cup of tea. When she returned, she saw a young couple cross the lobby with their new baby. They seemed to be floating on air, wearing wide, bright smiles and stopping a few times to look at their new child and then grin at one another with love. When they went out through the pneumatically opening front door, they were greeted by two older couples who Rosie had no doubt were the new grandparents. The adults gathered around the new mother, admiring and smiling and sharing their joy. Then they all got into a large, shiny black Cadillac Escalade and drove away.

"Have a wonderful life, little one," Rosie muttered to herself. Then she remembered the magazine she had stashed and took it out of the drawer. Thirty-five minutes later, she reached the last few pages of the magazine. There was a classified section that listed various gyms, equipment, diet supplements and a few personals. One little ad jumped out and grabbed Rosie's attention.

Wanted:
Mail order brides for farmers and miners.
Distant locations.
Inquiries to:
Women Pumping Iron
Box #596 - Spanish Wells
Eleuthera, Bahamas

It was five p.m. Nicole would be there in an hour. Rosie made a beeline for the gift shop where she bought a small box of lavender stationery with yellow daisies across the top of the page, and envelopes to match. She also bought five first-class overseas stamps.

Back at her desk, all was quiet. She carefully wrote five letters and addressed them to the address indicated in the ad in the Bahamas. Each letter, in different handwriting and with different stories and backgrounds, expressed keen interest in the mail order bride request. She signed them with her friend's names—Juliette Lobato, Freida Riggs, Gina Ferrari, Bonnie Apollo and Eva Kobva. The return address was the Residence.

Rosie sealed them, stamped them, and with a smile on her face, waved to her five friends as they gathered in the lobby while she dropped the letters into the hospital mailbox.

The next few weeks passed uneventfully. The hurricane season, which usually began in July, did not materialize. August brought two tropical depressions, but this year, the hurricane activity seemed to slip south and west into the Caribbean and Gulf. The heat and humidity of August slowly gave way to September's tolerable days and cooler nights. Routine at the Residence moved with it.

The six ladies usually went to church together most Sundays on a bus provided by the diocese. But this particular Sunday, after Mass, the ladies had made plans to have lunch and a cruise on the HENRIETTA III riverboat up the scenic northeast Cape Fear River. They invited Nicole along as their guest, so instead of going on the bus, they drove to Wilmington in the van.

Eva, who, after witnessing the atrocities perpetrated on the Jews of Europe by the Nazis and aided by the French Vichy government and many in Ukraine, gave up any belief in God or organized religion. But she went along to Sunday Mass to be with her friends. They all liked to hear Bishop Joseph Draper's homilies on the scriptures and his sermons that were usually timely and fairly political. Some of the views held by the church's new leader, Pope Francis, were at odds with Monsignor Draper's conservative views.

The congregation was basically conservative and Republican. The same could not be said for the six ladies. They all had, for the most part, a more liberal outlook and approach to life.

Rosie's husband had been active in the construction unions, and a leader in breaking down the racial walls of his carpentry trade. The dioceses, predominately Irish in its makeup, had been of little help on that matter.

None of Julie's divorces were recognized by the church. She didn't care. Her "deal," as she called it, was between her and God—not a bunch of male priests who were never married, much less the three husbands she had to deal with.

When Freida's husband, George, came back from Vietnam he stopped attending church. The horror of the war, prejudice encountered on base, and his eventual sterility and premature death from Agent Orange exposure hardened Freida to religion. Pope Francis gave her some renewed hope. In any case, she was still interested enough to see where the church might go.

Though raised by strict Italian-Catholic parents, Gina, having lived and worked on Broadway, in Las Vegas, and at the end of her careers, in Georgetown, had left that upbringing behind decades ago. When she came to the Residence, she went to confession just once. She sat in the confessional for more than an hour, relating as much of her life's sins as she could recall to an astonished priest. The poor man was overwhelmed by her narrative. He tried to stop her twice, suggesting that she take things a little at a time.

"I'm only gonna do this once, Father," she told him. "Then you'll absolve me and I'll be squared with God. After that, I promise, there won't be any need for me to see you, or any other priest again." From then on, he kept quiet until she was done.

Gina ended with contrition. "Oh, God, I am heartily sorry for my sins," she said, remembering her last confession, long ago in New York City's Saint Patrick's Cathedral.

The priest was silent for a long moment, unable to absorb all that he had heard. He decided to go by the book.

"God the Father of mercies, through the death and resurrection of His Son has reconciled the world to Himself and sent the Holy Spirit among us for the forgiveness of sins; through the ministry of the Church may God give you pardon and peace, and I absolve you from your sins in the name of the Father, and of the Son, and of the Holy Spirit. Give thanks to the Lord."

"I will," is all Gina said, and left the confessional.

Bonita went to mass for much the same reason as Eva—to be with friends, and for the social and community aspect of it.

Bonita Ortiz Apollo was born to a Latina mother and Greek father, in Ponce, Puerto Rico. Her mother was a Santera, a Priestess of Santería. The religion, an African and Caribbean form of Catholicism, was developed by slaves whose African religions were outlawed. They were forced to adapt and worship a new god and an accompanying army of saints. In doing so, they blended African rituals with baptism and Christian beliefs. After Bonita was born, her mother was diagnosed with a severe thyroid disorder and was unable to conceive, so she was an only child. Her father, a sea captain, practiced Greek Orthodoxy. When he was away at sea, her mother brought Bonita to the Santeria church. When he was home, he insisted that she attend his church. As a result, young Bonita's confusion led her away from both. Eventually, she became an agnostic.

She went to the University of Puerto Rico in San Juan where she got her BA in Liberal Arts and her Masters in Education. Her mother died shortly after that, and her father decided to move back to his hometown of Patras, Greece. Bonita did not want to do that. With the huge Puerto Rican influx into New York City in the 1960s, qualified bilingual teachers were in demand. She got a job teaching sixth grade in the Bronx. Bonita inherited the hypothyroid condition from her mother and was warned that she could probably not conceive. She led a quiet, fulfilled life. She married, but the doctors were correct and they had no children. Her husband, also a teacher, was from Charlotte, North Carolina. They retired there and he passed away three years ago. Her sister-in-law, who was active in various Catholic charities, suggested the Residence when Bonita showed symptoms of depression and admitted she was lonely.

That Sunday, after mass at Saint Simeon's RC church, Monsignor Draper, who noted that the six ladies and Nicole were not boarding the bus, asked Father Bernard why. He was told about the cruise. The bishop made a point of going to talk to them.

"Hello there, Ladies," he greeted as they gathered near the van. "I hear tell you are cruising this afternoon."

"Yes, Monsignor," Rosie told him. "It's the special Blackwater Adventure Cruise."

"What's that about?" he asked.

"The boat goes up the northeast Cape Fear River. Pretty wild up there," Bonita said.

"They say it looks like Wilmington was back in the sixteen-hundreds," Gina added.

"There's the old Rose Hill Plantation up that way," Freida told him.

"And a really nice lunch on board," Julie said. "It'll be grand."

"That sounds wonderful," the bishop agreed. "I wanted to tell you something. You all volunteer at the New Hanover Medical Center, right?" he asked.

"That we do," Rosie answered.

"Well, the diocese in Raleigh has received a wonderful donation. Several million dollars actually, and they have made an offer to build a special pediatric wing to the main hospital here. Some of the interest and work that you ladies and other residents at our home have contributed, especially to the children's area, played a part in the decision. So there are congratulations in order for you all. I just wanted you to know that. Now I don't want to keep you any longer and have you miss your fun day on the boat," he said.

"At our age, Monsignor, I imagine the fun boat sailed a long while ago," Gina answered with a wink and a grin. They all laughed, thanked the bishop for the information, and piled into the van. He stood and watched as Nicole started up the motor and drove away, perhaps a little faster than he might have liked. He made a mental note to talk to her about it before she came to him for his recommendation that was necessary for her to take her final vows.

Thirty minutes into the Blackwater Adventure Cruise, as the six ladies and Nicole sat on the open upper deck of the riverboat, a bend in the river took the city of Wilmington out of sight. The loudspeaker announced that lunch would be served shortly in the main dining room. The late September sky was clear. Deciduous trees along the riverbank were showing slight tinges of rust and yellow, but autumn was not in the air. This was a bright, early summer-like day.

"Bishop Draper seemed rather happy, didn't he?" Freida asked.

"Hey, getting a wing built at the hospital is a feather in his cap, for sure," Julie said.

"And, like he said, we had something to do with that," Eva said proudly. "With the kids, I mean."

"There's one cute little boy...I think his name is, yes, Daniel. I called him Danny and he told me his mother doesn't like that," Bonnie said. "I don't know why she would make such a rule. I mean..."

"Is there a story here, Bonnie?" Julia asked.

"Well, yes there is," she answered, slightly annoyed. She looked away at the boat's wake. Bonnie had a habit of drifting off point when telling a story. The other ladies let her go on, but not Julia.

"So?" Julia finally said.

"So, well, he held onto my hand as I read."

"That's nice," Julia told her.

"What was nice was that I felt, for a few moments, that he was, you know, my grandchild. It made me kind of sad, like I've missed something...Oh, I don't know. Never mind." There was a long moment of silence as the boat slipped through a placid stretch of river. A few large mansions were visible, set back from the shoreline among live oaks dripping with Spanish moss.

"I wouldn't be sad if someone a little older than Daniel, say around thirty or forty years, held my hand," Gina announced, breaking the silence. "And the rest of me."

A few of the ladies grinned and nodded. Nicole blushed and smiled to herself. There were times lately when she'd had similar thoughts. Even physical desire. It was confusing and thrilling. A life suppressing those feelings was, at times, unsettling.

"You know," Freida said, "all those years, when I had my career, I never thought I'd miss having...being a mother. A family. But now, sometimes..."

"Yeah. Sometimes I wish I'd had a few of those rug-rats myself," Gina admitted. "I'll be honest. I don't care to be an old maid, all alone."

"But we're not alone. I mean, we have each other," Rosie said as she spread her arms apart toward the others. Silence descended again as the women reflected on the fact that, with the exception of Rosie, all they had was each other.

"Listen, girls, motherhood's not all it's cracked up to be," Rosie said, trying to change the direction of what might become a downer conversation. "My daughter sends me a ticket to freeze my keester off in Boston once a year. And now, this year, she tells me she's found another Mister Right, a Harvard professor no less, who's taking her to Atlantis..."

"That disappeared eons ago," Bonnie interjected.

"Yeah, well, it's back as a huge resort on Paradise Island in the Bahamas, casino and all."

"They should invite you," Bonnie told her.

"Really, Bonnie?" Gina said. "Talk about a third wheel..."

"Who said anything about a wheel?" Bonnie asked, not understanding Gina's reference.

"That's kind of you, Bonnie," Rosie said, frowning slightly at Gina who rolled her eyes. "But I don't think that's a good idea. What burns me up is that I won't see my two grandsons this year."

"As I recall, don't they live pretty far away?" Julie asked.

"Los Angeles and Hawaii."

"Still, you're lucky to have them," Freida told Rosie.

"You know, sometimes I like to think of those little ones in the hospital as my own grandchildren," Bonnie admitted. Her voice was tinged with melancholy. "I feel that especially when we hold the babies who are crying."

"It would be nice to have a few of my own," Eva admitted whimsically. The tone of the conversation was getting to sound morose to Rosie.

"Well, Eva darling," Rosie said brightly, "maybe there's still time. I mean, that's why I got y'all those sexy Victoria's Secret goodies. Why don't you scope around this vessel and see if there are any eligible men to recruit? It's never too late, you know."

"You really think?" Eva said reflexively.

That brought a wave of lascivious laughter. Nicole blushed again, while at the same time imagining herself in one of those flimsy white teddies. Yes. Unsettling.

The group then settled down. They all gazed out at the passing scenery in silence, each, except Nicole, with their own, private thoughts and memories of passions, lost loves and opportunities long past.

Suddenly, the captain's voice came over the loudspeaker and broke the spell.

"Folks. Please give me your attention." The boat slowed and began to turn around. "I've just been informed by the Coast Guard and National Weather Service that a low is forming rapidly off the coast of the Carolinas. It could become a major storm. Possible hurricane force. We'll have time to get back to port and get you all home. Now, for your own safety, I'd appreciate everyone getting below decks and away from the railings. I'm going to pick up some speed in a few minutes. Your fares will be refunded. Sorry for this, but the weather is something we simply cannot control. Thanks for your cooperation."

Everyone above deck started for the staircase that led to the main cabin. As they descended, the passengers heard the engines rev up and felt the boat surge and then turn one hundred-eighty degrees back toward Wilmington.

CHAPTER ELEVEN

Something Happened
On The Way Home

The blue skies and sunshine were gone by the time they got into the van. It was three p.m. Nicole pulled out of the parking lot and turned on the radio to the Wilmington radio news station, WAAV, 980AM. The weather report was at the top of the news. A rare low pressure system, the result of a cold front that had dropped down rapidly and unexpectedly from the northeastern Atlantic over the warm Gulf Stream current, had formed and was rotating toward the coast. Heavy rain and strong winds, possibly hurricane force, were expected within an hour.

"We'll be home by then," Nicole announced, noting that there was heavier than normal traffic moving west, away from the coast. "I'll take Oleander over to Eastwood and across the bridge," she said.

"Maybe we should stay in town," Bonnie suggested. "The radio said it might be a hurricane."

"Well, I want to get home," Eva said emphatically.

Gina agreed. "The Residence is quite safe," she assured everyone. "It's been through several hurricanes. They build strong on the coast. Why, when I was working in Georgetown, up by Myrtle Beach, we were always snug as bugs in a rug in a storm."

"So then tell me why is all the traffic going the other way?" Bonnie asked.

"They don't live on the island. They're heading home early to beat the flooded roads," Julie answered.

The skies grew darker and the wind picked up a bit. The weather report on the radio now said that the storm had intensified and would make landfall in thirty to forty-five minutes. The vortex seemed to be heading for the Wilmington area. Residents were warned to keep off the roads and stay inside so that emergency vehicles could move quickly if needed.

"Isn't it something? Everything's a panic these days," Rosie commented nervously. "Always a crisis."

The van came to the end of Oleander Street. Nicole made a hard right turn onto Eastwood. The bridge to Wrightsville Beach was a half-mile ahead. The road ahead was eerily clear of traffic. "We'll be home in a few minutes, Ladies," Nicole announced.

Then it grew suddenly dark. Pitch black. The van stalled. The wind stopped. Silence. Frozen and disoriented, no one spoke. Nicole turned the ignition key. Nothing happened.

A musical, humming sound seemed to surround the van and permeate through the doors and windows. It was weirdly pleasant and soothing.

Slowly, out of the darkness, a multicolored, full-spectrum, rainbow-like illumination surrounded and enveloped the van. The vehicle began to shudder. Nicole grasped the steering wheel. The six ladies grabbed the seat backs, seat belts and each other. The steering wheel spun out of Nicole's hands. She pushed back against her seat. The sound and colored light grew more intense. The van began to shake violently.

The women and Nicole began to scream, but their cries were drowned out by the musical, humming sound that grew louder and increased in pitch. The light grew more intense; its brilliance made them all shut their eyes. They felt the sensation of the van being lifted up, off the road. It began to spin as it accelerated, higher.

Just as Rosie was about to scream, "Tornado!" there was an abrupt silence and total darkness. Fear trapped the word in her throat. They became aware of a strange whooshing sound, like air rushing through a wind tunnel. They were moving up at an impossible speed.

Then silence.

The road to the bridge was deserted.

The clouds rapidly dissipated, revealing blue skies and sunshine.

The van was gone!

CHAPTER TWELVE

Missing, Then Gone

Damage from the storm was minimal. Some power lines were downed by falling trees; a few small brooks overran their banks and quickly receded. There was little beach erosion. Local radio and television news reported several hundred outages and some minor damage. Thanks to the warnings from NOAA and the Coast Guard, there were no reported serious injuries. The speculation was that a sudden wind shear of upper cold air dropped into the warmer Gulfstream atmosphere, causing the violent, rapid disturbance as a mini-low developed. Its power might have spawned a tornado. That was being investigated.

By seven p.m., dinnertime, Father Bernard was concerned. Nicole and the six ladies had not returned from their luncheon cruise. He had called the cruise line, but their telephone was out.

At eight p.m., he called the Wilmington police to see if there had been any accident involving the van. They had no such report. By nine p.m., Father Bernard was a nervous wreck. He called Bishop Draper who recalled that he had talked to the ladies about the new hospital wing and had seen them drive off to the harbor for their cruise.

"They were looking forward to it," he told the priest.

"I fear something has happened, Monsignor. The police were busy, but took the time to check and said there was no report of a van in any accident. I was wondering...is it possible that you might inquire higher up?"

"I know the Commissioner and the Mayor, if that's what you're asking, Louis. Are you sure calling them is warranted? Maybe they stopped for dinner. Or the cruise boat took shelter in a safe harbor. There was enough warning to seek shelter. I heard no reports of injuries."

"Yes. I know all that. But I'm worried. Nicole Mallory is a very responsible novitiate. And there was a report of a possible tornado..."

"I didn't hear about that," the bishop said, now more concerned.

"Yes. It might have been in the vicinity near the bridge to Wrightsville Beach. That's only a mile from here."

"Oh, my. Yes. Of course. I'll get right on it, Louis. I'll call you back."

The investigation that followed the bishop's call about the missing van, and its seven occupants, began with a patrol car going to the harbor and physically locating the captain of the cruise boat. He reported that he had immediately returned to the dock and that all passengers disembarked. The parking lot was empty when he, and the crew, had secured the vessel and sought shelter. He did not remember the van, but did recall a group of older women up on the top deck, which was right below the bridge, when he announced that they were returning to port.

The search widened, and later that night, a traffic cam recording from the corner of Oleander and Eastwood showed the van in question turning onto Eastwood, heading east toward the bridge. Another camera in Wrightsville Beach showed that the van never crossed the bridge.

By the following morning, two items had made the local radio and TV news. There had been a tornado that touched down near the Wrightsville Island Bridge, and seven occupants of a van, who were residents of the Wilmington Parish Retirement Home for Ladies and last reported in that vicinity, were missing. So was the van.

When NOAA, the National Oceanic and Atmospheric Administration, announced that indeed, an EF4 tornado had briefly touched down in the area in question, the search widened. The time the tornado touch-down occurred coincided with the storm's sudden change of direction from westerly, one hundred-eighty degrees to due east. That meant that if the van had been swept up in the tornado's vortex, it was a relatively short distance to the ocean—a little more than a mile.

Simultaneous searches were organized on land, along the beaches and offshore. By mid-afternoon, using city, state police and military police, helicopters, Coast Guard vessels, search aircraft and hundreds of volunteers, a massive operation to locate the van and its passengers was underway. The story was picked up by TV networks and social media. By morning, it was being seen worldwide.

The six retired ladies and the young novitiate were identified. Families had been notified and flown to the area. Rosie's daughter Kate flew in from Boston with her boyfriend. Her sons were en route from L.A. and Hawaii. Nicole's parents came in from Elkhorn, Nebraska, with Nicole's older sister, Francis. Julie, Freida, Eva, Gina and Bonnie had no family.

Days of search turned up nothing. The speculation that the van had been hurled out to sea became a conclusion as the land search for miles around, in what is a fairly populated area, turned up nothing. Sophisticated underwater sonar, submersibles and cameras were employed. Two shipwrecks, previously undiscovered, were located. One of them, a slave ship sailing from Santa Domingo to Georgia that foundered with human cargo in 1760, and a WWII Liberty Ship carrying tanks and spare truck parts, torpedoed by a German U-Boat west of Bermuda.

But there was no sign of the van.

After five weeks, as November became December, the recovery effort tapered off. Rosie's and Nicole's families, who had remained in Wilmington, decided that all hope of recovery was gone. They met with Bishop Draper who sadly and reluctantly agreed with them.

The next Sunday, Bishop Draper and Cardinal Timothy Rush of the Raleigh Diocese celebrated a special Mass of Requiem for reasonable cause offered for several dead—in this case, the seven residents of the Wilmington Parish Retirement Home for Ladies. Father Bernard wore black vestments, while the cardinal and bishop dressed in purple robes. The church was packed, with an overflow of mourners outside, where the service was broadcast. News organizations from across America covered the event with their usual intrusiveness and repetitive speculation. Mass cards offered perpetual enrollment in the Society of the Little Flower that included the deceased in perpetual Mass and prayers offered each day by the Carmelites. The suggested offering was $25. Half of the proceeds would go to the Retirement Home.

Wilmington, America and the world moved on. Rosie's and Nicole's families returned to their homes. Four months later, as spring came to North Carolina, a small, marble monument, engraved with the names of the seven women, was dedicated on a rise of land overlooking the Atlantic in Wrightsville Beach.

The United States Naval Research Laboratory is headquartered on a vast campus along the Potomac River in Washington, D.C. Among other missions, it is the center for satellite tracking and various space research programs. Information, gathered from various facilities and tracking stations across the world, is fed into the main campus. In the United States, the Navy has several other locations in California, Mississippi, Florida, Maryland, Alabama and Virginia.

Three years, to the date, after the six ladies and Novitiate Nicole Mallory disappeared in the violent storm in Wilmington, a Chief Warrant Officer Five, and a Petty Officer, at the Blossom Point Naval Station for Space Technology, just south of Washington, D.C., were drawn by an alarm to the computer screen that showed data from satellite LL-945.9 in fixed orbit above the southeastern coast of the United States. It was early evening. That particular alarm and computer, which was programmed to indicate unidentified airborne objects off the southeastern United States, detected a disturbance—a small, unscheduled craft off the North Carolina coast.

The Petty Officer slid his chair on wheels over to the screen. He was joined by the Chief Warrant Officer, sliding over from the other direction.

"What have we got?" the Chief asked.

"Don't know yet. Can't determine size yet. Might just be noise. There's an electrical storm in the area."

"Okay. Whereabouts are we?"

"North Carolina. Off Wilmington."

The Chief studied the screen. "That's a pretty strong signal. Push in."

The Petty Officer turned to a nearby keyboard and typed in instructions that adjusted the satellite's optics to zoom closer to the area where the signal was indicated.

"That's damned close to the beach, Chief."

"And seems to be moving."

"Might be an emergency plane landing," the Chief speculated.

"Maybe. Or small boat. There are no immediate alerts on commercial or military activity."

"Drug runner, you think?"

"That's always possible. Not our concern."

"Push in some more," the Chief ordered.

The Petty Officer again adjusted the optics, but as he did so, the indication of the object began to break up and fade.

"We're losing it," the Chief said, annoyed. "Maybe looking for shelter," he mused. "Must be a drug run. What have we got in the area?"

The Petty Officer entered a few keystrokes and a list of military ships and planes in the area appeared in the corner of the screen.

"Destroyer. The Metz. It's that new DDG-1000 prototype undergoing tests. Fifty-three miles southeast of Wilmington. And there's an AWAC due to pass within ninety nautical miles in about fifteen minutes."

"What about the Coast Guard?"

The Petty Officer hit a few more keys. A list of Coast Guard vessels appeared just as the unidentified object disappeared.

"Forget it. It's gone." The Chief slid his chair back, away from the screen. "Probably just an anomaly."

"There are sunspots this week," the Petty Officer suggested. "What do you want me to report?"

"Just print out the log and send it up to the Captain at the end of the watch. I'll review it with her later."

The "anomaly" that was detected by the satellite scan program at the Blossom Point Naval Station for Space Technology was not sunspot activity or an electric storm disturbance. When the alarm went off, the sky around Eastwood Road, just east of the Wrightsville Beach Bridge, had rapidly grown dark. Menacing clouds roiled just off the beach. An east wind picked up, with gusts more than fifty miles an hour. The surf increased, with waves more than five feet high. That was when the satellite alarm first sounded. But then as suddenly as the indications of a storm had begun, the humidity dropped and all became eerily calm. Then, as the wind decreased, the disturbance began to fade on the Navy's computer screen.

A weird humming sound began to build. A brilliant white light emerged from the darkness above the road. Turning multicolored, it swirled like a frosty rainbow sherbet as it descended. When it touched the blacktop, the colors burst and scattered. The image disappeared from the Navy computer screen as the darkness above was gone and the colors disbursed. What was left was the Dioceses' 2003 eight-passenger Chevy Venture van, swerving and swaying wildly on the road in the exact spot it had vanished three years before.

CHAPTER FOURTEEN
A Knock On The Door

A matured Nicole Mallory gripped the steering wheel and drove confidently. She steadied the van and headed for the bridge. Her hair, once dull brown, was now shiny black, close-cropped, and tipped with flourishes of silver. She wore no makeup, yet her complexion was smooth and glowing. She was stunningly beautiful. Her clothing was simple and tailored—a fitted jacket made of beige, suede-like material, and similar dark brown slacks. Black, form-fitted boots completed her outfit.

Behind her, seated side by side in the van's first passenger row were Rosie, Julie and Freida. They were dressed in outfits similar to Nicole's. They too, had glowing, healthy complexions and bright eyes that took in the familiar surroundings. And, quite strangely, they appeared to be twenty or thirty years younger than the day they had disappeared in the storm.

At the same time, in the Residence, Father Bernard and Sammy Kim sat at the kitchen table having coffee, observing what had become an after-dinner ritual. Sister Mary Francis, obviously annoyed, loaded the industrial dishwasher tray with the evening's dishes, silverware and glasses. The fifth chef to be hired over the past three years, Bogdon Gruszniewski, was half-heartedly handing dishes to the nun.

"Could you move a little faster, Bogdon? I have an appointment with the diocese's accountant this evening."

"Washing dishes not chef's work, Sister Mary."

"Then you must think of it as God's work, Bogdon."

"Like you are baptizing dishes," Sammy told the chef, who was in no mood for jokes.

"I baptize you in there, busboy," Bogdon said, gesturing toward dishwashing machine.

"You wrong there," Sammy objected. "I'm head waiter."

"Then I put you in head first!"

"Please, gentlemen," Father Bernard begged, as he did almost every night since he'd hired this chef. "We all pitch in here, Bogdon."

"In Poland, bus boy do dishes."

"They have dishes in Poland?" Sammy asked. "From what you cook, I think they must eat from the floor."

Bogdon put down a large platter he had in hand and moved toward Sammy with a tightened fist. The chef was a large, beefy man. The blood vessels on his neck bulged.

Sister Mary Francis, who was a large and quite strong woman herself, grabbed him by the arm. "I said I have an appointment, Bogdon. You two are grown men acting like children."

Bogdon hesitated. Sammy looked down at his coffee cup.

The two men, who seemed to taunt each other from the day they met, actually liked one another. Both being immigrants was a common bond. The animosity was partially to break the monotony of the work, and because they learned to enjoy seeing how long it took before Father Bernard and Sister Mary Francis got emotionally, and then physically, involved. They imagined it brightened up what the waiter and chef perceived as a quiet, and often boring, existence that these two humble servants of the church lived.

But this evening, the drama was interrupted by a loud, insistent knock on the outside, rear kitchen door. Father Bernard got up and walked toward the door.

"Okay, guys. Let's all just relax." He opened the door. Nicole stood there, smiling broadly with anticipation.

"Hello, Father," she said, waiting for him to embrace her. But the priest did not recognize Nicole. She had changed so dramatically.

"Hello, my dear. What can I do for you?" Nicole stood there, smiling at the puzzled priest. A thought emerged in Father Louis Bernard's mind. *Could it be? Impossible.* Yet it persisted.

At that moment, Sister Mary Francis came up behind Father Bernard. She was holding a small stack of coffee cups.

"What's going on, Louis?" she asked. Then she saw Nicole. Her heart skipped several beats and she drew in a deep breath. "Oh!" she exclaimed, as she dropped the cups. "Oh, praise be to God!" She pushed Father Bernard aside and swept Nicole up into her strong arms. She was trembling. "Oh! Oh!" was all she could say. Finally she said, "Nicole! Our Nicole has come home!"

"Nicole!?" Father Bernard exclaimed. "Yes. Of course! Nicole!" He fell to his knees, crossing himself. "Dear sweet Lord. Thank You! Thank You for..." He stopped and stood up. "Come, Nicole. Come in." He took her hand. Sister Mary Francis took the other. They guided her into the kitchen while everyone spoke at once.

"What happened to you, child?" Sister Mary asked.

"Where have you been?" Father Bernard asked.

"What you do with ladies?" Sammy asked.

"Yes! Of course. The ladies?" Sister Mary asked. "For God's sake, where are the ladies?"

"They are all fine. We are all okay. We've had... It's a long story. Sort of an adventure." The shock of Nicole's suddenly showing up finally sunk in. Sister Mary broke down in tears.

"Thank God. We didn't know what... We thought you all were..."

"Blown out to sea in a tornado," the priest said.

"I think maybe kidnapped," Sammy added. "But no ransom demand."

"We feared the worst, child," Sister Mary admitted.

"Lost all hope," Father Bernard added.

"FBI was here." Sammy looked at a confused Chef Bogdon. "Good thing I have green card."

"I have papers, busboy. Who is this pretty lady?" Bogdon asked.

"Nicole...Nicole Mallory. Was, she is, our novitiate. This is Bogdon Grusza... Gruznnyskeuw...Uh..."

"Gruszniewski," Bogdon interrupted. "I am here for two months and still Father cannot say my name. Nice to meet you, Miss Nicole."

"Bogdon is our new chef," Father Louis told Nicole.

"We have five chefs since you and ladies check out," Sammy told her. "This one is Polish."

"Enough already about chefs," Sister Mary said. "For God's sake, Nicole, tell us...where are Rosie, Julie, Eva, Bonita, Freida and Gina? Where are our ladies?"

"Well now," Nicole began. "Rosie, Julia and Freida are just outside. In the van. Let me get them." She turned to the rear kitchen door.

"And what about Eva, Gina and Bonita?" Sister called after her.

"Not to worry. They're just fine."

"But where are they?"

"Like I said, it's a long story. Now just wait. I'll be right back." Nicole walked quickly out the door to the van that was parked near the wall, in the shadows of the Residence.

"That novitiate, she grow up nice," Sammy said.

"It's a miracle," Sister Mary said softly, crossing herself while looking upward to Heaven.

"Amen," Father Louis said. He turned to Sammy and Bogdon. "And I want you two to stop bickering all the time. It's quite annoying."

"He starts," Sammy complained.

"He makes fun because I don't know America."

"Immigrants gonna ruin the country."

"Will you stop it?! Please?"

At that moment, Nicole came back into the kitchen. Trailing behind her, in single file, were Rosie, Julie and Freida. Sister Mary and Father Louis came toward them with open arms. They both stopped abruptly as Nicole stepped aside.

"Oh, boy!" Sammy announced. "You ladies must have some really big adventure."

Rosie, Julie and Freida, looking years younger and smiling, were very, very pregnant!

Father Bernard and Sister Mary Francis were stunned, emotionally rocked, confused and dumbfounded all at once. They could not take their gaze away—first from the three fairly familiar, but younger faces and secondly, their protruding bellies. It just did not compute. Father Bernard finally broke the silence.

"Is that?... Is it?... Are you really...? Rosie?"

"Julie? Freida?" Sister Mary uttered. "You look like you're...O, my Lord. You're so much younger and..."

"And having babies!" Sammy blurted out. "Looks like soon to me!"

The awkward silence of incomprehension returned. This time it was broken by Bogdon, who stepped forward, wiped his right hand on his grease-stained white apron, and extended it in greeting.

"May I introduce? I am Chef Bogdon Gruszniewski. Americans cannot say my name so please to call me Bogdon."

The three women shook hands with Bogdon, each announcing how pleased they were to meet Mister Gruszniewski, pronouncing his name perfectly. His face exploded in a broad smile.

"I like these women. Smart. And pretty. Where you from?"

Sister Mary, who had gathered her composure, stepped in front of the chef. "Not now, Bogdon." She embraced each of the women silently, and then stepped back, smiling broadly and kindly at them.

"My dear Rosie, Julie and Freida. I apologize for my...for our, reaction.

This is... Well it's quite wonderful that you are home. And, and uh, looking so. So...younger? It's a..."

"A miracle, Sister Mary?" Rosie asked.

"It is, isn't it, Sister?" Nicole added.

"Oh, yes. Surely a miracle. A wonderful, blessed miracle. Isn't it, Father Bernard?"

"Of course. Of course. Come," he gestured, "sit down. All of you." He led them to the kitchen table as Bogdon cleared away the cups and plates.

"You like some tea?" Sammy asked. "We have nice Heavenly Delight herbal."

"That would be lovely, Sammy," Freida told him. He smiled.

"That's your favorite. Talk loud so I can hear story," he said as he went to fill the kettle and put it on the stove.

Bogdon and Father Bernard quickly gathered more chairs around the table. They all took chairs, except Sammy, who turned a flame up under the kettle and went to the cabinet where the tea was stored. Julie remained standing. She waited for a moment until everyone had adjusted their chairs and settled.

"What happened to us," Julie stood and began, "will be a difficult story for you to believe. But as you can see, with your own eyes, we are here, and yet we are not who we were three years ago to this very day. Since Rosie was, in a very real sense, responsible for all that has happened...well, maybe not everything that happened, well, sort of after it happened... Well, anyway, we thought it best that she be the one to tell about it. Rosie?" Julie sat down.

Rosie, whose expression was that of the cat that had been caught eating the canary, blushed a bit and smiled. Father Bernard, seated next to her, made a funny, squeaking sound from deep in his throat. Had his mouth been open it would have sounded like "Uh-huh?" Rosie reached over and patted his folded hands.

"Where to begin?" she said softly.

"I don't know," the priest said.

"That's rhetorical, Louis," Sister Mary Francis scolded. "Start at the beginning, dear. That's usually best."

"Yes. The beginning," Rosie agreed. "Okay. First, let me assure you that Gina, Eva and Bonnie are quite well, and safe, and happy. We were recently in touch with them and although they..."

Father Bernard could not contain himself. He shook his head as if trying to bring reality into focus. "Please, Rosie!" he said. "I can't stand it anymore. What in God's name happened to all of you? Where have you been?"

"Well, Father, that's not really the beginning," she said, "but to answer your question, I've been on Marlino; Julie lives on Gimm; last year Freida moved to Roonio nine with Jinko. We three still reside in our Milky Way Galaxy. Eva is in the Centauras-A Galaxy, on a planet, well, actually twin planets whose names are really not translatable. We've decided to call them Ying and Yang." She smiled at what she thought might be amusing to Father Bernard and Sister Mary. They didn't react. They minds were now in a place beyond understanding what Rosie was relating, or in what language. "Bonnie is in the Markarian Galaxy," she continued. "It a fairly new place to explore for the Marlinons. Oh, that's my home now. Marlino. I told you that. And finally, Gina, lucky girl, has signed on as a humanoid entertainer on an Orbalidinian intergalactic cruise ship. She's dancing up a storm, she told us, like in the old days in Vegas."

"America is very big place," Bogdon announced, impressed.

Father Bernard and Sister May Francis sat in silence, slowly moving their gaze from Rosie to Julie to Freida, wondering who had gone insane, the ladies or themselves, or the whole world?

"Well, it's not quite America I was talking about," Rosie told him.

Freida, who had been fairly quiet so far, saw their confusion. "If I may, Rosie?" Freida said. Rosie nodded. "Look," Freida began, "we figured that initially this kind of information would make no sense to you. Why should it? I guess almost everyone on this planet believes we are alone in the universe. It's only been a few hundred years that the concept that there might be other life out there crept into our Parochial brains and lexicon. But we are here, as witnesses, to tell you that everything Rosie said is true. These places that she spoke of are planets, systems, stars and galaxies. They are named by those who inhabit them."

"Dear God," Sister Mary muttered.

"Yes. Well, some believe that, Sister. And some don't. But that's another discussion we might have someday. Anyway, first you must grasp the concept that what we call the vast universe is real and actually way beyond our earthly idea of vast. And, as some have proposed, it is filled with, actually teeming with, life. These names that Rosie told you are what we call the beings and places. We made them up from sounds we heard, or that are telepathed to us, or, in some cases, the appearance of things we remembered from going to planetariums here on Earth along with help from Bonnie and Eva, who were once teachers. Obviously, as you might imagine, the humanoids, and other, let's say, species that we have met do not speak English. Many are travelers whose experience of the universe makes our concept of it seem pathetically primitive."

Sister Mary and Father Bernard were numb. Freida's instinct was correct. They had no ability to comprehend what she had just communicated to them.

The water kettle whistled, indicating it had reached a boil. The sound jarred Father Bernard to focus.

"Ok, uh, then what you are saying," the priest began, "is that you, what, flew...traveled somehow to other stars and planets? That Eva and Bonnie and Gina have gone off to other galaxies?"

"Exactly, Father!" Nicole said enthusiastically. "Stars and planets and galaxies. It all began when Rosie answered the ad."

"What ad?" Sister asked.

"For mail-order brides," Rosie said, smiling and lifting her eyebrows as though she were a child pleading guilty to a prank, which, in fact, she was. "It was in *Women Pumping Iron*."

Father Bernard made that sound again. But this time it came out as a high-pitched whimper of confusion. "Huh?" And then softly, he asked, "Pumping Iron?"

"It's a magazine I discovered at the hospital when we were volunteering. I saw this ad and sent away...you know...to kind of brighten things up a bit. Everyone seemed sort of bored. Anyway, it was an ad for mail-order brides."

"In distant locations," Freida said.

"For miners and farmers," Julie added.

"The thing was, well..." Rosie again smiled slyly, "the ad didn't say how distant they really were."

"And how distant was that?" Sister asked.

"Kind of very far," Rosie admitted.

"And then some," Freida said.

"Light years, actually," Nicole informed her former superiors.

Father Bernard shook his head again as he tried to find a place in his brain to put Nicole's description of light years as far. To his mind, and beliefs, the concept of light years might as well have been mythology.

"All right. Enough! Is this your idea of some kind of weird joke, ladies?" the suddenly pragmatic Sister Mary Francis asked. She felt it had all gone too far. She had convinced herself that they all took off on some extended holiday during the storm three years ago. "What you are talking about...All this space travel stuff? It's a bad joke. People were worried. Distraught. For God's sake, we thought you all were dead. I want to know what happened." She was so intent on ending what she believed to be a charade, and the fact that the ladies were seated and their bellies were out of sight, that she forgot about their appearing to be pregnant.

"This is not a joke, Sister," Freida said, pointing up toward the ceiling. "What we're saying is that the ad that Rosie answered was from up there."

"Ahh... You go to mountains," Bogdon said. Up to this point he was bursting with questions because he could not quite grasp where the ladies had actually gone.

"You go to Canada?" Sammy asked as he brought a tray with the tea, milk and sugar to the table.

"Space!" Rosie said firmly. "Why don't you listen? We went into space. The Milky Way. The stars. Planets. Galaxies. We boldly went to where no Earth humans had gone before!"

"You went into space?" Sister Mary Francis said slowly.

"Yes," Rosie told her. "To be precise, across our galaxy. Across the Milky Way."

"But how did you do that? I mean how could it be?" Father Bernard could not process the information.

"You see, Earth is on the outside edge of our galaxy," Julie explained. "The Marlinons...the ones who picked us up, live way on the other side."

"My husband was the one who placed the ad," Rosie admitted.

"But your husband passed away years ago," the confused priest said.

"Dr. Cohestle is my new husband."

"Ah-hah!" Sammy said as he passed around the teacups. "You marry plastic surgeon! He make you young faces."

"No, Sammy, dear," Rosie corrected. "He's a chemist, actually."

"This is craziness," Father Bernard said.

"No, Father," Sister Mary told him, "it seems clear to me." She had decided to let the game play out. "They've married space people."

"Space people, Sister?! Are you serious?"

"Sister is right, Father," Nicole told him. "We were picked up by a spaceship from a planet called Marlino."

"It's in the Virgo system," Julie said. "It's pretty far in terms of light years; well, that's relative, I guess. Their sun is a star they call Boorin. Hydra's the system I live in. I can tell you, it blew my mind. I mean when we realized we were actually on a spaceship...well..."

"We were very upset and confused," Freida admitted. "Really frightened. I mean, who wouldn't be?" But her tone of voice was filled with excitement.

"Dr. Cohestle was charming," Rosie said. "I think I fell in love with him then and there. Anyway, he had placed the ad as an agent for others. Like it said—miners and farmers. I was the first to respond to it, so naturally he came and got us."

"Naturally," Sister Mary said sarcastically.

"We were discombobulated," Freida said.

"I was scared, but it was surely wondrous!" Nicole admitted.

"So the old ladies go on spaceship," Bogdon muttered, almost to himself, but they all heard. He was still trying to catch up on some words that he didn't quite understand.

"Of course, when Dr. Cohestle learned about what Rosie had innocently done," Freida said, "and he offered to return us to Earth immediately. And immediately I said yes."

"Me too," Julie admitted.

"But Bonita..." Rosie said. "You know how she is. She became very curious. I mean it's not every day you wind up on a spaceship."

"That very true," Sammy agreed.

"Eva was also in no rush to leave," Julie chimed in. "She started asking about the ship and planets and where we might be going."

"And Gina," Nicole added. "Gina wanted to know about the men who were waiting for us."

"What happened then, slowly but surely," Rosie went on, "was that we came to realize that what we were being offered was, well, something very unique."

"I can understand that," Sister Mary said softly, playing the game.

"A different life from the one we had here, Father," Julie told the priest. "A chance at a fantastical adventure. Nothing close to it in our quiet lives. Well, maybe it wasn't so quiet for all of us. I mean, Eva had the war in Europe, and Gina was a showgirl in Vegas and a, uh, madam at the Sunrise Inn, but imagine the prospect of meeting all kinds of other beings. And some who were not humanoid, as the good doctor explained. Uncountable worlds. Cultures. Civilizations. Beliefs. And eventually," Julie said, rising and patting her swollen stomach, "something we all, other than Rosie, had missed here on Earth. Having children."

At that moment, at the sight of Julie's pregnancy, Sister Mary Francis felt a chill run down her spine. The idea that these three ladies were telling the truth moved her to shudder and silently pray for God's help.

Also, at that moment, the Destroyer USS Metz, a new DDG-1000 class upgraded prototype, was on its third shakedown cruise, heading due south through a sea of light swells, closing in on the port of Wilmington. The captain, a twenty-two-year veteran of Iraq One, Two and Afghanistan, had received an order to investigate an unknown vessel, or possible electrical anomaly, as the Commander of the Blossom Point Naval Station for Space Technology had put it. He was in his observation chair on the bridge when the first officer brought him a mug of fresh, hot, black coffee.

"Thanks, Bob," the captain said, taking the mug. He sipped the coffee. "Nice and hot. At least we know the coffee urns work," he joked.

"Among a few other things, sir. We've been trying to raise that unidentified on long range and from the satellite downlink. So far, nada."

"I'm not surprised. Those guys in Space Tech can't wait for an alien invasion. They hope every UFO blip is men from Mars."

"We're zeroing in. Wilmington is ten minutes down the pike. Do we launch a chopper?"

The captain finished his coffee. "Not yet. Let's settle off a few miles and poke around with the upgraded radar and sonar packages."

"Okay, Skipper. Probably drugs, huh?"

"Oh yeah. More than probably." The captain slipped off his chair. "I'm going to get a refill. Take the bridge."

"Aye, aye sir." The first officer took the chair. "Back down to twenty knots," he told the helmsman, "and change course to one-five-nine."

"Twenty knots; one-five-niner," the helmsman repeated. He then punched a few buttons on the console in front of him and adjusted steering to the new course.

Back at the Residence, the door from the dining room swung open and two of the residents, Lynn Ferrari, age sixty-six, and Debra Dix, age seventy-one, came rushing into the kitchen. The two women, who were known for making night visits to the freezer for ice cream, stopped short when they were confronted by the gathering at the kitchen table.

"Oh, dear!" Lynn uttered. She was embarrassed.

Debra was not. "Father, Sister, Sammy, Bogdon...working late? Or are we interrupting a private...?" She stopped and stared at the three younger women who were seated at the table. Her jaw dropped; her eyes widened. She took off her trifocals and rubbed her eyes. "Is that Rosie?" she muttered softly from the back of her throat.

"What did you say?" Lynn asked.

Debra Dix was very bright. And athletic. She had worked her way up from park ranger at the Great Smoky Mountain National Park on the North Carolina side of the Tennessee-North Carolina border to promotions and management posts at the Grand Canyon, Yellowstone and Gettysburg National Parks. But her love was always the mountains where her career began. So at the end of her career, she returned, worked three years and retired. Debra, like many of the women at the Residence, was a widow. She met her husband of forty-four years after he mustered out of the Marines in 1970. He had fought in Vietnam and had been exposed to Agent Orange. He'd died quickly of pancreatic cancer four years ago. Before that, they had traveled extensively. Also, like so many residents, they had no children.

"Jesus!" Debra said, ignoring Lynn's question. She put her glasses back on and looked directly at Rosie. "Can that be you?"

"Who can be who?" Lynn asked, frustrated. "What are you talking about?"

Debra raised her right hand and pointed. "Rosie!"

Lynn Ferrari's gaze followed to where Debra's finger was pointing. She was confused to see it was a young looking woman sitting with Father and Sister being called Rosie, a forgotten contemporary. "Rosie? Rosie Conlon?" she asked. "Are you crazy, Deb?"

Lynn Ferrari's last job had been as a reporter on The Fayetteville Observer, *North Carolina's oldest newspaper that is still published. It was started in 1816 and survived Union General William T. Sherman's march to the sea during the Civil War.*

Her career as a journalist began as a cub reporter for the New York Post *after graduating from the City College of New York with a BA in English. Her father was an editor on* Life *magazine and got her the job through his contacts. Lynn married, had two daughters, and became a stay-at-home-mom. She kept her finger in the journalism pie doing features for local New Jersey papers. Her husband, Leopold, whom she met through her cousin Angie from New Jersey, owned and operated two eighteen-wheeler tractor-trailers with his best friend Don Freeman. Both men drove.*

With her girls grown, and out of the house, Lynn went back to work full-time for the Newark Star-Ledger. *What she didn't know was that Leopold and Don were running a side business of smuggling cigarettes up from Virginia for a local Mafia family. On a trip up from Virginia to Wisconsin, Leopold's truck was pulled over by federal agents from the U.S. Department of Justice's Bureau of Alcohol, Tobacco, Firearms, and*

Explosives at the Kentucky border and searched. He was sentenced to seven-and-a-half years under federal sentencing guidelines in the medium security federal correctional institution in Bennettsville, North Carolina. Lynn sold their house in New Jersey and moved to Charlotte to be close to Leopold while he served his time. He served his full sentence. But when he came out, he revealed that he was a bitter and changed man who showed none of that whenever she visited him. He was convinced that he had been set up. They argued constantly. Within less than a year, they were divorced.

Lynn stayed in Charlotte where she had found a job writing features for the Charlotte Sun Times. *Leopold went back to New Jersey where he got involved in smuggling again. This time he was a victim of a hijacking during which he was fatally wounded.*

Lynn stayed in Charlotte for several years and then took the job on The Fayetteville Observer. *She retired to the Residence three years ago. Her daughters and grandchildren visited her once a year. She was a quiet, introspective person who was secretly writing a novel based on her husband's illegal activities.*

Rosie, Julie and Freida simultaneously slid their chairs back and stood up.

"Julia...Freida..." Debra whispered. Lynn heard her.

"No, Deb. Look, they're pregnant!" Lynn exclaimed. "They can't be..."

"I can see that they're pregnant," Debra scolded. "I'm not blind."

Father Bernard attempted to ignore the fact that Debra thought she had recognized Rosie, and that the three ladies had stood up and revealed their condition as though it was natural and acceptable.

"Well now, Lynn and Debra," he said cheerfully. "These are some possibly new residents."

"For God's sake, Father, they're pregnant and..." Debra fired back.

"Wait a minute," Lynn interrupted. She stepped toward Nicole. "I know...Why that's...you're Nicole!" she gasped.

Nicole's only response was to smile. Lynn frowned and came closer to the table. She squinted and looked at the four strangers for a long, silent moment. Her frown became a smile that broke out into a huge grin.

"Yes! Nicole. I can see that. My God, what happened to you?" she asked as she hugged the novitiate.

Meanwhile, Debra came closer to the three pregnant women. "Rosie? Julie? Freida? Yes! That is you hiding behind those younger faces."

"Yes, Deb, it's us," Rosie said and she stepped around the table and embraced the older woman. "We're home."

"Oh, my dear Lord!" Lynn shouted as the realization finally sunk in. "It's them! They're home! Wait 'till I tell everyone!" She turned and ran out of the kitchen.

"Wait, Lynn!" Father Bernard called out. But she was already at the door and through it.

"Now we're in for it," Sister Mary Francis moaned. Father Bernard sat down and stared into his empty tea cup.

"More tea, Father?" Sammy asked.

"I think maybe a glass of brandy for Father would be better," Bogdon suggested.

The Metz was at stop-engines in a calm sea as its new, hi-tech MFR, Multi-Function Radar, scanned the sea and horizon for 360 degrees. It launched an AUV, an Autonomous Underwater Vehicle, for a detailed sonar probe of the ocean floor. The search had been going on for an hour. The captain and first officer studied the readouts being sent up from the battle room below onto two large screens on the bridge.

"That's the final sweep, sir," the first officer confirmed. "No space creatures in the area," he said with a smirk.

"I'm shocked," the captain responded sarcastically. "Okay. Report to Norcom and then let's get back to our mission. So much for today's war of the worlds. Tomorrow they'll probably have us looking for Godzilla."

"Aye, aye, sir." The first officer turned to the seaman at the helm. "Return to course two hundred degrees north-northeast. Thirty knots ahead."

As the Metz pulled away, a large section of the ocean floor moved slightly. A blue glow that outlined a huge teardrop shaped object beneath the sandy bottom appeared, followed by a rainbow flash around its edges.

And then it was gone.

CHAPTER SEVENTEEN

Q & A

The tables in the dining room had been moved to the side near the windows, and the chairs set up in four neat rows. All of the residents sat there, facing Rosie, Julia and Freida who were seated in front of them on a sofa that Sammy and Bogdon had moved in from the lounge. Luckily, no one had been out and about when Lynn took off from the kitchen to spread the word.

At Freida's urging, Father Bernard and Sister Mary Francis had rushed to gather everyone as quickly as possible before word leaked out beyond the walls of the Residence. Sammy and Bogdon pitched in, going room to room, in many cases waking up those who were already in bed.

Initially, the reunion with their three disappeared, and presumed dead friends, was highly emotional. Tears were shed. Embraces, long and tight, lingered as the residents were overwhelmed. At first, they found it difficult to believe the miracle they held in their arms, and then, unwilling to let go for fear that what they had lost three years ago in the storm would not be real. After fifteen minutes of cries of delight and innumerable questions, Father Bernard clapped his hands to get everyone's attention.

"Ladies. Please. We all have such joy in our hearts this wonderful night. The best way to answer all your questions is to stay as calm as possible. So please be seated and let us first hear what has happened to Rosanne, Juliette and Freida, in their own words. Please. Let us all sit down and listen."

The ladies silently agreed and took their seats. They ranged in age from four in their late fifties, to most in their late sixties and early seventies. Two were in their eighties. There was a lot of life's experience and wisdom in the room. All of these women were either widowed, divorced or had never married. All had gone through menopause decades ago. Few had children, grandchildren or extended families. Those who did were mostly estranged from them. Although they came from diverse backgrounds and experiences, at this stage of their lives they had made the similar decision not to live out their remaining days alone. The Residence gave them a comfortable home, care and companionship.

Father Bernard, Sister Mary and Nicole stood off to the side. Sammy and Bogdon, who had helped set up the room, were in the kitchen preparing coffee, tea and a snack of pound cake and butter cookies for what the staff knew would be a long evening.

As in the kitchen, Julia and Freida chose Rosie to start telling their story. She stood up, gesturing with her hands spread apart, and immediately explained, in a calm voice, that Eva, Gina and Bonita were well and thriving.

"I will tell you where they are shortly, but right away let me say that they are not in a, uh, in a family way. Pregnant, that is, as we three obviously are."

In spite of the priest's plea, there were immediately a dozen questions flying at Rosie.

"How did that happen?"

"How could that possibly happen?"

"Who are your husbands?"

"Where are your husbands?"

"Were you kidnapped?"

Sister Mary began to step forward, with her arms poised to wave and her mouth opening to stop the questioning. But Nicole stopped her, and then stepped in front of Rosie. She put her fingers to her mouth and blew out a loud whistle that silenced the room.

"Ladies," she began, in a voice they did not connect with the quiet, shy and inexperienced teenage novitiate they knew three years ago. A lovely, mature young woman, with a commanding presence, stood before them. "Our story is going to be hard to believe. Three years have passed and you were all told that we were dead. You must be bursting to know everything. We understand that, and you will have answers. But you must believe that it is best told by us, in sequence. There will be time, days and weeks, ahead, when every question will be answered to your satisfaction. Now please, if you can hold off and give Rosie your attention that will be best."

Nicole stepped back. The room was quiet. The residents settled in their chairs. A few were not happy to have been scolded by someone more than fifty years their junior.

"So," Rosie began again, smiling, "like I said, your friends, Eva, Gina and Bonita are well, thriving, happy and not pregnant. Obviously, we three are well and thriving and pregnant. And I speak for all of us when I say, we are very happy. Now to the beginning..."

Rosie explained her mischief in answering the ad, their abduction and decision, as she put it, "to continue with the adventure." She did not immediately get into the names of beings, humanoid and other, planets, systems and galaxies.

"A lot of what happened after that is, well, sort of technical in that they, I mean the people, uh, humanoids who placed the ad, had to be sure we were able to travel into space. So they had to physically check us out."

One thing, unknown to the audience, was that while Rosie spoke, Julia, Freida and Nicole were communicating with her telepathically. They were feeding her the thoughts and feelings that they were able to pick up from the residents, staff and management who were there.. It was an ability they had decided to keep to themselves for as long as they were on Earth. Unspoken questions, some of them gynecological, popped up. Three of the residents wondered if this was the same thing that had happened to other people who, over the years, maintained they were taken by aliens and reported being "probed."

"The physical exam was really simple. They had this wand kind of instrument that they passed in front of us. In case you're wondering, we were all dressed. The results showed we would be able to travel, with certain, as they put it, adjustments."

Julie picked up a thought from a resident named Isabella Johansson who wondered if the adjustments were surgical alterations that somehow allowed them to get pregnant.

"These adjustments," Rosie continued, hearing Isabella's thought forwarded by Julie, "were molecular—actually, more on a cellular basis. Putting it another way, our bodies were cleansed of the pollutants and poisons humankind has put into our air, water and soil, and thus, into what we breathe, drink and eat. The adjustments purified our bodies and strengthened us. As a result, our organs, systems, blood, tissue and bones were rejuvenated to a state of well-being that an untainted environment would have given us naturally."

While Rosie continued to explain, Julie, Freida and Nicole picked up a wave of jealousy, and some anger, from several residents who felt cheated out of what might have been better health and longer lives had the planet not been polluted. Others thought back on husbands and loved ones who had died young and wondered if such processing would have saved lives.

Some of the women felt shame for not having spoken up against the polluters and those who denied that the planet was warming from carbon emissions.

Rosie got those thoughts and feelings, but there was nothing she could say to assuage them. It would do no good to tell how other humanoids in the Universe had realized the potential of extinction these problems contained, and solved them. She quickly moved on to how they were taken to Marlino; how Dr. Cohestle introduced them to the humanoid males from other planets who were waiting for them; how, during the first year, she and Julie and Freida fell in love and found mates while Eva, Gina and Bonita did not, and, when offered, chose to travel. Then she paused because that was as far as they had gotten with Father Bernard, Sister Mary, Sammy and Bogdon before Debra and Lynn came into the kitchen.

At that point, the four travelers rapidly and silently communicated as to what to do next. They decided that rather than impart detailed information, they would now open the floor to questions. Their reasoning was that there were so many amazing things they had seen and learned, and beings that they had met, that they felt Earth humans would not be prepared to comprehend, or accept, that kind of information. This was based on their initial hesitancy to believe some of what their eyes, ears and hearts told them was heretofore impossible. The reality, the truth, about who they were, where they lived, and their current place in the development of humanoid life, might be incomprehensible , or even frightening, to a religious, close-minded, Parochial world.

Abigail Rubin, an eighty-two-year-old woman who had been at the Residence longest, was the first to stand when Father Bernard opened the floor to questions.

Abigail was a kind of celebrity at the Residence. She had enlisted in the Army at the age of twenty, during the Korean War. She remained in service for thirty-five years and retired as a full colonel. Her second career, as she called it, was philanthropy. Three weeks after retirement, fate stepped into her life when she bought a winning lottery ticket that, after taxes, gave her a cool $6,773,487.26. When she reached the age of seventy-eight, she had spent down all of that money, the income from it, and half of her pension by giving college scholarships to deserving veterans. She had been awarded the Medal of Freedom by President William Jefferson Clinton. She never married, though she had many proposals after her bonanza. She had no children of her own. She maintained that those recipients of her scholarships were all her children.

The three women got up from the sofa to answer questions.

"How did you get younger?" Abbie, as Abigail was called, asked.

"That was a result of the processing," Julie answered. "Dr. Cohestle said it was possible; that it might happen, but since the Marlinons experience processing differently, what would happen to humanoids was inconclusive, Abbie. It took some time, about three months as I recall, before we began to notice any outward physical changes."

"My mate, my husband," Rosie explained, "his name is Cohestle, he's sort of what we might call a medical professional here, so I call him doctor... Anyway, he explained that in our case, the processing took some time to initiate certain chemical and physiological changes in our bodies. So we were rejuvenated internally, so to speak, and that allowed us to travel in space. It just took a little longer to actually manifest that rejuvenation externally."

"But, in my case," Nicole added, "because I am, well, younger," she smiled, "I required less processing. I seem to be aging normally."

"You've aged beautifully, dear," Abbie told her.

"Were you scared, Jule?" Carol Walkley stood and asked Julie. They had been good friends. She was the only resident who called Julie "Jule."

Originally from Gary, Indiana, Carol Walkley had worked in a steel mill there as the first woman Melter, the person who made the decision when to tap the molten steel from the electric arc furnaces. When the mill shut down in 1980, she became a union organizer and moved to Gardendale, Alabama, to work there in the union office of the USW (United Steelworkers). She was sixty-eight, and never married. She carried the nickname of Bunny, but never explained why to the residents.

"Oh yeah, Bunny," Julie answered. "You bet I was scared. But those folks on the ship were really nice. I mean they didn't exactly look like us, but close enough so that part of it wasn't scary. I mean they didn't look like the movies make people from space look. And they spoke English, which made it kind of easier. And then when Bonnie began to ask lots of questions and the Marlinons began to show us some of what we might see and do, well, it was so darn interesting... I mean really awesome, Bunny, so I guess I just forgot to be scared."

"I can imagine you would, Jule," Carol said. "You look great. I envy you. All of you." A low murmur of agreement rose from several of the residents.

A resident named Allison Sterner stood up. She was a sixty-five-year-old widow from Tennessee who had lost her husband and two children in a tornado many years ago. She kept the farm, but never remarried. Six years ago she sold it. She was one of the women whose thoughts about speaking out against those who were polluting the planet and affecting the weather were picked up by Rosie, Julie, Freida and Nicole. She had flashed back on the F-5 twister that had taken her family.

"You said that the processing that these, uh, space creatures..."

"They're called Marlinons, dear," Rosie corrected Allison, politely. "I'm actually a Marlinon myself now. "

"Okay. Whatever. So was it this processing that made it possible for you all to conceive?"

"We think so," Freida answered. "It rejuvenated us, like Doc Cohestle said, but it also sort of reversed the aging process. In other words, things started to work again that had shut down. I guess all of us here have experienced menopause. Well, not you, Father," she said, smiling at him.

"Not me," Sammy added.

"Me too," Bogdon agreed.

"But our getting pregnant wasn't planned. It sort of just happened," Freida admitted. "It was quite a surprise."

"A very pleasant surprise," Julie agreed.

"Why did you come back?" a voice from the last row asked. The woman, tall and attractive, stood up. She was someone that the travelers did not know.

"A good question. You must be new here," Rosie remarked.

"About two-and-a-half years. I'm Lois Carlson. I'm from Asheville. I've heard so much about the way y'all just vanished. It was scary...I mean I kept thinkin' well, whatever happened to y'all might happen again. I found that downright disturbin' for a while. But then, most people stopped talking about it and we all forgot."

"Except today," Sister Mary Francis interjected. "We always say a special prayer on the anniversary. That was today. At dinner."

Lois Carlson was one of those people who never strayed far from her roots. She was born, raised and schooled in the town of Woodfin, North Carolina, north of Asheville. She was a tall, awkward, gangly girl who morphed into a long-legged, shapely, Blue Ridge Mountain beauty. She attended the University of North Carolina, Asheville, earning a Bachelor of Science Degree in Forestry Management. During that time, her closest girlfriend and roommate urged her to enter the Miss Asheville contest, which to her surprise, she won. That led to the Miss North Carolina pageant, which she did not win. But as a result, she had the pick of any young

man on campus, or for that matter, in the state. Yet she never married.
Some rejected suitors spread rumors that she preferred the company of
women to men. The fact was that she was interested in neither gender.
Perhaps she was just a-sexual. No matter, she decided to devote her life
to the preservation of the forest, and species therein. She joined the National
Park Service, eventually working in the Biological Resource Management
Division (BRMD), focusing on ecosystem restoration and management
in the Great Smoky Mountain National Park, a few miles from her birth-
place. Her areas of expertise were pest management, invasive species,
and threatened and endangered species.

"Yes, Sister Mary. That is surely true. It was in my thoughts today.
Well, anyway," Lois Carlson went on, "from what I hear so far, y'all been
havin' a ball out there in space. So, like I said, why'd you come back?"

"That's an important question, Lois," Freida answered. "Nice to meet
you. Coming back has to do with rules, you might call them, out there
in space among the travelers. One of the most important rules, we
learned after we three got pregnant, is that, whenever possible, babies
conceived from inter-humanoid, mixed marriages we might say here,
should be born on the mother's home planet."

"Experience has taught all the known travelers, like the Marlinons,
that doing so is for the infant's protection," Rosie explained. "They've
found the survival rate is much higher that way." There was a long
moment of silence as the word *survival* sunk in.

CHAPTER EIGHTEEN

Where Do We Go From Here?

The Q & A went on well into the night. Whenever the subject matter came around to things that were personal, such as what their husbands were like, or could some of the residents join them—the four women deferred direct answers to those questions to when their situation in the next few weeks became safer. What this meant was that their presence had to be kept secret. If word got out that four of the seven missing ladies, presumed dead, were actually alive, it would gain immediate national attention. If where they claimed to have been "taken" was exposed, doubts, interrogations, quarantine and accusations, from lying to dementia, would be proposed and an investigation instigated. Certainly the local and state police would jump in, as well as a bunch of self-serving politicians—especially the Washington grandstanders in Congress. Add that to the fact that three women in their seventies were pregnant, and in a Catholic Retirement Home, and then certainly, total media pandemonium would ensue. The residents and staff understood and promised to keep the secret.

Well past midnight, Rosie, Julie and Freida, wearing borrowed nightgowns, robes and slippers from residents, and Nicole, barefoot and wearing jeans and a polo shirt borrowed from Sammy, relaxed on the porch in wicker chairs. It was a cool autumn night with no moon and a brilliant display of the heavens above. The women were not chilled, nor tired. During the Q & A, they had explained that their rejuvenated health did not require as much rest as before. Father Bernard and Sister Mary were with them, dressed warmer and more tired, but still quite excited at the ladies' homecoming and story.

"I think everyone accepted it very well. Far easier than I did," Father admitted.

"I thought they might be jealous," Sister said. "Certainly there were doubts at first. But your descriptions and, well, your condition, clinched things."

"Of course we imagined there would be an initial shock, but we figured, after all, they are our friends," Freida said.

"And we were right," Julie added.

"God moves in such wondrous ways," Sister Mary commented wistfully.

"Yes, He does," the priest agreed. He noticed that Nicole was gazing up at the stars. She had a faint, peaceful smile on her face. He was about to ask about God out there among those beings they had met, but Rosie, sensing that was coming, interrupted his thoughts.

"We need your help, Father...Sister Mary," Rosie said firmly.

"Yes. Of course. What can we do?" Father asked.

"We are all due to give birth in about three weeks. That's assuming the gestation is like it would be on Earth."

"Could it be different?" Sister asked.

"Possibly. But so far, so good," Julie offered. "Doc Cohestle thinks it should be okay."

"That's good. And afterwards, how will you go...uh, I mean how will you get back home?" Father Bernard asked, gesturing to the starry, autumn night sky.

Nicole looked anxiously at Rosie and sent her a message, reminding her to be careful. But Rosie was way ahead of the young woman.

"Oh, they'll come and pick us up," Rosie said casually.

"I see. Well, in the morning I'll make arrangements at Sisters of Mercy Hospital in Raleigh and..."

"That's not exactly what we had in mind, Father," Julie said, interrupting him.

"We'd like to have our babies right here," Rosie clarified.

"Not in a hospital?" Sister asked.

"It's like we said before. Please remember. This must all be kept a secret, Father," Rosie said firmly.

"I don't understand. You're going to give birth. You three look young enough to be mothers. I mean we know you're not really young... but, I guess you are, and so who would know?"

"We just can't take that risk," Freida said.

"But then where? The care you will get in a hospital is certainly far better than..."

Rosie cut him off. "It can't happen, Father Bernard. You see, well, the babies might not be exactly what the hospital is used to."

"What does that mean, Rosie?" Sister Mary asked.

"The fact is that our husbands...well, they're sort of different and so—"

It was Father Bernard's turn to interrupt. "Different? What do you mean, different?"

"Let's just say, for now, it's best done privately," Nicole began to explain, "If the media ever found out..."

"We discussed that before," Sister Mary interrupted. "What can be so wrong with three fortyish women having babies?"

"It could become a media circus," Nicole said, finishing her thought.

"Nicole is right. It's too risky," Rosie added. "Imagine, three middle-aged, single women from a Catholic Residence having babies? You would have to explain that. And who are the fathers? Where are they? In outer space? Really, Father? Our babies would have no peace. We would be questioned. Perhaps ostracized. The church would be ridiculed. The Vatican would—"

Father Bernard raised his hands in surrender. "Okay. Okay. I get it. But having your babies here? We'll need help. Doctors, equipment..."

"And the residents?" Sister Mary asked, concerned. "Can they all really keep it a secret? Some go out to the movies and museums. Some have families that visit. We can't control all that."

"They've promised to keep our secret," Nicole said.

"I don't think we can count on that. You heard what Lois Carlson said; that she envies you all. I think that..." Father Bernard paused as he teetered on a decision. They all waited. "Okay. Here's what has to happen. We speak to Monsignor Draper. He has discretionary funds and connections. I pray he will understand."

The four women silently exchanged their concerns about expanding the circle of those who knew about them. It was something that they, along with Eva, Gina and Bonnie had discussed at length. They knew coming back to Earth to give birth would be difficult to keep a secret. But if the bishop, who at times took their confession, would treat this situation the same way, with his vow of the seal of confession, then he might facilitate everything required. There was much of their story that they had not yet dared to reveal.

Bishop Joseph Draper had not been told why Father Bernard wanted this meeting, only that it was urgent. The Monsignor respected the priest for the excellent job he did at the Residence, and for his management skills. They were good friends, and when alone, quite informal.

When the four women came into his study, he greeted them warmly as strangers and graciously offered them to sit on the sofa and chairs placed around a mahogany coffee table that matched his large desk. Once settled in, Father Bernard warned the bishop, before the four women spoke, that what he was about to hear was remarkable, but true.

After hearing the ladies' story, Bishop Joseph Draper, who was usually a jolly, soft-spoken man, took on the demeanor of a testy U.S. Senator. The sixty-year-old Monsignor was irritated and flabbergasted, but at the same time grasped the consequences this event would, if publicized, affect much of the church's dogma, ceremony and teachings. He was deeply concerned. His mind raced to find the words. Father Bernard, who by now had not only accepted the facts, but found them strangely uplifting, sensed the bishop's concern.

"Fascinating, isn't it, Joe?" the priest said, breaking the moment of silence in the room.

"Yes, Louis. To say the least. Good grief. I find this unbelievable. And yet, I see the truth of it before me and must accept what these lovely ladies say. The fact is that I recognize them, young as they now appear, from the last time we met...the day they disappeared." He took a deep breath and let it out quickly. "This is, well, Earth-shaking." He was excited. Of course we must keep this under wraps. No doubt about that. You are all correct. It would rock the world. It's absolutely amazing!" He then smiled and adjusted back toward his usual controlled demeanor. "It's wonderful to have you back, ladies. And to hear, to see, that you are well and...and...here." He chuckled. "So? These husbands of yours? Are they Catholic? At least Christian?" It was the first thing that had come to mind once he had accepted the story. He was immediately sorry he had asked. The ladies picked up his regret.

"You understand that they're from other planets, Monsignor Draper," Rosie said.

"Our Earth is not the center of the Universe," Julie added.

"Like we told you, it is vast. And filled with all kinds of...well, beings and civilizations and histories and, of course, beliefs."

"To answer your question, Monsignor," Nicole said, "so far, in our three years of limited travel, limited that is, compared to Eva, Gina and Bonita, we have not encountered any Catholics."

"Or Jews, Muslims, Hindus, Bahia, Shinto, Buddhists... well, maybe some close to Buddhists," Rosie quickly added. Although the ladies' answers were not said sarcastically, but rather informatively, the bishop felt he was being corrected as though he was a student in high school.

"Well, yes," he answered quickly, "not having been out there, you all do have me at a disadvantage."

"I'm sorry, Bishop Draper," Rosie told him. "I guess in our desire to explain such wonders, we might sound a little, well, arrogant. We don't mean to. You can surely imagine what a shock it was to see the reality that we, on Earth, are not alone in the Universe. Life is everywhere out there, beyond the imagination."

"What Rosie says is true, Monsignor," Nicole said. "We have learned to believe that life here is unique. But we now know we are not the only life that exists. So many of our core beliefs, religious, ethnic, nationalistic...well frankly, as we suddenly and clearly understood, so much of that was simply wrong."

"They have no faith? No belief in God?" the bishop asked.

"Some do," Freida answered. "I had converted to Reform Judaism years ago, but now, well, honestly I have no belief in man-made, organized religion. No offense, bishop, and there are such organized beliefs out there, but for me, well, I have yet to absorb, much less codify such beliefs. But for many that we've met so far, they view everything differently."

"Differently how?"

"Possibly as many ways as there are planets and systems," she told him. "We four have only visited a few. Bishop, there are millions! Perhaps billions."

"Billions?!" Bishop Draper exclaimed.

"Maybe even more," Nicole told him. "There are galaxies yet to be explored by travelers like the Marlinons. Even they have seen only seen a tiny part of this one, our Milky Way."

Father Bernard's concern was dealing with the problems of the present that confronted them, not a discussion of religion in the Universe. "Can you help with this, Joe?" he asked with some urgency. "Any ideas?"

"Well, ladies, I gather, compared to the circles you've been moving in for the past three years, my domain is somewhat smaller. And very Catholic. What you're suggesting is for me to conspire with you. To ask favors. To commit funds. To, quite honestly, risk exposing the church to...to God knows what. You're asking for the protection of the Church for, you'll excuse me, for what could be perceived as a joke—a science fiction tale that could give the enemies of our church damaging ammunition with which to hurt and discredit us."

"But it's not fiction!" Nicole said, frustrated. "Oh! I knew this would happen. For God's sake, look at them, Monsignor!" she said, pointing to the three pregnant women. "They are in their seventies and due to give birth in a few weeks. What further proof do you need?"

"I don't need proof, young lady. I believe you," Bishop Draper told her. "You are, were, what...a Novitiate? You know there are many who would wish our church and our country ill. They could turn this into a nightmare." There was no doubt that Bishop Draper was upset. "Today there is plastic surgery to hide aging, fetal implants, hormone treatments, cloning... Science plays with creation like a child with matches. There are things that we are against. There is doctrine, scriptures, liturgy, saints, baptism, catechism, confession..."

"Nicole, dear," Father Bernard interrupted, "what Monsignor is saying is reasonable. Most people think things like UFOs and life beyond Earth are nonsense. As I recall, bishop, you were once quite outspoken about mankind's place in the Universe."

"That was in the context of Jesus as God's only Son. An atheist reporter asked me if there is life on other planets would God have had a Son on every one of them."

"Or daughters?" Nicole asked.

"You forget that I am a Catholic Priest," Bishop Draper told her. "You are, well, you were a Novitiate. We believe that Jesus is God's only Son."

"But now I know that is *soooo* narrow-minded!"

"Nicole!" Rosie chided. "Monsignor Draper is right insofar as his experience goes. Please, let's deal with the problems at hand." She turned to the bishop. "You are correct, Monsignor. Our realities are now different from yours. We need your help. I suppose the question is, how we can prove our story to your satisfaction?"

"Is there a spaceship?" he asked.

"We were uh, just dropped off," Julie said quickly.

"Even if we prove it, their husbands aren't Catholic," Nicole said. Her tone was firm, but calmer.

"My dear Nicole," Bishop Draper said softly, like a priest might to a troubled parishioner. "You misunderstand me. I would never withhold aid and comfort to those in need, no matter who they were. Above all else, I am a priest."

"I'm sorry, Monsignor," Nicole said, pausing for a moment. "I do have an idea. The ladies are going to need medical help and a safe facility. Perhaps you know someone who could examine them. That might provide the proof you need." The bishop thought for a moment. The ladies read his thoughts, but kept quiet. Rosie winked at Nicole and sent her a "good idea" thought.

"Jimmy Bowmeister," Bishop Draper said. "Doctor Jimmy. He's a friend. What you call an OB/GYN."

"Can he be trusted?" Rosie asked.

"I've heard his confessions for more than twenty years. If I can keep his secrets, he can darn well keep mine."

Everyone laughed. Tension melted. Hope was in the air.

Sister Mary Francis was skeptical about the Monsignor's offer to investigate the matter further. But Father Bernard dismissed her negativity. He was encouraged by the bishop's offer to talk to his friend, Dr. Bowmeister. They were having coffee in the Residence office after dinner.

"They are going to meet tomorrow," he told the nun. "After the doctor examines the ladies, I'm sure things will move forward. I don't see any other possible outcome."

"You forget how conservative Bishop Draper is. He's quite adamant about allowing gay marriage. Imagine how he must feel about the ladies being married, or as they say, mated, to...to whom? Or to what, he must think? So don't get your hopes up, Louis. He's a political person. It wouldn't be the first time he avoided controversy or commitment beyond his vows."

Out on the porch, a very different conversation was happening. The three ladies were convinced that once examined, the bishop would come on board and help. Nicole was not so sure. She was aware that although she had barely finished high school, and the processing had not seemed to change her aging or physical development, it had somehow increased her intellect well beyond that of a far older woman. She had been the most affected by the discovery of a Universe teeming with life. While the ladies still held on to some Earth-human ideals, theories and memories, she had discarded almost all of hers. She fully enjoyed her sense of physical, emotional and intellectual power.

"I don't trust the bishop," she said quietly, glancing around to be sure no one was listening. Most of the residents were in their rooms watching TV. Some had gone to the movies or out to dinner. None were on the porch. "He's a conservative. What we revealed to him today really rocked his world."

"That may be true," Julie said, "but facts are facts. When that doctor, what's his name?"

"Bowmeister. Jimmy, he called him," Nicole told her.

"Yes, Bowmeister. Sounds German. Anyway, when he examines us, well, we know he's in for a few surprises."

"To say the least," Rosie said and lifted an eyebrow.

"But watch out," Nicole warned. "What he discovers might really spook the bishop."

"That's true," Rosie agreed. "We'll just have to wait and see. That brings me to another problem."

"Problem? You feeling okay?" Julie asked.

"Oh, yes. I'm fine. He's getting bigger every day," she said, tapping her belly. It was larger than the others. "It's my daughter and grandsons. I don't think it's fair anymore to let them think I'm dead and gone."

"You're not dead," Freida said. "But, in a way, you are gone. I mean, once we deliver, we're out of here. Right?"

"Absolutely," Rosie assured her. "But I want them to know. And I want them to share this wonderful event with me. They are my family, after all. So they'll be his family too."

"Don't you think that's dangerous," Nicole suggested. "I wouldn't dare tell my family. They would do anything to keep me here, including telling the world. Remember there are others involved, especially the Marlinons."

"Of course. Secrets will be kept. And I understand how you feel about your family, dear," Rosie said. "That's your choice, and you're most likely correct. But just as I'm about to give birth to my half-Marlinon son, I gave birth to my daughter, and she to my grandsons. They have a right to know they have a brother and uncle, don't you think?" Nicole shook her head, but said nothing.

"You should do what you think is right, Rosie," Julie told her friend. "I have no family, so I don't have that problem."

"Nor I," Freida added. "Whatever you decide, I'll accept."

"The question I have is how do I do it?" Rosie asked. They all kept their thoughts to themselves and pondered the problem. Finally, Nicole spoke up.

"I'm the obvious one to do it. I'll go and tell them in person. First your daughter. Cambridge, right?" Rosie nodded. "And the two boys?"

"Last I knew one was in California. Los Angeles, I think. And the other in Hawaii. Actually Maui. That's where he was when we left."

"Then an extended road trip is in order," Nicole said, getting up. "I'll need some money. Practicing that vow of poverty left me a pauper."

"Money's not a problem," Julie said. "I had a conversation with Father Bernard and asked him to do a little checking. It seems no one here ever notified Social Security, the bank or the brokerage where I had my investments about my, so-called, uh, disappearance. I imagine you two," she said, looking at Rosie and Freida, "are in the same boat. Father said he'd look into it discreetly. In any case, we've got some money."

"That may be, Julie," Nicole told her, "but your walking into the bank after three years is going to look strange. And if anyone there remembers our being sucked up into the tornado and thrown out to sea—not your everyday event—then the cat's out of the bag."

"You're right," Julie admitted. "So what do we do?"

"We ask for a loan from Abigail Rubin. She did win the lottery once, after all. Five or six million, I think."

"Six," Freida confirmed. "She gave most of it away."

"Most, but not all I think," Nicole said.

"Well, let's see. I'll ask her," Julie offered. "As far as our accounts go, I think we should keep it quiet until the good doctor Bowmeister convinces the bishop that we're on the up and up. Then we can find a lawyer to deal with that."

"My grandson Herbie, the one in Los Angeles, is a lawyer. My goodness, he must be twenty-seven by now," Rosie mused. "Maybe more."

"That works," Freida said. "What does the other one do?"

"Alex? He's a year younger. I'm not sure exactly. I think he was some kind of engineer or scientist. He went to work on a climate project in Hawaii. Molokai, I think. That's near Maui. Bananas..."

"Did you say he was bananas?" Julie asked.

"No. No... The job was about bananas. They grow them on Molokai. Anyway, he liked it there so much, he stayed nearby on Maui."

"I've always dreamt of going to Hawaii," Nicole said.

"The last time I was in Boston, my daughter showed me pictures of where Alex lives," Rosie told her. "It's beautiful. Tropical, like your farm on Roonio nine, Freida."

"Lots of people go to Maui on their honeymoon, Nicole," Julie said teasingly. "Is your Alex married, Rosie?"

"He wasn't three years ago."

The three women looked at Nicole and smiled. "What?" she asked. They didn't answer. She smiled back at them. "Playing matchmakers again? Like you did with that transport pilot from Gimm, Julie?"

"He was cute. We mated well," Julie answered.

"He was seven feet tall!" Nicole, who was five-foot-two, responded. "He would have crushed me if..." She hesitated and blushed.

"Don't knock it until you've tried it, honey," Julie told her, with a knowing wink.

CHAPTER TWENTY-ONE
A Doctor In The House

Bishop Draper poured a tall Scotch neat for his friend, Dr. Jimmy Bowmeister. It was a little after one o'clock on an unusually warm day for October. The OB/GYN was a gruff, self-assured man in his mid-fifties. They were in the bishop's residence, a comfortable cottage, three blocks from the church and only a block away from the Cape Fear riverfront shops and restaurants.

"Easy does it, Joe. I can still get nine holes in this afternoon."

Bishop Draper squirted a little seltzer into the glass. As he carried it, and a martini for himself, over to where the doctor sat at a small table next to a window, Mrs. Carol DePaulo, the bishop's dour house-keeper, came into the room with a tray of sandwiches and coffee. She eyed the drinks and frowned.

"Hello, Dr. Bowmeister," she said.

"Good to see you, Mrs. DePaulo. How're you these days?"

"Good enough not to have to visit you," she answered in such a way that Dr. Bowmeister wasn't sure if it was her little joke or an insult. She placed the tray on the table as the bishop arrived with the drinks and sat down.

"Thank you, Mrs. DePaulo," he said.

"Shall I pour coffee?" she asked.

"Not now. As you can see, we're having drinks." Carol DePaulo looked at her watch, frowned again and shook her head disapprovingly.

"I can see," she said, as she walked toward the door. "A little early in the day if you ask me," she muttered, just loud enough for the men to hear as she closed the door behind her.

"She's some piece of work, Joe," the doctor said.

"You don't know the half of it, Jimmy. But she's got a heart of gold."

The doctor raised his glass. "To Mrs. DePaulo and her golden heart. May it keep ticking forever."

"Good health, and God bless," the bishop responded. They clinked glasses, and then savored a long sip. The doc reached for a ham and Swiss cheese on a roll and took a hefty bite.

"So, what's up, Joe?" he asked as he munched.

"First off, Jimmy, I will have to ask you to perform an act of faith."

"Would that act require my checkbook?"

"No checks today. I need your solemn oath that what you see today will forever remain a secret."

"Is it your health, Joe?" he asked, concerned.

"I'm fine. Your word, Jimmy?"

"You have it, Monsignor."

"Good." Bishop Draper looked at his watch. "We've got a little time. Forget about those nine holes. Eat and drink up. And if what I show you today proves to be true, you may not have time for golf for quite a while."

The bishop took another long sip from his martini and picked up a sandwich from the tray. Dr. Bowmeister swallowed what he was chewing and had more Scotch. He set down the glass.

"So, you want to tell me about it?"

"Have another swallow of that Scotch, and then be prepared to hear the wackiest story you've *ever* heard. Guaranteed."

Two hours later, Bishop Draper and Dr. Bowmeister were in Father Bernard's office in the Residence. They had come from the nurse's office and first aid room where the doctor had examined the three ladies. Rosie, Julie and Freida sat on the sofa. Sister Mary Francis was in a chair next to them. Father Bernard had brought in two chairs from the dining room for the doctor and the bishop. Nicole preferred to stand next to the sofa. Father went to sit behind his desk as everyone settled in place.

Dr. Bowmeister smiled at the ladies who were smiling back at him, glowing with health and joy. He shook his head and nervously scratched his eyebrows, his demeanor, best described as stunned.

"So, Jimmy?" the bishop asked anxiously. "What do you think?"

"I think..." He paused, searching for the right medical words while trying to keep what he was really feeling, confusion and awe to himself. "I think that if the rest of the story checks out, well, then Joe, I think I've seen it all. It's downright incredible."

"So, they're pregnant?"

"Oh, yes. No doubt. These lovely ladies are indeed very pregnant."

"You're certain?"

"Joe. Please. I've been doing this for twenty-five years. They are pregnant and very near term. At their age, that is if they are really as old as you've told me..."

"They are, doctor!" Nicole said firmly.

"Absolutely," Sister Mary concurred.

"Well then, I don't understand...I mean, I know what you've told me, space and all that, but they shouldn't be."

"But we are, aren't we, doctor?" Rosie asked.

"You most certainly are Miss, uh, Mrs..."

"Mrs. Cohestle. But please just call me Rosie."

"Yes, you are, Rosie. Sitting right here in front of me. But, Jesus, Joe," he said, turning to the bishop. "Space? Planets? Galaxy? I'm trying to wrap my head around it. To understand..."

"Aren't we all, Jimmy? So, what do we do?"

"I have to do some tests. Sonograms, blood, amniocenteses. A complete work-up. And quickly."

"Can you do that here?" Nicole asked.

"No."

"How about your office?" Father Bernard asked.

"Not really. I know you want to keep this quiet, right?"

"Absolutely," the bishop said quickly.

"We must!" Freida added emphatically.

"Well then, okay. I'll need equipment, machines, a lab... Maybe some expertise I don't have."

"So what you're saying is that we will need more people who will have to know?" Julie asked. She passed her concern silently to Nicole, Rosie and Julie.

"What about the new wing at the Hanover Regional Medical Center, Bishop Draper?" Rosie asked. "You mentioned that to us after mass on the day we, uh, we left?"

"I remember that day. Yes. Well, almost. The official opening is scheduled for January second."

"That's not a bad idea, Joe. It has pretty much everything that I need there," Dr. Bowmeister said. "But is there any way we can get in and keep it quiet?"

The question forced Bishop Draper to commit before he was prepared to do so. The dilemma was that without the equipment, a final determination couldn't be made. And if the ladies' story proved to be true, they would need a private location to give birth and all that entailed. The new wing might just do the trick.

All eyes in the room were on Bishop Draper as he sat, looking down at the carpet, slowly nodding his head. He felt a rush of adrenaline rise up his spine. Was it panic, fear, or something else? He took a deep breath.

"It's possible," he said softly. He looked up and saw everyone looking at him. "It will take more people getting involved," he continued, stronger, "and, God willing, a great deal of luck." Everyone in the room was smiling. He felt the adrenaline rush again; only this time, he knew it was not panic or fear. It was excitement and joy.

Abigail Rubin was more than delighted to help finance Nicole's trip to Boston. But, she insisted that it was not a loan. However, if possible, she asked that it be considered as a down payment for her taking a trip to Marlino someday. Rosie couldn't promise that would happen, but assured Abby that they would make every effort on her behalf.

Rosie discussed getting in touch with her daughter with Father Bernard and Sister Mary Francis. Both were concerned about how Kate Conlon might react. The thought occurred to them that her hearing a voice on a phone, telling a fantastic story, could be construed as a prank or sick joke. And the fact that she lived so far away, perhaps in haste, Kate might contact the police. That was worrisome. But both the priest and nun agreed that Rosie's family had the right to know she was alive and well.

They also discussed Rosie calling one, or both, of her grandsons. That presented a secrecy problem as well. Would they believe her? How had their lives changed in three years? And Rosie couldn't even be sure that her daughter still lived at the same address. Perhaps she had moved. Or maybe married the Harvard professor she'd gone with to Atlantis that last Christmas and New Year's before the Marlinons showed up. Rosie knew that they had still been seeing each other when the ladies departed.

Nicole did some research. She contacted the Cambridge Board of Education, informing them that she was calling from the Wilmington Parish Retirement Home for Ladies. If anyone traced the call, they would find out that was true. She inquired if Kate Conlon worked at the chancellor's office. Yes, Kate was an employee. If, for some reason, the call was mentioned to Kate, and she called the Residence, Father Bernard was prepared to say they had discovered some of Rosie's clothes in storage and were wondering if Kate wanted them.

The final decision, and safest compromise, was for Nicole to go to Cambridge and meet Kate Conlon in person. She was to take a picture of her and Rosie together, holding a Wilmington newspaper to confirm that the photo was current. As further proof, Rosie gave Nicole a handwritten letter with a few facts about Kate that only Rosie would know, and recorded a short video on a smart phone that Allison Sterner, the widow from Tennessee, loaned to her, saying, "No one calls me anyway. I just use it in case of an emergency."

With the finances covered, and a plan agreed upon, Father Bernard rented a Honda Civic at Avis in Wilmington for Nicole to drive to Charlotte Friday afternoon. She stayed overnight at the Airport Ramada and took the eight o'clock, the first direct flight to Boston, the next morning. Being accustomed to travel at near light speed these past three years, Nicole experienced a strange sensation as the Boeing 575-200 lifted off the runway. She had never flown in an Earth-human aircraft before that. The comparative slow speed of takeoff, and the roar of the jet engines at full thrust to gain altitude, made her uneasy. The pull of gravity startled her for a moment. But by the time the plane reached cruising speed, she realized what was happening. She adapted and relaxed.

Three hours later, Nicole paid the cab driver in front of Kate Conlon Legum's apartment on Pearl Street, in Cambridge, Massachusetts. The front door of the apartment house was locked. A key, or buzzing up to an apartment, was required to get in. Nicole had planned for that possibility and as a contingency she had bought a few large stuffed animals and some magazines at the airport gift shop. They were in a large brown paper bag. When a tenant approached the front door, she came up behind him, struggling with the bulky bag. The man, in his mid-thirties, took out his key and opened the front door that led into the lobby.

"Could you hold that, please," Nicole begged, with both arms wrapped around the bag as though it was heavy. He held the door open for her. As she entered past him, she smiled coyly and said thanks. He went to the elevator. She feigned going to get her mail until he got into the elevator and the doors closed.

Kate Conlon's name and apartment, 4-C, was listed on the building's directory above the mailboxes. She set aside her brown paper bag, went to the elevator, and waited for it to come back to the lobby.

When Nicole got out on the fourth floor, she saw that there were only eight apartments. It was eleven-fifteen in the morning. She easily found 4-C in the middle of the hallway. The name Conlon was above the doorbell. She pushed the button, and to her surprise, a man opened the door—the same man who had let her into the building. Remembering her from a few minutes ago, he was as confused as she.

"Hi," was all he could manage.

"Oh, uh, hi. Is this four C?" she asked, looking away, up and down the hallway.

"Yes. Didn't I just let you in..."

"Kate Conlon. I'm looking for Kate Conlon," Nicole said quickly. "I thought this was her apartment."

"It is. Who are you?" Nicole was relieved. She picked up a few of his thoughts and put two and two together. *He's the Harvard professor. Maybe they did get married.*

"Oh, well, I'm a friend of her...uh, you see, it's a little complicated. I'm from Wilmington, North Carolina, and..."

"Arthur? Who is that?" a woman's voice from behind him asked.

Arthur stepped aside. Kate Conlon, looking much like the picture Rosie had shown Nicole from her holiday visit to Cambridge five years ago, appeared. "Did you say Wilmington?" Kate asked.

"Yes, Miss Conlon. From the Wilmington Parish Retirement Home for Ladies. May I come in?" Kate's spine tingled. Her face flushed.

"Yes. Of course," she said, gesturing for Nicole to come in. Arthur stepped aside, wondering where their mysterious visitor had put her large bag of groceries.

The apartment was a modest, but neat, one-bedroom with a service-able kitchen, living room/dining room and one bathroom. It was simply furnished with contemporary pieces. Kate led Nicole into the living room.

"May I sit down?" Nicole asked. Kate gestured toward a cushioned chair near the sofa. Nicole sat down. Kate and Arthur remained standing. The moment was awkward and tense.

"So you're from the, uh, the place where my mother...What can we do for you, Miss...?"

"I'm Nicole. Nicole Mallory. I used to work there." Nicole paused. She had rehearsed for this moment, and knew that the message, no matter how precisely delivered, would not be immediately accepted. And now, her words did not come easily. She realized that Kate, who was forty-eight, looked to be the same age as her mother, Rosie. Maybe younger.

"Well, you see," Nicole continued, "I was actually a novitiate at the Residence."

"I see," Kate said. Nicole saw Kate Conlon frown. She sensed the sadness Rosie's daughter felt. "And what can we do for you? I mean, why are you here?" Kate was still standing.

Nicole smiled. "It's really more of what I can do for you," Nicole told Kate, taking control of the moment. "Won't you sit down? It's a rather long story, but one that I am certain you will find both interesting and delightful."

A half-hour later, after showing Kate the letter, Nicole took out the cell phone that Allison Sterner had loaned to her, and showed Kate and Arthur the picture of her and Rosie, and another of the three pregnant ladies together, taken yesterday. The clincher was the video recording of Rosie, proudly showing her swollen belly as she delivered a message to Kate.

"My darling. I am so sorry for what my disappearing must have done to you and the boys. By now, Nicole has explained that it was my foolish prank that got us into...well, that made all this happen. That being said, if you can please, please, forgive me, and know that I am fine and that what is happening is for me, for us, simply wonderful. I want you and the boys to be here, in Wilmington, with me. Nicole can make the arrangements. I love you all, and miss you terribly. We are happy and well and living a fantastic experience. Please come to me. I love you so very much."

Kate broke down weeping. Arthur sat down and held her in his arms. He was crying too. The rest of the day was spent making plans and reservations. Rosie's grandsons, Herbie and Alex, were called. Kate told them that a special memorial was being held in Wilmington, and that they absolutely had to attend. Herbie, who had turned twenty-eight, and recently gotten engaged, wanted to bring his fiancée, Mara Walkley. Kate told him that as much as he wanted to bring her, this was for immediate family only. "It will only be a day or two," she told him. Alex, a year younger than Herbie, still lived in Maui, and was single. They would all meet in Wilmington in a week. Although Kate and Arthur were not married, Kate insisted that Arthur come with her. Having seen Kate's reaction to the situation, and not willing to leave Arthur behind to possibly leak the story, Nicole did not object.

CHAPTER TWENTY-THREE
Church Politics

The same day that Nicole left for Boston, Father Bernard, Bishop Draper and Dr. Bowmeister visited the new pediatric wing of the Hanover Regional Medical Center. The building stood apart from the main hospital and was only connected by a narrow footbridge in the third floor and an underground tunnel, so it was barely a wing. In fact it had its own loading dock and service elevator.

The administrator for new the pediatric center was Father Colm Malone, a conservative priest who had earned a Bachelor of Science in Hospital Management at Trinity College, Dublin, Ireland. He was a member of the Columban Fathers, and had extensive hospital management experience in South Korea. He had been at the main hospital for the past two years during construction of the wing. He referred to it as his, "Baby for Babies."

Before having a look at the new facility, the three men paid a surprise visit to Father Malone. They had to be sure that if they were to use a portion of the wing for the births, there would be trusted personnel and airtight security available. To that end, the administrator's cooperation was critical.

Father Malone greeted the three unexpected visitors enthusiastically. He knew Dr. Bowmeister as a respected OB/GYN who had privileges at the hospital, and Father Bernard from the women at the Residence who regularly volunteered. However, it was not often that Bishop Draper paid the hospital, or him, a visit. They settled in a conference room adjacent to Father Malone's small office. After pleasantries, the bishop got down to business. It had been decided that at this point, they would not give Father Malone the real story.

"Well, okay then, Colm," Bishop Draper said, clapping his hands together twice, "there's a definite reason why we're here today."

"I figured that much, Monsignor," Malone said. "You three walked in looking like you're on a mission."

"On a mission from God, Father," Bishop Draper said, doing a pretty good imitation of John Belushi and Dan Aykroyd in *The Blues Brothers* movie. Everyone in the room, except Father Bernard, got the joke and laughed. "But seriously, Colm," Bishop Draper went on, "we're here to ask a big favor."

"Whatever I can do, Monsignor."

"Good. Good. So, Dr. Bowmeister here, our friend Jimmy, has a few patients who require certain facilities, like those in the new wing, during the next few weeks."

"What about the main hospital? I mean, we're not to open until January."

"No, Colm. That just won't do."

"And why is that?" the priest asked suspiciously.

"They're famous. Sort of celebrities," Dr. Bowmeister answered, expressing a prearranged reason. "It's all got to be handled with the utmost care and secrecy."

"I don't understand," Father Malone said.

"These women, well, they aren't married, and they refused to have abortions," Father Bernard said, knowing Malone, a pro-lifer to the core, would approve. "I'm sure you understand."

"Of course. I wish every woman felt that way."

"We all do, Colm," Bishop Draper agreed. "Lord knows that. And, fortunately, the children are already spoken for by wealthy and loving families."

Father Malone nodded approvingly, but took a moment to think. Dr. Bowmeister added the final touch.

"The other thing is, Father, that two of these births may be a little difficult. Thanks to you, the new wing is state of the art. And, as you may remember, I recommended some of the new hi-tech equipment. It's exactly what I'll need to ensure positive and successful outcomes for these women."

"What do you need?" Father Malone asked.

Dr. Bowmeister leaned forward and looked into Father Malone's eyes. "Just two things, Father. Line up a small, experienced and trustworthy staff of obstetric and pediatric people for me to meet with in a few days, and keep this project to yourself. I'll give you most of the names that I think fit the bill. But I don't know any of the new technicians you've hired. We'll need a few of those for sonograms, CT scans and the latest blood and amniocentesis workups available. They don't need to know the reason for all this just yet. When you get it all together, I'll brief them myself."

Father Malone leaned back in his chair and nodded his head knowingly.

"This is highly irregular," he said, looking directly at Bishop Draper. The priest's expression and tone of voice left little to the imagination. The bishop had seen and heard it before. Politics was on the table. You don't get to be a bishop, and head of a dioceses, without understanding the nuances of politics.

"I know, Colm. And don't think it won't be deeply appreciated by me and, of course, the families of these wayward young ladies, one of whom, by the way, is related to Cardinal Antonio Napoli."

"The Undersecretary of State of the Vatican?"

"One and the same, Colm. And the man closest to Cardinal Poricelli."

"The one who prepares the lists of titles for the Holy Father?"

"Well, yes. That's part of Cardinal Poricelli's portfolio. But we both know that the titles Bishop and Archbishop, and even Cardinal, are one and the same. We are all bishops. But a title is a title, and some carry more, shall I say, influence? In any case, Colm, Cardinals Napoli and Poricelli are good men to have on your side."

Father Bernard nodded his agreement. Jimmy Bowmeister looked interested. Bishop Draper smiled. There was a moment of silence. Father Malone smiled back.

"When do you want to meet your team, Dr. Bowmeister?"

"As soon as possible. My patients are due to give birth within the next two weeks. I have to run some tests. In fact, is it possible to give us a little tour now? I'd like to see what I think you once described in a meeting as the heart of the wing. I believe it's on the third floor."

"The heart is correct, doctor. The wing was designed around a safe and efficient flow that is keyed to what happens on the third floor. That's where everything we are pledged to do is concentrated. It's where all of our leading-edge obstetrics and pediatrics are focused."

CHAPTER TWENTY-FOUR
Into The Wing

That night, a laundry truck drove up to the service and delivery dock at the rear of the new wing. It was a little before midnight. It carefully turned around and backed up to the loading dock platform.

Sammy Kim, who was driving, had borrowed the truck from his friend Lee, who drove it for the service that laundered the bed linens, tablecloths and napkins from the Residence. Sammy, and Chef Bogdon, got out of the cab and looked around. As arranged by Father Malone, the steel rollup door to the loading dock had been retracted. Inside, one light near the elevator was on. The two men walked to the rear of the truck, jumped up on onto the platform, and opened the rear doors. Seated inside, next to three large laundry hampers on wheels, were Father Bernard, Rosie, Julie and Freida. The three women wore slacks, light sweaters and flats. Nicole, still in Cambridge, was assisting Kate with travel arrangements to Wilmington for her sons, and Arthur.

Sammy, not familiar with the length of the truck, had left it a little short of the platform. The two men had to help the ladies and the priest to bridge the gap onto the platform. Once there, Father Bernard went to the elevator and pressed the call button. The floor indicator above the door showed that the elevator was on the third floor. It started to come down, showing it went from three to two.

"Okay," Father Bernard called out softly. "Let's get going."

Sammy pushed the hampers out to the rear of the truck, while Bogdon grabbed them and swung them onto the platform.

"You go first, Miss Rosie," Sammy said after the three hampers were off the truck. He held out his hand. Rosie took it. Bogdon was at her other side. She took his hand. Both men slipped their free hands behind Rosie's knees and clasped hands, making a seat.

"You lean back, Miss Rosie," Sammy told her.

"We have you good," Bogdon added.

As she leaned back, the two men lifted her up and into the laundry hamper. There was a clean white sheet in it.

"That was easy," she said. "You two are strong." Sammy smiled.

"You as light as a feather," Bogdon told her.

"I may be," she told them, "but this guy in here sure isn't," she said, patting her large belly.

"I guess you'll have a look-see at how big he really is tonight," the priest said. "The sheet is there to hide you, in the off chance we run into anyone." She pulled the sheet around her.

As Bogdon and Sammy helped Julie and then Freida into their hampers, the elevator arrived. "I'll wheel Miss Rosie to the elevator and hold it," Father told Sammy and Bogdon. "You guys wheel Miss Julie's and Miss Freida's chariots over there. Don't forget to tell them about the sheets."

When Father Bernard got to the elevator, he found a young man in a white laboratory coat standing inside. His hand was on the button to hold the doors open.

"Hi, Father. I'm Dr. Leslie Weiss." He put his hand out to shake. The priest took it. The doctor, no more than thirty, Father Bernard guessed, shook hands. The young doctor's hand had a strong grip.

"Louis Bernard. Nice to meet you, doctor." The priest took his hand away quickly. "The others are coming now."

Rosie grabbed the sides of the hamper and slowly stood up. "I'm Rosanne Conlon, doctor. Nice to meet you." They shook hands. Father Bernard noticed that Dr. Weiss's firm grip didn't bother Rosie. The doctor stared at her belly. "He's a big boy," Rosie said. Dr. Weiss just nodded, keeping his thought that this baby was enormous, to himself. Rosie picked up the thought, but said nothing. She sat down and pulled the sheet up around her.

"I'll see what's keeping them," Father Bernard said. He walked back to the platform, rubbing his aching hand and wondering why Rosie hadn't even flinched when Dr. Weiss shook her hand.

Julie and Freida were settling into their hampers when Father got to the platform. They were sitting down, but their sheets had to be unfolded. Sammy and Bogdon were doing that, but arguing about which way to do it.

"You take right side, Sammy. I have left."

"You have right. That my left. No...other way."

"My right or your right?"

"Okay. Enough." Father Bernard stepped in between them, and pointing to the correct sides of the sheet, got things straightened out and unfolded. "There's a Dr. Leslie Weiss waiting at the elevator with Rosie."

"Doctor Wizze? Must be smart doctor," Bogdon said.

"Not wise, like wise guy. Weisss." Father hissed the ss's, correcting the Polish Chef. "His name is Weiss. And watch out if you shake hands with him. He's got a grip like bear trap."

"I do that in Parchew Forest," Bogdon announced proudly.

"Shake hands?" Sammy asked.

"No, busboy. Trap bear."

Julie, who by now had picked up on the language and word games Sammy played with Bogdon, stood up in her hamper.

"You were in forest without clothes, Bogdon?" she asked.

Sammy laughed. "Bogdon Gruszniewski is naked bear hunter," he said, pointing at the chef.

"Some American names are hard for me." Bogdon repeated "Weiss" three times softly to himself.

"Enough of this, please," Father Bernard pleaded. "We have to get going."

Sammy and Bogdon each took a hamper and rolled them toward the elevator. When they got there Dr. Weiss introduced himself. When he took Bogdon's hand, Bogdon was prepared and squeezed back, winking at Sammy. Dr. Weiss did not react. The ladies then popped their heads out from beneath their sheets to say hello. Afterward, Dr. Weiss stepped away to a nearby wall and flipped a switch. The steel door to the loading dock's platform quietly rolled down into place. When it reached the floor and stopped, the light went out. He stepped back to the large freight elevator where the hampers had been moved in. Sammy, Bogdon and Father Bernard were standing behind them.

"There should be no one in the building, except a few of Dr. Bowmeister's team," Dr. Weiss said. "Everything's ready upstairs. This the most exciting day of my career. I'm honored to be part of the team. I mean, I can't imagine what we're going to learn and experience. I mean, what I understand, like where these ladies have been and what happened to them..."

"I think we might want to get going, doctor," Father Bernard suggested. "You're closest to the buttons."

"Oh? Oh, yes. Sorry. Just so excited." As he turned and pressed the third-floor button, Sammy looked at Bogdon and rolled his eyes as if to say, *I'm glad he's not my doctor.*

Bogdon nodded and closed his eyes momentarily, agreeing.

The new wing was in the final throes of construction, with the dedication and grand opening scheduled a mere two-and-a-half months away. All of the furnishings were set. The examination, labor, delivery and operating rooms were complete with the latest equipment, including CT, PET and MRI scanners. They had all been tuned and tested. A state-

of-the-art pediatric intensive care unit was up and functioning, as well as a regular pediatric unit, capable of handling more than thirty infants. The labs were equipped, and during the day, training sessions were underway. The plan was for most of the medical staff to come over from the old pediatric unit in the main building, but they were being supplemented with technical people for the new equipment. During the day, a few painters, carpenters and electricians were still putting on finishing touches. They would be out by the end of the next week.

Dr. Bowmeister met the elevator as the doors opened onto the third floor.

"The space ladies are here!" Dr. Weiss announced brightly, sweeping his hand toward the hampers with a flourish. As though on cue, the three ladies popped their heads up. "Delivered, safe and sound," Weiss went on as if he had personally brought them from the Residence. Dr. Bowmeister was a bit embarrassed by the young doctor's enthusiasm. But he was a sharp, knowledgeable radiologist—the best in the area as far as Bowmeister was concerned. And he could be trusted to keep the secret. The ladies took it all in and smiled, waving hello.

"Yes. Well that's fine, Leslie. We've got a lot to do, and only a few hours to do it, so let's get moving. There's a lounge down the hall," he said, pointing. "I've got my nurse and physician's assistant from my office waiting there."

Father Bernard picked up on the doctor's cue and signaled for Sammy and Bogdon to start pushing the hampers out of the elevator and down the hallway.

"I worked in hospital once," Bogdon told Sammy as they rolled along.

"As what? Brain surgeon?"

"No. Helper."

"You were a brain surgeon's helper?" Father Bernard asked, surprised. There were giggles from the ladies in the hampers.

"No, Father. I was helper in kitchen."

"Oh... I see," Father said, not aware of what the ladies found amusing. "Well, here's the lounge." They rolled past the door that Dr. Weiss held open. The ladies were carefully helped out of the hampers. Dr. Bowmeister made the introductions. His nurse, Judy Lennard, was forty-five.

Five years ago she had retired from the Navy, after twenty years of service. During her career that began as a seaman recruit fresh out of high school, and with education and special training, she rose to the rank to Master Chief Petty Officer and Nursing Supervisor of the Walter Reed Bethesda's Department of Obstetrics and Gynecology. She ended her career there. Dr. Bowmeister had been a pro-bono visiting physician at Walter Reed where they met and had a brief affair. Judy was single. The doctor was not. They remained friends. When she retired, he offered her a job in Wilmington. But their affair was never continued.

Dr. Bowmeister's PA, Harold Watanabe, was thirty-four—a fourth-generation Japanese-American.

Harold Watanabe had attended Cornell's famed veterinary school, and graduated into a crowded veterinary job market. He worked a few low-paying jobs in his hometown of Fayetteville, North Carolina, where his parents had a chicken farm in Grays Creek, south of Fayetteville. He saw no future in veterinary medicine, so he enrolled in the Physician's Assistant Graduate program at Methodist University and got his Masters of Medical Science Degree in Physician Assistant Studies. He moved to Wilmington after school and got a job in Dr. Bowmeister's practice. His goal was to save enough money to go to the University of North Carolina's Chapel Hill School of Medicine. Three months ago, Dr. Bowmeister, who knew how talented and devoted to medicine Harold was, offered to help him, professionally and financially, in getting into that school. The deal was, that Harold put one more year into the practice, and promise to come back to the practice after his residency for at least three years. The young man jumped at the deal. His application was now pending at Chapel Hill.

Before they were separated for individual exams, Nurse Judy Lennard drew three vials of blood from each of the women. It would be analyzed in the wing's hematology lab tomorrow, as soon as Dr. Bowmeister decided on which Hematologist and technician he would approach to join their team.

After drawing the blood, labeling and storing it, Judy took Rosie to ultrasound. Dr. Weiss took Julie for an MRI scan. Dr. Bowmeister and Harold Watanabe took Freida to one of the exam rooms that they had prepared for amniocentesis.

Father Bernard settled down in the lounge. Sammy and Bogdon went back to the truck and moved it away from the hospital wing. The priest would call Sammy on his cell phone when the exams were finished.

In the ultrasound, or sonogram room, Nurse Judy exposed Rosie's belly and rubbed gel on it. Dr. Bowmeister had set the Doppler wand so that Judy could record the heartbeat as well as the baby's image. She moved the Doppler and watched the monitor. The sound of the baby's heartbeat filled the room. It was strong and fast. Faster than any Judy had every heard. It worried her, but that was not what worried her the most. The ultrasound image of the baby showed a humanoid boy in a strange fetal position. It took her several moments to realize that the baby's knees, normally tucked near the stomach in fetal position, were actually up beyond his head. His body was the full length of his thighs. To call him a big boy was a gross understatement.

Around the same time, Dr. Weiss was watching the screen as the

MRI on Julie was underway. CT and PET scans are normally not used during pregnancy, unless an abnormality is suspected or indicated, because they employ radiation that might harm the baby. But MRIs are deemed safe. At first glance, the image of the baby on the monitor looked normal. It was a humanoid female, slightly small in size for the ninth month. But then Dr. Weiss began to notice the unusually thick and oddly muscular legs of the girl. Normal infants don't have that much muscle development or mass. Her arms were also extremely well developed and muscular. And she seemed to be alert, with an expression on her face that made him believe she could see him. In fact, for a moment, he thought he heard her say hello.

Dr. Bowmeister and Harold Watanabe were having an adventure of their own doing the amniocentesis on Freida. Ultrasound was required to guide the long needle used to withdraw amino fluid protecting the infant. All had gone well. Freida's baby, also a girl, looked normal, and was quiet. Her eyes were shut. But when the needle was inserted into the amino sac, her eyes opened and her head turned toward where the needle had entered. Dr. Bowmeister observed that and proceeded very slowly to draw fluid. Then, with a lightning-quick movement, the baby reached out her hand and grasped the needle above the point. When Dr. Bowmeister tried to withdraw it, he could not. The baby then reached for the needle with her other hand and grasping it, bent it to an L shape. After that, she released it, allowing him to take it out, slowly and carefully. The baby then went back into her original position and closed her eyes. A slight smile grew on her lips, and then passed. Freida was smiling too.

CHAPTER TWENTY-FIVE
Reunion

When Kate Conlon saw her mother, she burst into tears and rushed to embrace her. Both women sobbed and rocked back and forth with cries of "Oh, my God," and "I love you," and "I'm so happy to see you...I missed you so much..." They cried and laughed and let their hearts flow. It was not so much a, 'You've come back from the dead,' thing as it was the realization of how much they loved each other and how grateful they were to be able to say that which had not been said for a long time, well before Rosie disappeared.

When they finally separated, Kate stepped back, still holding Rosie's hands in hers. She looked at her mother's belly and then up to her face.

"Mom! You're younger than me."

"No, no, my darling. I'm seventy-six now. I've just been, sort of..." *How to put it?* "The people we went with, they stopped the aging process we have here on Earth. And then, it seems, once in a while, it gets reversed a bit." She stroked her belly. "And look what that caused," Rosie said, chuckling. "Quite the result, huh?"

"I'm amazed. God, you look so wonderful!"

They were in Rosie's room. Sister Mary Francis had set up vacant rooms for the three ladies and Nicole in the basement of the Residence. They had been used by the staff before Hurricane Diana flooded it and trashed the building, back in 1984, when it was a resort hotel.

"The boys will be here tonight," Kate told Rosie who had sat down on the bed. Carrying the baby had become more and more of a strain. "Alex came from Hawaii and they're flying together from Los Angeles. They had to go to Atlanta and get a commuter to here. It's the best connection they could make."

"Yes. Nicole told me. You're sure they don't know...I mean, you didn't say anything after Nicole left Cambridge. Yes?"

"Of course not."

"And your boyfriend?"

"Arthur? He's not said a word. I swear."

"You don't have to swear, sweetheart." Rosie tapped the bed. "Come. Sit beside me." Kate sat down. Rosie put her arm around her daughter. "I want to apologize for what I put you through. But I also need to be honest. When we were, well, I guess taken is the word, our friend Gina...she was once an entertainer in Las Vegas. A dancer. She's doing that now on an Orbalidinian intergalactic cruise ship and..."

"A what?" Kate interrupted.

"It's like a cruise ship here only...I'll explain later. Anyway, she used to say we were snatched. You know, like yanked up off the Earth. It's kind of what happened. But there was nothing violent about it. Just fast. And when the leader of the Marlino ship, Dr. Cohestle, he's my mate...when he heard how it was my silly prank that made all that happen...Nicole did tell you about the magazine ad I answered?"

"Yes. And some of your other pranks. You called this man your mate. Are you married?"

"Not exactly in the Earth-humanoid sense. I mean not religiously or with promises of death do us part. Their life span is quite different from ours. Mine may have changed too. Only time will tell. But we are what they call bonded, so married is just as good a description. Anyway, I was saying, Dr. Cohestle immediately offered to return us. But Gina sort of got curious about the ship and the other Marlinons.

Then another crewmember, an Orbalidinian, expressed interest in her. And she was sort of eying him herself."

"So why didn't you come back?" Kate asked, missing the relevance of Gina's suitor.

"Let me explain it this way. The last time you were here, Katie— that was what, eight years ago when Dad died and I moved into the Residence?"

"Nine," Kate answered quickly, sensing that her mother was about to blame her for something. "But we saw you, Mom. You came to Cambridge for the holidays. I mean, after all, I was working and the boys were..."

"Please, sweetheart. I'm not accusing you of anything. I know all that. You had your life and I had mine. And when you met Arthur, the year before we left, I understood it was important that you go away with him. I was happy for you. And I'm really happy to see you two are still together. And the boys? They were far away with their new jobs and new friends. That's the way it should be."

"Arthur can't wait to meet you."

"Me too. But I wanted this private time with you, and later with my grandsons. I think when you're older, you'll understand better. So, what happened on the ship was, at first, we all said yes. We wanted to go back. But Julie, you'll meet her later. She's pregnant too. She's mated to humanoid Chgool-Biner from Gimm. Would you believe six-foot-eight? Dr. Cohestle, my humanoid mate? He's a bit over six-three. And he's one of the shorter Marlinons. It's because of gravity. On Gimm, it's even less than on Marlino. But where Freida lives, on Roonio nine, the gravity is incredibly strong. She had a tough time adjusting."

"Mom? I haven't the slightest idea what you're talking about."

Rosie smiled and hugged Kate close to her. "Of course you don't. We'll explain it all over the next week or so."

Kate sat up. "Okay. So you were saying that this doctor...?"

"Cohestle. My mate. Yes. He offered to send us back immediately. But Gina was talking to this Orbalidinian and then a few of the girls, my friends, they became interested in the ship and the crew and, well, the idea of taking a trip. You know, life around here was pretty boring. It's why I tried to liven it up sometimes."

"Well, you certainly did, Mom."

"I suppose. But as you'll see, what happened has literally taken us from being six aging, single, bored, maybe even discarded, present company excluded, women, to three mothers-to-be with fascinating lives. And now we're three intergalactic travelers!" Rosie withdrew her arm from around Kate's shoulder and stood up slowly. "This guy," she said, touching her large belly, "is getting bigger by the hour. Now, let's meet this young man of yours."

While Kate introduced Rosie to Arthur, and then went on to meet Julie and Freida, Nicole and Father Bernard drove to the Wilmington International Airport to meet Herbie and Alex Legum's plane. The boys had kept their father's name. Alex had flown to L.A. on Hawaiian Air the night before, and met his brother at Los Angeles International. They then flew together to Atlanta on an early morning Delta 747, transferred to a Delta commuter to Wilmington, and were scheduled to arrive at 5:10 p.m. Father Bernard wore his Roman collar and black suit. Nicole, to keep up appearances, put on her old, black novitiate outfit that Sister Mary Francis had kept with the hope that someday the young novitiate might return. She wore no makeup, and to play down her good looks, put on a pair of horned rimmed granny reading glasses she'd borrowed from resident Debra Dix.

Father Bernard wheedled gate passes from the Delta counter clerk after telling Nicole, "She has the map of Ireland on her face. Must be Catholic." When they greeted the two young men, as they came off the plane, their attitude toward the arrivals was friendly and solicitous. They welcomed them and expressed their sorrow for the loss of their grandmother.

While waiting for their luggage, the young men were concerned that they might be asked to speak at the memorial service. Neither felt up to that task.

"Only if you wish," Father Bernard told them, finding it uncomfortable that keeping up the surprise required some fibbing. Until now, he hadn't considered how much more obfuscation he might have to present to the world to keep the visit and births secret until now. "We don't expect a large crowd," he told Rosie's grandsons, surprised at how smoothly the falsehood came out. "Aside from your grandmother, the other missing women had no close family."

"As is the case for most of our residents," Nicole added.

Nicole drove the Residence's new van. The old one that the space travelers returned in was parked in the three-car garage under the basement. No one had driven it since they had arrived. Father Bernard inquired about the men's lives in California and Hawaii. When Herbie said he was a lawyer, the priest asked what kind.

"I work for CBS Television in the contracts department."

"Oh. That's nice."

"Do you know about wills and estates?" Father asked.

"Yes. Why?"

"Well, it seems some of the missing ladies, your grandma Roseanne included, had bank accounts. No one stopped their social security checks and pension payments. A few of the others owned stock and bonds. Dividends were deposited. None of the brokers called. I was wondering if you might have a look into that?" the priest asked.

"I'm not a member of the North Carolina bar," Herbie told him, "but I can check with some of my associates and see if I can identify someone for you here."

"That would be wonderful."

"What do you do in Hawaii?" Nicole asked Alex, who was sitting next to her in the front passenger seat.

"I live on Maui, I'm a chemist. I'm working on developing new hydroponic farming techniques."

"That sounds interesting," she said, looking over and smiling. He was a youngish-looking, handsome young man. Alex smiled back.

"Did you know my grandmother?"

"Yes. A wonderful woman."

Traffic was light. The rest of the ride went quickly. They arrived at the Residence close to 6:30 p.m. Close to sunset. When Father Bernard, Nicole, Herbie and Alex entered the dining room, it appeared to be empty. The lights were dim. Nicole and the priest slowed, letting Herbie and Alex walk slightly ahead of them. Then Herbie saw his mother and Arthur Baumgartner standing with a nun and two pregnant women next to the wall of sliding glass doors that looked out on the ocean. Alex, on the other hand, noticed what his mind said was impossible. One very pregnant woman, whom he knew had to be, but couldn't be, his grandmother, Roseanne. While Herbie waved to his mother, Alex ran to his grandmother and hugged her as best he could, considering the size of her belly.

"Oh, oh, oh, oh yeah, oh yeah..." was all he said, loudly, over and over. Herbie looked at his brother and froze. The pregnant woman Alex was hugging was smiling at him. It was a smile he knew. He looked back at his mother. She was nodding and saying, "Yes!" vigorously. He joined his brother and grandmother, wrapping his arms around them both, he began to cry tears of joy.

Father Bernard found the dimmer switch and turned the dining room lights up. Sammy and Bogdon wheeled out a cart with coffee, tea and a strawberry shortcake that Bogdon had baked and decorated for the occasion. He had bought a small, plastic toy spaceship and placed it on top. Introductions were made and they all sat down at a table that had been formed by putting three of the regular dining room tables together. Herbie and Alex, still slightly dazed, were full of questions. Rosie, Julie, Freida, and from time to time, Nicole, explained their adventure, as they had before to everyone else at the table. It took nearly half an hour.

Sister Mary Francis then got up and opened the dining room doors. All of the residents, who had been waiting outside, filed in. They took chairs and placed them in a circle around the triple table. When every-one was settled, Nicole got up and clapped her hands for their attention.

"You all know something about what happened to us, and why, and you must have many questions. You also know that, obviously, there have been physical changes and, should I say, events?" A wave of laughter filled the room. "Yes. Big events. Or as we say on Earth, blessed events." There was a smattering of applause. "We have not talked much about specifically where we have been, and what we four, and Gina, Eva and Bonita have been doing. That is aside from one obvious activity." She smiled and gestured toward the three pregnant women. "But now that Rosie's family is here, it is time to fill everyone in on our, what we call, our adventure. Obviously, it is more than that. Even words like *fantastic* and *unbelievable* do not do it justice. So we ask you to clear your minds of as much science fiction as you can, and just listen. Each of these ladies will tell you where they have been, and what they have done. After that, I'll fill you in on where Gina, Eva and Bonnie are, and what they have been up to, as far as we knew, when we left to come here to Earth. Rosie?"

Rosie stood. She held onto the back of her chair for support. Nicole left the room to get something from the old van parked under the basement.

"It's so nice to see all of you together again. Since we came back, as you may know, we've been busy and haven't had much time to spend here. So, first of all, let me thank you for keeping our secret. We are eternally grateful." She bowed to the audience—a strange gesture. "That is one way we say thank you on my new home planet of Marlino. Before I get into my personal adventure, I want to introduce you to my family; the ones I left so abruptly back here on Earth. They have been wonderful in accepting what happened, and maybe not so happy that I was the cause of what I thought was a little prank. It turned out to be, well..." Rosie patted her ample belly, "...not so little." That brought some laughs. She introduced Kate, Arthur, Herbie and Alex. They stood, and there was polite applause.

"My grandsons just arrived this evening so forgive me if I repeat some of what you may already know." She paused and gathered her thoughts.

"Okay. So, I live on a planet called Marlino. Translating the language of the Marlinons, it sounds like that in English. It's beyond the star system we call Virgo, so from Earth's point of view, let's say it's in the Virgo system. That's like how we refer to Earth's place in what we call the Solar System—*Sol* being Latin for sun. Both of our stars and planets are in what we call The Milky Way Galaxy, but Marlino is across, and a bit on the other side and closer to the galaxy center.

Earth is more on the edge of the galaxy. It might sound close, but the distances are almost beyond comprehension. Until," she quickly added, "one has the ability to travel as the Marlinons do. And don't ask me how they do it. I haven't a clue." There was laughter. "The Marlinon sun is a star they call Boorin. My mate, that's the definition most of the humanoids we've met use for males and females who cohabitate, is named Cohestle. His work and rank would be equivalent to a PhD here, so he's Dr. Cohestle to me. Actually, he's a chemist—to be more precise, a molecular and biological chemist. The Marlinons are travelers. Since they perfected space travel...that was about fifteen of our millennia ago, they have visited more than three hundred systems and three times that number of planets that contain and sustain what we call life. So when you think of the millions of stars and planets in our galaxy, and the millions of galaxies in what we call the universe, well, dear ladies and," she looked at Father Bernard, Arthur, Sammy and Bogdon seated at her table, "gentlemen, there's a whole lot of life out there. We are not alone. To some people, that might seem scary, or impossible. The movies certainly try to portray our galaxy and universe as teeming with horrible, violent beings who want to eat us or take all our water or enslave us. That's all nonsense. All those we've met, humanoid and others, are what you and I would call peaceful and pleasant. They may look different, and live differently, and do things we do and don't do differently, but they are alive, thinking, caring, even loving beings. That's been my experience and I am honored to have the privilege of knowing them." Rosie got emotional for a moment. Her eyes began to tear up a bit. She dabbed them with a napkin from the table.

"To travel in space, our bodies had to be adjusted. Processed, if you will. We explained that to you and how, in our case, the processing initiated certain chemical and physiological changes in our bodies. So we were, in a sense, rejuvenated internally, and that allowed us to travel in space at the speeds required to move around our galaxy. It took a little longer for the processing to cause our external rejuvenation; getting to look younger. And, a bit more to return our ability to reproduce."

Rosie moved on to how they were taken to Marlino and how they met the humanoid males from other planets who had interest in Earth-human women. During that time, Nicole quietly returned to the room, signaling silently to Rosie that she had what she'd gone to the van to get.

"Julie and Freida will fill you in on their adventures and Nicole will tell you about Gina, Eva and Bonita. Within a few months on Marlino..." she hesitated again... "You have to imagine that days and nights and time—weeks, months...It's all different than here. The processing helped us adjust to that situation as well. Dr. Cohestle was charming. I think I started to fall for him on the trip back to Marlino. He was kind and caring. And he seemed to take a special interest in me because I was the one who had answered the ad. He told me that playing pranks was a very Marlinon trait. As I've learned about them, I agree. My late husband, here on Earth, was that way too. Maybe I saw a little of him in Dr. Cohestle." Rosie shrugged and smiled at her daughter. Kate smiled back and nodded.

"About two Earth-months after we landed, Dr. Cohestle proposed mating to me. By then, we had adjusted to the planet and the reality of what had happened to us, where we were and the possibilities of what lay ahead." Rosie looked over at her grandchildren. She sensed a thought in both their minds. *'Why did you come back?'*

"Just a few more things before I talk about my life on Marlino. Coming back here to have our babies, as we told you, has to do with what you might call a humanoid space-traveler rule. There are many. This is one of the most important. It states that whenever possible, babies conceived from inter-humanoid, or mixed-mating should be

born on the mother's home planet. That rule evolved from the experience of many known travelers, like the Marlinons. They found that
it is best for the infant's protection and viability."

Rosie smiled at her grandsons and winked. Their thoughts conveyed
that somehow she had read their minds. She let a thought float back
to them affirming their suspicion. At the same time, Nicole sent her
one reminding her that telepathy was to be kept secret.

"One more thing and then we'll get on with the show. We use the
word *humanoid*. We refer to ourselves as Earth-humanoids. Marlinons
are humanoid. It doesn't mean that most of them, Marlinon, and
those from other planets and systems, look like us. Many of them
don't, exactly. But they have what they call commonality. That's a
translation. Others simply refer to our kind of carbon-based life in
words that translate into 'Of the People.' Something like many of the
Native American tribes called themselves. It's even in the preamble of
the United States Constitution. We the People..." There was a murmur
of recognition and surprise.

"We share many of the same characteristics." Rosie pointed to her
belly. "We share a large component of our DNA—Deoxyribonucleic
acid, and RNA—Ribonucleic acid. I won't get too technical, but remember, my mate is a chemist. So, there are two types of DNA—Genomic
and Mitochondrial. In the systems, worlds, moons and asteroids that
the Marlinons have explored so far, humanoid DNA and RNA is, more
or less, the same. It points to a theory, just a theory, that humanoid
life, though it may evolve differently depending on a planet's environment, might have a common source. With that mind-bending concept
to keep you awake tonight, let's go on to Marlino. Nicole?"

Nicole stood up and walked to the dining room wall that was made
up of the glass sliding doors. She carried what looked like a small
satchel that turned out to be the handbag that Julie was carrying the
day they were snatched. In it was an octagonal device, about nine

inches across and four inches high. It had what looked like a glass eye, but was in fact, a soft translucent membrane, on three sides of the octagon.

By now it was dark outside. A moonless night. Nicole asked for the lights to be dimmed. Sammy got up and did that. She placed the device on a table closest to the glass sliding doors and touched her right forefinger to the top of the device. A brilliant, panoramic, three-dimensional image immediately appeared on the glass across its entire width. It was an image of the planet Marlino. Two moons, one tinted red, like Mars, and the other silvery metallic in texture and smaller than the red one. They both circled the planet. Marlino appeared to be as round as Earth, but the image had no reference to determine its size. It was cloudless. There was what looked like water mingled with several large land masses. Part of the land was white. It seemed to be covered with snow, or ice. The picture was taken on the day side of the planet. There was a definite blue tint to the daylight. As the planet drew closer, the view moved to the night side where lights emerged that seemed to indicate cities. There were hundreds of them, all perfectly round with totally dark centers.

"This is how Marlino, and its two moons, appeared to us as we approached after our trip across the galaxy from Earth," Rosie Conlon said aloud, narrating. "Marlino is about thirty percent smaller than Earth. The red moon is farther away and has a very slow rotation and wide orbit. It's called in English, fire. The smaller moon has no rotation, and a faster orbit. It's called shine." The image was now on the surface of the planet skimming over patches of water and ice; land and snow.

"Marlino's sun is farther away than Earth is from ours. Its atmosphere is basically argon and nitrogen, with very little oxygen and carbon dioxide. It was breathable for us for very short periods of time, but it caused headaches, dizziness and nausea. Not a sustainable atmosphere for Earth-humanoids. The Marlinons supplied us with breathing devices."

An image of Rosie taking off her breathing mask and taking a deep breath appeared. She was on some kind of patio made of a shiny, coal-black substance. She was wearing what looked like a parka, ski pants and furry boots. She rolled up her sleeve and showed a bump in the crook of her elbow.

"Because I chose to stay on Marlino, my mate, Dr. Cohestle, designed an implant that allows me to breathe the atmosphere." The picture then showed Rosie squatting down and leaping up nearly ten feet into the air. In the background, the landscape was mostly bare and spotted with clumps of snow and ice and the suggestion of a few trees that looked like leafless acacias.

"Adjusting to the forty percent lesser gravity took some time. But it was fun. I didn't do much of this after I realized I was pregnant. You can see that the land is pretty bare. There is some vegetation and a few hardy animals and insects. But much of the planet's surface is crystallized water. Solid like ice or powdery like snow. It's clean. No carbon emission in their air. The sunlight reaching the planet is much more on the ultraviolet spectrum than Earth's. Although some life flourishes on the planet's surface, almost all of Marlino industry and agriculture is below, closer to the planet's hot magma core. It supplies warmth and almost infinite energy. Their technology reflects evolutionary expertise for survival under these conditions. It is testament to the tenacity of intelligent life to adapt, procreate and protect the humanoid species."

The images were back in the air, flying over one of the circular cities. The architecture was stunning, angular, glittering and esthetically pleasing. The dark, circular centers were made up of a series of tunnel openings, Rosie explained, that led down deep below the surface where so much of the Marlinon activity took place.

"But almost all Marlinons who work below, choose to live on the surface," Rosie said, as images of her home were projected. It was a neat, single-story, bunker-like structure made of the same coal-black substance seen earlier. Inside, it was a spacious, open dwelling, bathed in soft purple and blue light. The severe furnishings were offset by colorful human touches of flowers, pillows, drapes and paintings.

"My mate lived alone. What some might call a man-cave? But I did some poking around and found places that made, what shall I say, softer and colorful things," Rosie quipped. There were chuckles from the audience. "And notice how high the doorways are? You see, because the gravity is less on Marlino, less than forty percent of Earth's, the people are much taller than most of us. Dr. Cohestle is short for his kind. He is six-foot-three. His mother's family had several mixed-matings with humanoids from larger, heavier gravity planets."

The next image was that of Rosie, dressed in what might be a comfortable black caftan trimmed with gold. She was in the kitchen with appliances that appeared familiar.

"I had my mate build this kitchen for me. It took me several weeks to figure out how their foods related to ours. But I did. No meat—just all kinds of vegetables, fruits and several hundred varieties of crustaceans and fish that they raise in lakes and rivers down below. He likes my cooking. With my implant, I breathe normally, and my skin is ionized to protect me from ultraviolet exposure. I've been down below. It's extremely interesting. But Cohestle and I prefer to be above and see the sun and moons and stars—blue, red and silver."

The final image was of Rosie, smiling off camera to an unseen Dr. Cohestle. "I have a good life with a man who loves me and whom I have grown to love. That's it."

"Lights please, Sammy," Nicole said, standing. There was applause. The dining room lights came on. Herbie and Alex were standing, grinning and clapping. *Who is this woman?* they thought. Rosie heard them and her heart swelled. Kate got up and embraced her mother. More tears.

"Julie Lobato's story is next, and then Freida Riggs." Nicole announced. "I have images of their homes too. Afterward, I will speak a bit and then take questions." Nothing was said as to why there were no images of any Marlinons, but the four visitors heard it was on everyone's mind.

Julie did not go into the beginning of the journey, only to say that for a while she was not happy about Rosie's prank answering the ad in *Women Pumping Iron*.

"But once we were on the Marlinon ship, and Rosie's hubby-to-be offered to return us, Gina looked around and kind of got us interested. I mean, there we were, out in space, looking back at the Earth like astronauts. Jesus!" She looked over at Father Bernard. "Sorry, Father. Just an earthly expression of amazement."

"Of course. He's always with us, Julie," the priest said, with a nod.

"There are some out there who would differ with you, Father, but I'll leave that discussion for another time." She winked at him and turned back to the audience.

"However, ladies, I can tell you about someone who was definitely with us—a six-foot, eight-inch, humanoid navigator named Yan-Ar-Betch. I've been attracted to tall men all my life. And as some of you gals here know, I even married three of them. So this man was, as the saying goes, tall, dark and damned handsome. He smiled at me. Now today, I may look younger than my current seventy-four years," she said, tapping her pregnant belly. "However, then I was a real seventy-one and having something like this little one in here was far behind me. But I did feel a tingle. And mind you, this was before the processing, and way before our hormones, estrogen and ovaries kicked back in." That brought a wave of laughter and a blush on Father Bernard's face.

"Now you know I'm not prone to be shy. And those of you who knew me back then...well, you knew I was a compulsive gambler. So I smiled back at the hunk. Damned if he didn't come over to me and take my hand in his. I gotta tell you that something flowed between us...something I had never felt in my life, three marriages and all. All I knew, at that moment, was that I was not interested in coming back here. Anyway, as you've heard, we all freely chose to stay. We got processed then and there, on the ship. It didn't hurt. No discomfort. No symptoms that anything had happened except we were full of energy, like teenagers with raging hormones, and a brain that seemed to take everything in and understand it. I mean, the ship and the humanoids on it and the heavens outside around us, which was breathtaking. Imagine what you see from down here on a clear, dark, starry night and multiply that times one hundred. One thousand. It was like we suddenly understood that we belonged out there among it all."

Julie stopped for a moment, looked down and touched her belly. She patted it gently. A caress. "She just moved. It's a girl. Anyway, so we went on to Marlino and as Rosie said, spent some months learning, adjusting and meeting perspective humanoid mates. Rosie wound up with Dr. Cohestle. I never strayed far from my Yan-Ar-Betch, the navigator. I called him Yanar. Betch is his father's name. Did I say he isn't from Marlino?"

Lynn Ferrari, the semi-retired journalist from New Jersey, who was about to turn seventy, was seated in the front row close to Julie. They had been friends. "No, you didn't, Julie," she said.

"Thanks, Lynn. Well, he isn't. But his mother is. Yanar was born on Marlino, in keeping with the rule of birth on mother's home planet. But then they moved to Gimm, his father's planet, when it was clear his genetics were predominantly Gimmish. That's in the system we call Hydra. Gimm is the fourth planet out from their sun, whose name is impossible for me to pronounce, but it translates into our word 'life.' It's larger than our sun. Yanar and I mated on Marlino and moved to Gimm for a year. We lived on his family farm. He traveled on and off as a navigator until I got pregnant. That's about it." She looked over at Nicole. "I guess we can go to the images now, Nicole."

"Sammy? Lights again, please," Nicole asked. The Korean-American started to get up from his chair, but Bogdon got up faster.

"I do it, Miss Nicole," the chef announced as he quickly walked to the light switch and turned down the dimmer.

Sammy frowned and muttered something under his breath that ended with the word "Poland."

With the room darkened, Nicole operated the octagonal projection device and Julie narrated the images that appeared on the sliding glass doors. The first was on the shore of a small lake. It could have been in New Hampshire or Vermont. The water was blue and clear. The image suddenly moved up over the lake and landed on the far shore. It was hard to tell the distance. The shore was lined with very tall trees. Many had large, diaphanous leaves with a variety of flowers of many different colors. The camera recording the picture then moved up and over the trees. Several large and brilliantly colored birds were flushed out of the trees and flew away from the camera. A few slim, but large, monkey-like animals popped their heads up from the tree-tops as the camera passed. Beyond the trees, the camera panned down, revealing acres and acres of cleared forest with rich, black soil that held row upon row of large, blue-green leafy plants.

"Gimm is a planet as close to tropical Earth," Julie began, "in terms of weather, plant and animal life, as I've seen so far. Yanar tells me he has seen several like it, but maintains that Gimm is the most beautiful. All I can say is look and judge for yourselves. The forests teem with life. The soil is fertile. There are many springs and large aquifers beneath the surface. The rainfall is mostly in the evening. Betch, Yanar's dad, grows five kinds of what we would call fruit. They are big and luscious, like melons and pineapples. As Gimm farms go, Betch says his is average. My guess is, it's about a square mile. I don't know how many acres that might be."

"Six-hundred forty," Debra Dix, who was once a senior official in the National Park Service, called out.

"Thanks, Debbie. I guess that's a lot. You may have noticed that things like the trees and leaves and birds and those curious monkey-type characters popping up, are all kind of large. Like I said, my Yanar is six-foot-eight. His father is seven-foot-five. Yanar is smaller because his mother is small, even for a Marlinon. Gimm's gravity is even less than Marlino's. About half of Earth's. So these are tall folks."

At that point, the camera settled to the ground. The lens turned and showed that it was Julie who was operating it. She was taking a "selfie," wearing shorts, a halter-type top and shoes that conformed to the shape of her feet.

"Yes. That was me shooting these pictures. The gravity allows me to take some pretty high leaps. But I've learned how to adjust. Low gravity on Gimm is why so many things on the planet are big, compared to Earth, that is."

The images that followed showed wooden farm buildings, some neat machinery and a few large animals that looked something like light brown, furry water buffalo, grazing in a field of tall grass. The image then moved inside one of the buildings. The rooms were spacious, clean and nicely furnished with what might pass for an Early American style blended with Danish Modern—the doorways were high, as were the ceilings. And as with Rosie's home, there was no sign of humanoids.

"This is where Yanar and I live on the farm." The camera moved to a room that was obviously a nursery. "And this is what I will bring our daughter home to."

The image then cut away and showed Gimm from space. The planet was green with patches of blue-green water. As the camera moved toward the horizon, the vegetation began to wane, until it was sparse, and the topography was mostly scrub bush and desert. There was very little sunlight on that part of the planet.

"There is an odd situation on Gimm. It has one moon that is in a fixed orbit, synchronized with the planet's rotation. It is always in the same place, relative to the planet. That means it blocks seventy to eighty percent of sunlight to that portion of Gimm, making it an uninhabitable desert." The last image showed the moon and the planet from a distance. The glass sliding door wall went dark.

"Lights, please," Nicole called out. Bogdon, who had stood by the dimmer, dialed it up.

"Where are the mates?" Isabella Johannsen asked.

"What do the people look like?" Abigail Rubin called out.

"Please be patient, everyone," a frustrated Nicole answered. "As I said before, after Rosie, Julia and Freida speak, we will answer your questions as best we can. Freida, you're next."

Freida Riggs had a different story to tell. The retired violinist did not meet her future mate on the spaceship. During the trip to Marlino, and in the days after their arrival, Dr. Cohestle interviewed the ladies, asking about their Earth lives...what they did there; did they have children, family, jobs? It was, he said, necessary to be able to match them up with perspective mates, should they decide to explore that option. There was no pressure to do that.

Among other things, Freida told him about her late husband, their life in the military and her musical career. Later, after they had been on Marlino for a few months getting oriented and adapting to their new reality, the climate on the planet's surface and below, and the concept of possibly becoming mail order mates, Freida and the other three ladies, Gina, Eva and Bonita were asked to consider being introduced to a group of humanoid males from Marlino and other planets.

"Dr. Cohestle took credit for coming up with the ad for mail order brides," Freida told the audience. "He had picked up the idea from a web site, www.hotrrussianbrides.com, that some other space travelers had had success with. When the time arrived for us to meet the humanoid males, who had come to Marlino seeking mates, we made it clear that since we had been the brunt of Rosie's little game, the idea of being a bride to some, well, kind of strange humanoid, didn't sit well with us...at least not with Gina, Eva, Bonnie and me.

By then, Rosie and Dr. Cohestle, and Julie and Yanar the navigator, seemed fairly well set on being with each other, or at least giving it a chance. I know that sounds weird, but by then, we had absorbed the scope of the galaxy, being light years from Earth and how extraordinary our adventure really was. Dr. Cohestle was very understanding. Apparently this method had worked a few times in the past with women from the Middle and Near East and Africa. They were mostly young women looking to escape poverty or religious oppression. The ad that Rosie answered was the first time he had tried it in North America."

In spite of Nicole's announcement about questions, Allison Carlson, the widow from Tennessee, could not help herself. She jumped to her feet.

"Freida!" she called out. "Are you saying that women have been abducted from Earth before?" Nicole immediately stepped away from the projection machine to answer Allison, but Freida held up her hand and sent her a silent message that she wanted to handle this now.

"We asked that there be no questions until we are finished talking and showing you something about our lives, Allison," Freida said. "Otherwise, we could be here for days answering things that we can tell you first. And, more important, we are all due soon. So we don't have time to spend. Here's all that we can say about what you just asked, Allison dear. Yes. The Marlinons and other humanoid travelers have been here before. Probably for centuries. Like we told you, our Milky Way Galaxy, and surely the Universe, is teeming with intelligent life. Much of it is humanoid. The word you used, *abducted*, sounds like a Hollywood horror movie. The travelers don't abduct. There are rules; regulations if you wish. Nor do they eat us, blow up our cities, infect us with deadly viruses, or any other ludicrous, fantasy speculations or presentations of what extraterrestrial life might be. No one has been abducted, but there are some, like us, who when presented with the choice, have opted to leave Earth. For several, the conditions where they were living were so dangerous or hopeless or prejudiced that the offer of a different life was a no-brainer. I don't have to tell you that there are millions of human females, children and adults on this planet who are oppressed, starving, sick, brutalized, raped, enslaved, denied education and ruled under primitive tribal or ancient religious systems by cruel male despots."

Freida paused to gather her thoughts and composure. In a way, having seen some of the galaxy and how humanoid people lived in harmony and respect with one another, she felt sorry for the residents in the room, as she was for so many of her sisters on Earth. She realized how angry and scolding she might sound to the residents.

"I'm sorry. Sometimes I tend to rant. Let me answer Allison's question directly. No human being has been forcibly removed or harmed by any space travelers that we are aware of. Those who decided they did not want to leave Earth were returned with implanted memories that were designed to seem real, but were dreams. In time, those memories will fade."

"You mean like their bodies were being probed?" Allison asked.

"Yes. And what some call out-of-body experiences or travel to another plane of consciousness."

"Thanks, Freida." Allison sat down. The room was quiet.

"You're welcome, Allison. So, the four of us, Gina, Eva, Bonnie and I met with nine prospective mates. It was an informal dinner that Dr. Cohestle arranged in his home on Marlino's surface. Rosie, Julie and Nicole did not attend. The male humanoids were interesting and polite. They all had basic Earth-human characteristics. A few had gone to the trouble of learning some English. Two who were interested in Bonita, learned some Spanish. They had all studied information and images about our planet and several cultures, religions, races and ethnicities. And, around that time, we were all beginning to reverse age. It was a pleasant affair.

"To make a long story short, by the end of the evening, the four of us had a good idea of who we might like to see again. We met after the dinner to compare notes. Fortunately, there were no conflicts. The reality of mating was still something we weren't sure about. But, I had met a male that I found interesting. His name is Jinko. He's a miner. If Julie's Yanar was tall, dark and handsome, my Jinko was short, squat, muscular, dark and, to me, quite handsome. And he loves music. He knew I played the violin. He had one made for me and gave it to me as a gift. It was a quality instrument. Jinko lives on a huge planet named Roonio nine. It is three times the size of Earth and has four times the Earth gravity. Three weeks after that dinner, after meeting with him several times, I agreed to become Jinko's mate. Bogdon? Can you turn off the lights? Nicole?"

Bogdon, who had remained next to the dimmer switch, lowered the lights. Nicole then turned on the projector. The sliding glass doors were immediately filled with an image of a huge, brownish planet with three moons circling it. Two of the moons were small and irregular in shape. One looked fairly round until about one third of it was revealed to be an enormous crater, the result of a massive collision with another space object. Another was oblong with jagged, black mountain peaks. It tumbled slowly as it orbited. The third, a much larger moon, was farther away from the planet than the other two. It was pockmarked with craters. Its mountains were worn and rounded. A wide chasm cut diagonally across from north to south as though a gigantic being with a huge knife had tried to slice the moon in two, but did not succeed.

"Roonio nine is located in what Earth astronomers call the Perseus constellation, or star system," Freida began, narrating. "Perseus was the Greek god who cut off the head of Medusa. To the ancient Greeks, the constellation showed him holding it in his hand. Well, the brightest star there, Dr. Cohestle told me, is one Earth-humans call Mirfak. It means elbow in Arabic, and is the brightest star in the constellation, as seen from Earth. Mirfak's real name, given by the Chertack people, Jinko's people whom I now live with, translates into 'light of life.' It's a yellow-white supergiant, about five thousand times stronger than Earth's sun."

The image began to move rapidly toward the dusty planet. Treeless mountains, valleys and wide barren plains began to be defined. There was no indication of water on the surface.

"I tell you all this because Roonio nine is the fifth planet out in our system, and when I knew I was coming back here to give birth, I wanted to be accurate about my new home. That way, after we leave, you can kind of look up into the night sky, find Perseus, then bright Mirfak, and wave hello." That remark brought laughter.

"Roonio nine is pretty hot. And very dry. My first husband and I were once in the Negev Desert in Israel. This planet is like that dry-hot. There are many aquifers deep below the surface, and some ice on the poles, but not enough water to maintain much agriculture above ground in the open. They have developed marvelous hydroponic systems that produce a variety of high-quality food. They import seeds from other planets. And since there is not much surface animal life, Roonio nine imports some protein food as well. The population if the planet is quite small in relation to its size. It has a breathable atmosphere of nitrogen, oxygen, argon, carbon dioxide and helium. Most important, there is an almost inexhaustible and varied mineral supply, including the much sought after fifteen rare earths. As I understand it, they are used for electronics by many advanced peoples, civilizations and travelers. They are greatly valued here on Earth."

The camera passed over a small city whose structures were all low to the ground; two or three stories at most. They looked like metallic bunkers. They had no windows or doors.

"Our home on Roonio nine is not far from what might be called a nice-sized town, or small city. This one is Pelldar-four. The names I tell you are my poor English translations. Much of the Chertak language is guttural and still difficult for me to pronounce. Also, they tend to describe things differently than we might."

The image changed to what looked like a Texas ranching spread. It was built on a small plateau that seemed to have been dug out of the mountain behind it. The main structure was, like the town, metallic, without windows or doors. Adjacent to it were several smaller buildings. Beyond them, up against the mountain, were what appeared to be corrals. As the camera moved closer, the corrals were seen to be outdoor storage areas where mounds of different colored rocks, crystals and shiny black nuggets were stacked in neat piles. Nestled next to the smaller buildings were large pieces of machinery similar to backhoes, bulldozers and trucks. They had no tires or wheels, but sat on top of what looked like large fans.

"My Jinko is a miner, and this is where we live," Freida announced proudly. "It is very close to the mines that Jinko and his brothers own and operate. The smaller buildings are where some of the workers live, and where certain rare and volatile minerals are initially processed. The machinery you see is for mining and transport to nearby mills, smelters and forges. This is our home..."

The image was inside the main house. In contrast to the hard, metallic exterior, the inside had curved, plaster walls painted in warm colors—browns, tans, oranges and yellows. The furnishings in the main room had metal frames, but were all upholstered in beautifully woven fabrics. Tables were made of translucent, multicolored glass. There were no visible lamps or any direct lighting source. Yet the room glowed in warm light that somehow emanated from the walls, ceiling and floor as though it was part of the material. The doorway to another room, a dining area, was rather low—not more than five feet high. All of the doors were that height. A few more rooms were explored. One of them held several musical instruments, including a beautiful violin.

"Jinko lived here alone, and when he decided to seek a mate, he had it fixed up. As you can see, he did a beautiful job. He works hard, my mate, and cares for me, as I care for him. It is a good life—actually, quite wonderful. We are happy there. I believe I am a very lucky woman."

The lights came up. Freida sat down between Rosie and Julie. Nicole turned off the projection device and made her way to the main table. Bogdon made his way back to his chair next to Sammy. Once everyone was settled, all eyes focused on Nicole as she faced the residents.

"Before we take your questions, let me relate a little about what I've been up to these past three years. My traveling companions have pretty well covered how, thanks to Rosanne Conlon, our Rosie, we arrived on the Marlinon vessel and what happened to them after that. I had no interest in finding a mate. I was a nineteen-year-old novitiate from Elkhorn, Nebraska. Arriving on a planet two hundred light years from Earth was not on my radar. I had no idea what a light year was, much less what or where Virgo was. Suffice it to say, I went along with the six ladies' decision because somehow, according to my job description at the time, I felt responsible for them."

She looked over at Sister Mary Francis and Father Bernard who both smiled and nodded approvingly.

"I stayed with them on Marlino for nearly an Earth year. By then, Freida had left with Jinko for Roonio nine, while Eva had gone off on intergalactic travel to Centauras A with a handsome, adventurous devil from planet Bilenial in the Epsilon Aurigae system. Last time I saw them, they were just friends and had not mated."

Nicole saw confused expressions on the residents' faces.

"Don't ask. Let's just say Eva met a guy who was a traveler and they went off to another galaxy to have a look-see. Gina also met a guy. A traveler and entertainer. His name is Clafebb. That's my translation of how it sounds. He's from a planet called Orbaldinia in the star Castor system. That's in the Gemini constellation. Orbalidinians are travelers who run, what you might call, intergalactic cruise ships. Gina, who was a dancer in Las Vegas during her Earth-life, is perform- ing again. Last I heard they were off to the galaxy in Andromeda, still just friends who do a song and dance act together. And Bonnie, Bonita, went off with a guy, not mated, who was from... I'm going to run this by you quickly. You don't have to memorize it. There's no test later. The guy is a Marlinon navigator, like Julie's mate, Yanar. His name is Jing-Ar-Mainz. Jingar. He's a really nice guy who went out of his way to learn Spanish. That impressed Bonnie. He's smart, adven- turous, kind, and nearly seven feet tall. They are, as far as I know, not mates, but she chose to travel with him. Last I heard they were entering a pretty far out Markarian Galaxy to explore its central blue star."

More totally blank stares.

"Okay. So after a year, Dr. Cohestle got me a berth aboard a Marlinon trading vessel and I've been hopping around our galaxy, visiting all kinds of planets; meeting many humanoids; and exploring many civilizations. I took some of the images you saw on Marlino, Gimm and Roonio nine. And, no, I haven't met, nor have I looked for, a mate. I'm only twenty-two and I there is much of the Universe that I want to see. That's it for me. Questions?"

As almost everyone's hands shot up, Rosie, Julie and Freida stood up and joined Nicole in front of the residents.

"How do you stay in touch with each other?"

"Mostly through the Marlinon communication systems," Rosie answered. "Because my mate, Dr. Cohestle, is a traveler, he has access to intra-galaxy and inter-galaxy communications. But some are few and far between."

"Because I travel extensively," Nicole added, "I pick up info and forward it back to Rosie, Julia and Freida. But the others, off to other galaxies, are sometimes out of touch for long periods of time. Intergalactic communication can be quite iffy at times."

"You all mentioned humanoids, but there are no images of any of them. Not even your mates. Why?"

The ladies and Nicole shot their thoughts back and forth. They had discussed this question and were not completely in agreement as to how to answer. Finally, Nicole telepathed to the others that she would take it on.

"Up front, let me say that we all don't agree about this. I won't reveal anyone's individual position, but I can say that we are evenly divided. On the question, we did decide that unless we were one hundred percent agreed, we would refrain from that aspect of our lives. The rationale of the two of us who did not think it wise to show mates or other beings, humanoid or otherwise, nor animals we encountered, was that Earth, and please don't take this personally, that people on

Earth are not ready to accept the facts that such things exist." She looked over at Father Bernard. "Some of what we saw throws a very different light on what we call organized religion. There is faith. There is recognition of what we call humanity; being cognizant of life, death, love, procreation, conservation, sharing...many of those human traits that religion and civilized people profess on Earth, but are yet unable to deliver. Even just knowing, with certainty, that we are not alone in this galaxy, much less the Universe, would upset many, many apple carts. That, in fact, will be a burden for all of you to bear, and we hope, keep to yourselves. Be mindful of how cynically those who answered ads, and chose to return, were treated when they spoke of extraterrestrial experiences. In this case, two of us have decided that less is better. Next question?"

"How does it feel to get younger?"

"We don't feel younger," Julie answered, "in the sense I think you mean. Our bodies have rejuvenated and reactivated, but our knowledge and experience remains with us."

Julie then started to say something about increased brain activity and usage up from ten percent to nearly eighty, but Freida silently warned her not to. That would be intimidating.

"The best way I can put it is that we have experienced not only physical change, but that our whole outlook on life has evolved."

"Are there any more humanoids, as you say, looking for mates from Earth?"

"I imagine there are," Rosie answered. "But the Marlinons have taken a hiatus while they see how things work out with our group."

"What things?"

"Our being older than the women they previously encountered. What our offspring might be. How difficult it is to bear young on this home planet. Things like that."

"So you're like test cases?"

"I guess you can say that," Nicole interjected, "because the Marlinons didn't factor in the possibility of a senior prankster personality like Rosie's." That got some laughs.

"How did they place the ad?"

"Through the Internet. Personals in several magazines are free as long as they are not salacious."

"Freida? Why are there no windows or doors in your home?"

"Well, there are doors that give us access from beneath the house. You see, because of the dry and hot conditions on the surface, there are often large and powerful dust storms. As I said before, our water comes from aquifers far below the surface. Our power comes from a place even deeper. It's geothermal."

"If we can't see any of the humanoids, what about the others you mentioned. I think you said non-carbon based?"

"Humanoids like the Marlinon, Gimmian, Chertak, Bileneal and Orbalidinian that we all met," Nicole answered, "are, like us, carbon based. We share most characteristics and, as we said, DNA and RNA, more or less. Some chromosomes are different, but not beyond compatibility. You ask what the non-humanoids are like? Different, but not radically like sci-fi movies portray. Some are carbon based, but more like batrachians. Some are crystalline. Others I've met are hybrid humanoid and feline. There's been a lot of mixing and evolving going on out there, but the more the Marlinons and others travel, the more it seems that there is a common source. We humanoids seem to be related genetically in some fashion."

"You mean created?" Father Bernard asked.

"I'm honestly not as sure of that premise as I once was, Father," Nicole said. "Let me end on these thoughts as you all seem to have the same questions, posed differently. What are they, the beings we've met out there? How do they live and how do we fit in? Here on Earth, we frown on racial, ethnic and religious inter-marriage. We erect fences and borders. We teach our children to hate. We allow starvation. We deny marriage to gay couples. We deny women the right to control their own reproductive processes. We fight over territory, money, beliefs. We maim, starve, rape and kill one another. Out there, for the most part, the beings, humanoid and otherwise, do not. So, in a very real sense, we on Earth do not belong out there...yet. They have accepted the seven of us, and others from Earth, because as individuals, we do not carry the virus of hatred and bigotry. What we learned that first year was that to join the universe of travelers, Earth-humanoids must first figure out how they, and their planet, can survive peacefully. The behavior now practiced on Earth will not be welcomed by civilized beings that have nurtured their planets and have been at peace for millennia."

There may have been more questions, but there were no more raised hands. Nicole's last statement was a sobering indictment of the Earth-human race. Rosie joined her family. Father Bernard and Sister Mary Francis got up. Julie and Freida left. The residents filed out of the dining room quietly. When they had all left, Sammy and Bogdon cleaned off the main table, put the chairs back in place, and set up the room for breakfast.

The next morning, Dr. Bowmeister sat silently at the mahogany reading table in the Residence library with Nicole, Dr. Weiss, the OB/GYN resident, Nurse Judy Lennard and PA Harold Watanabe. They were waiting for Bishop Draper. After securing access to the new hospital wing's third floor, the library had become a makeshift operations center. This morning, the team had a new member, Dr. Ivan Altschuler, a medical geneticist specializing in genetic diagnosis and treatment of genetic disorders. His PhD, earned at Harvard, was in molecular genetics; his dissertation, published in the New England Journal of Medicine dealt with new processes in Cytogenetics, which is the study of the structure and function of cells; in particular, chromosomes. Dr. Bowmeister had brought him into the group after seeing the disturbing results of the blood and amniocentesis tests they had done on the three ladies last week.

The bishop arrived with apologies for being late. Father Bernard was with him. The teenage daughter of a congregant family had been in a bad car accident and he had to pay a last rites visit to the hospital. He was obviously disturbed.

"The child was only sixteen. Her boyfriend, just eighteen, had his license for a week. He had been drinking. He survived. I really have no satisfactory answer for parents when they ask me why. To tell them to have faith rarely is an immediate answer to that kind of tragedy

and heartbreak. And to call it God's will is, to me, woefully inade-
quate." He saw that his dilemma caused discomfort to the others in
the room. "Well, we all have our tasks in this life. That was mine this
morning. Let's talk about yours. You said you have some test results."

"That we do, Monsignor," Dr. Bowmeister began. "You know Dr. Weiss,
Nurse Lennard and my PA, Harold Watanabe. Let me introduce Dr.
Ivan Altschuler. He's on board as our expert geneticist." The doctor
rose and reached over to shake the bishop's hand.

"Good to meet you, doctor. Are you an MD?"

"PhD. Good to meet you, Bishop."

"Yes. So, Jimmy, how are our ladies?"

"Physically, they're solid," Bowmeister answered.

"But I can hear that you're concerned."

"The amniocentesis showed discrepancies," Dr. Weiss said.

"Does that mean that there is something wrong?" Nicole asked.

"It's the babies," Dr. Weiss continued. "The amniotic fluid contains
antibodies and cells that we can't identify."

At that moment, there was a commotion in the hallway outside
the library. Sister Mary's voice was heard.

"And I said there is a meeting going on. You will have to wait!"
Then the door burst open. Sister Mary Francis was backing into the
room. She was being pushed by a tall, middle-aged, fiftyish, stout
woman dressed in a white nurse's uniform, white shoes, black cape
and a white nurse's cap. She was carrying a small black suitcase. Sister
Mary had hold of the front of the nurse's cape.

"Will someone instruct this person to release me?!" the nurse
shouted. Dr. Bowmeister jumped to his feet.

"It's okay, Sister," he called out. "This is Nurse Allison Tracy. I asked
her to meet us here."

"Well, somebody ought to have told me," Sister Mary grumbled. "I
don't like strangers poking around here, especially with the, you know
who, visiting with us."

"You're right," Father Bernard said. "It's my fault. I should have told you when Dr. Bowmeister called this morning. It's just that after last night, well, I was sort of discombobulated."

"Well, please combobulate yourself, Father. It's most important, as they say, to keep me in the loop."

"I will. I surely will," Father Bernard assured her.

"May I get to work, doctor?" Nurse Tracy asked, directing her request to Dr. Bowmeister. "Where are my patients?"

"Of course. First let me introduce... This is Sister Mary Francis, Father Bernard, Doctor..."

"Hello, everyone," Nurse Tracy said, with a condescending nod, cutting him off. "My patients, doctor?"

"Of course," the doctor said. "Sister, would you please show the, uh, Nurse Tracy to the ladies downstairs?"

"Rosie is with her family."

"Then Julie and Freida first. Please. And tell them all we'll be down for a visit in a little while." Sister Mary huffed out an okay. Nurse Tracy took her by the elbow.

"Okay, Sister. Let's get to work!" Sister Mary pulled her arm away.

"Hands off. I'm not one of your patients."

"Of course not. How could you be? You're a nun."

"This way," Sister said, turning abruptly to the door. Nurse Tracy marched past her. Sister Mary looked back at the people at the table, rolled her eyes and shook her head as if to say, *This is getting out of hand...* She closed the library door behind her, not gently.

"Who is this person?" the bishop asked.

"Allison Tracy. The best OB/GYN Nurse Practitioner I've ever known," Dr. Weiss answered.

"Is she going to be a problem?" Father Bernard asked. "She seems a little intense."

"I'd trust her with my life," Dr. Bowmeister told the priest. "She's the best. And she knows how to keep a secret."

Everyone in the room settled down.

Having heard that the reports presented questions, Nicole was anxious. "You were saying, Dr. Weiss? About the babies?"

"I've studied the slides," Dr. Altschuler said in response to Nicole's query. "I am concerned. I wish we knew more about the fathers. At least if I had some of their blood and tissue samples..."

"But we don't. We're flying blind," Dr. Weiss interrupted. "The babies could be in danger. The mothers too."

There was a long, silent moment. The faces of everyone showed worry; all except Nicole, who gazed out the window at the Atlantic Ocean. The tide was receding and there was a chilly, on-shore breeze that caused the waves to break earlier and higher than normal.

"Do you know anyone who has a boat?" she asked no one in particular at the table.

"There's a guy I've been out with, fishing with friends," Harold Watanabe told her. "He's a charter. Knows the waters. Not too expensive."

No one in the room asked Nicole what she was up to. But somehow they knew it must have had something to do with the test results.

CHAPTER THIRTY-THREE
A Dive, A Kick And A Blip

Three days later, Charter Captain Dave Butts eased back on the throttle of his twenty-eight-foot Boston Whaler, aptly named the *Butt-In*. The twin 250 Yamaha four-stroke engines slowed the boat until it was barely moving forward in the light swells. He was steering from the flying bridge. It was another unusually warm autumn day. He turned and glanced below to the stern where the young lady, who had chartered him for the day, was making adjustments to her scuba equipment.

Butts, a surly, weatherworn fifty-five-year-old, was a retired Master Chief Petty Officer who had served his entire Navy career on submarines. He was born six years after the first U.S. nuclear submarine, the USS Nautilus, was commissioned. He spent his thirty years of service onboard various nuclear subs in the American fleet.

"We're on your numbers, ma'am," he called down to her. She was finishing strapping a weird-looking electronic device onto her right arm. She waved a thumbs-up up at him. He cut the engines, double-checked the GPS and his depth gauge/fish-finder. They were over a reef, fifteen meters, or about fifty feet below. He dropped anchor and then slipped down the steel ladder to the deck.

"How long you gonna be down there?" he asked.

Nicole was adjusting her mouthpiece and testing her regulator. She took the mouthpiece out. "Maybe a half-hour. No more unless you're hiding a decompression chamber somewhere on board," she joked.

"I'm not." Butts was serious. "And I'm only doin' this, I mean, lettin' you go down alone, 'cause Doc Bowmeister and the bishop vouched for you bein' certified and all..."

"I appreciate that, Captain Butts."

"I ain't no Captain. Most I made was Master Chief."

"Well, as far as I'm concerned, you're the captain of this vessel." He smiled and threw her a quick salute. She finished adjusting her flippers and put on her mask. "I'm good to go." Nicole picked up a shiny metallic case she had on the deck. She opened it. Butts saw it was filled with bricks.

"What's that for?"

"It's a case for the coral samples I have to gather. The bricks are just weight to let me carry it down. Dr. Bowmeister did tell you I work for NOAA, right?"

"Yeah. Marine biologist," he said.

"Okay. So, the increased water temps and polluted sediment have caused some outbreaks of Atlantic White Pox Disease up and down the coast. I'm going to have a look around and get some samples, especially the Elk Horn Coral, for our lab in Woods Hole, Massachusetts. I'll leave the bricks behind." She moved to the side of the boat, near the stern.

"Now you take care, young lady. This far out, there could be some nasty sharks. Hammerheads and..." Before he finished his admonition, she was over the side and gone. "...tigers just off the reef."

Back at the Residence, everyone had settled in to await the births, all under the watchful eyes of Nurse Allison Tracy. She had turned out to be a tremendous asset, keeping the three ladies comfortable and watching their diets. She supervised the meals Bogdon prepared precisely to the instructions Drs. Weiss and Bowmeister prescribed. Both he and Sammy quickly learned not to cross her. She had little to no sense of humor. She insisted on checking temps and blood pressure every six hours and made sure that the expectant mothers took two naps a day—no excuses.

The very experienced nurse had also made her peace with Sister Mary Francis, with apologies. She explained that once assigned to a case, she was totally committed and focused on her patients' care.

"As I am on those in our little flock here," Sister Mary told her.

"Understood and respected," was Nurse Tracy's response. And since then, their run-in outside the library was forgotten and they were, if not buddies, polite, respectful and helpful to one another.

On the day that Nicole was diving off the *Butt-In*, Kate Conlon, and Herbie and Alex Legum, borrowed Father Bernard's car and drove into Wilmington. Herbie's mission was to meet with an officer of Wells Fargo Bank, and then Morgan Stanley Brokerage. He had power of attorney documents that he drew up and backdated four years, from Rosie, Julie and Freida. Kate and Alex went to do some shopping for gifts—infant stuff and some new clothing for the ladies.

Herbie had no problem settling matters on the accounts. His story was that the ladies' wills had finally been discovered and he was in the process of getting their estates into probate. The final accounting showed that the three ladies, collectively, had several hundred thousand dollars in liquid assets. He left the accounts active and intact at both financial institutions. He would be in touch.

Since it was a nice day, the ladies were on the porch, playing Mahjong with Lynn Ferrari, the retired journalist from New Jersey. Eva had taught them the game when she first came to the Residence. A few of the other residents were nearby, reading or playing cards. Nurse

Tracy sat slightly away from the square bridge table, between Rosie and Julie, watching. Freida taught her that the word for that was kibitzing. As the Mahjong tiles were thrown and picked, the player called out the name of the tile she threw.

"Four crack," Julie said, throwing and picking a tile from the wall.

"Two crack," Rosie said, doing the same.

"Do the green dragons go with the bams?" Lynn asked.

"Green dragons live on Hillet," Rosie said with a wink.

"What's a Hillet?" Lynn asked. "I don't remember that tile."

"What's a dragon?" Nurse Tracy asked. Lynn held up a blue square with a wiggly line inscribed on it.

"That's like a dragon, but it's called soap, dear. They go with dots. The red dragon goes with cracks and the green dragon goes with bams," Julie informed her.

"You have to speak Chinese to play. I'll never get the hang of this," Lynn said, frustrated.

"Of course you will. Dr. Cohestle made me a set. He learned how to play in about twenty minutes. Of course he could read my mi..." She stopped herself.

"Of course he can read," Freida said quickly.

Arthur Baumgartner, Kate Conlon's boyfriend, was lounging nearby, reading the newspaper. He had a good idea that Rosie was going to say "read my mind." Julie picked up his thought and looked over at him. He quickly looked down at the newspaper, but she knew what he was thinking. He would bear watching.

"What are they like?" Nurse Tracy asked.

"Who?" Freida asked back.

"Your husbands...mates, as you call them."

"They're darling. Perfectly normal humanoids," Freida answered.

"Sweet," Julie said.

"Loving," Rosie added.

"And hardworking," Freida said. "My Jinko puts in long daylights at the mines."

"But what are they *like*? You know…"

"You mean physically?"

"Well… Yes."

Rosie patted her stomach. "As you can see, Nurse Tracy, they're quite human."

Freida, Julie and Lynn laughed. The residents at the nearby card table joined them. Nurse Tracy shook her head.

"Not like that. I mean how do they…?"

Suddenly, Rosie doubled over in pain. In a flash, Nurse Tracy was on her feet.

"Oh! Oh my God!" Rosie moaned.

"You've had a baby before, Rosie," the nurse said. "Does it feel like it's time?"

"How do I know? I never had a Marlinon baby. Oh Jesus! She's moving."

The nurse took out her cell phone. "I'm calling Dr. Bowmeister and Dr. Weiss." Then, as quickly as the pain came, it was gone. Rosie relaxed.

"No, wait," she said as she took a deep breath. "Wait. It's okay. It's passed. I feel fine."

"Maybe we should get the doctor anyway," Arthur suggested as he got up and came over to the table.

"She said she's fine," Julie said quickly, reading his thoughts. *He was considering calling a friend of his at CNN in Atlanta, telling him he had a big story. They could get a TV crew down to Wilmington quickly. It might even land him the producing job he craved.*

"It was just a false alarm, Arthur," Rosie said with conviction. "I had plenty of those with my Kate."

"Nevertheless," Nurse Tracy said, "I'll see what Dr. Bowmeister thinks about seeing you tomorrow. But if it happens again, we're out of here."

They resumed the game. Julie made a mental note to have a talk with Arthur. Rosie and Freida picked up on it and sent back a message: "Let's all have a chat with him!"

After forty-five minutes underwater, Dave Butts was worried. He was up on the flying bridge, scanning the area and checking his watch. He was a certified diver and had scuba gear on board. He decided to give the NOAA marine biologist ten more minutes. If she was a no-show, he would go down after her.

Below, Nicole was swimming up from the deep trench east of the reef. She had paid a visit to the Marlinon spacecraft, still buried beneath the sea floor. It had moved slightly so she could access an entry portal. Three minutes later, as she read his thoughts, Nicole emerged off the stern and waved at a relieved Dave Butts. He helped her climb aboard, noting that as she swung the shiny metal case onto the deck, it seemed much lighter in her hand. He guessed that the coral she had gathered was not the thick, heavy kind.

A half-hour earlier, the Blossom Point Naval Station for Space Technology had received a call from the Southeastern office of the United States Geological Survey regarding a mild underwater disturbance off the North Carolina coast, near Wilmington. They were asked to aim the optics on their satellite LL-945.9, still in fixed orbit above the southeastern coast of the United States, on specific coordinates. This was the same area that the Navy had dispatched the new DDG-1000 class Destroyer, USS Metz, to investigate what was eventually deemed an anomaly earlier that month. The crew had used Multi-Function Radar and an AUV, Autonomous Underwater Vehicle, to survey the area above and below the ocean. They had found nothing.

What Dave Butts didn't know was that at that moment, as Nicole began to remove her wet suit, and he started the engines and retrieved the anchor, the Navy satellite, scanning the area, saw and zoomed into a tiny dot off the southern North Carolina coast. It was quickly identified, through an NSA computer search, as the charter fishing vessel, *Butt-In*; home port—Wilmington, North Carolina.

Back at the Blossom Point Naval Station for Space Technology the data and NSA identification gathered had the attention of the same Chief Warrant Officer Five, and Petty Officer who had been involved of the so-called anomaly investigation a few weeks ago. They both sat at the main console studying the image of the *Butt-In* heading for port, and the data regarding the vessel.

"What do you think, Harry?" the Petty Officer asked.

"I'm thinking that's the same place and same burst of high energy. That's no anomaly, Lou."

"Agreed. Someone's playing games. Let's see if the Coast Guard can nail it this time." Harry reached for the hotline phone and called the U.S. Coast Guard Command Center in Washington, D.C. He entered his section code and was immediately patched into the Intelligence and Criminal Investigations Section.

An hour later, as the *Butt-In* backed into her slip at the South Harbor Marina, two Coast Guard investigators, Chris Block and Annie Mallory, watched from their unmarked, 2011 black Subaru Forester.

"There's only one passenger," Chris Block said as he observed Nicole shake hands with Captain Butts.

"She doesn't look like much of a fisherman to me," Annie Mallory commented as she peered through a monocular. "Pretty though."

"Check out the scuba gear on the deck. She must have been diving."

"Maybe. There's a reef out where they were spotted. But she's leaving it on the boat."

"Rented?"

"Could be. Or hers and she's coming back."

"Which one do we check out?" Block asked.

"The girl's going to a van. She's got some kind of metal case with her. You hang in here and keep an eye on the captain," Mallory told her partner. "I'll follow her."

"And then what?"

"See what he does. Call me and I'll pick you up."

"How about I follow her? I mean, I'm already behind the wheel and the seat's adjusted for me."

"Because a woman hanging around this marina will stand out more than a man, and, because she may go somewhere that's all female, and, because I'm your boss and I don't feel like hanging around here."

Block, a pudgy forty-three-year-old black man, reluctantly got out of the SUV as Mallory, a slightly older, tall, freckled redhead, got out of the front passenger side and walked around to the driver's side.

"What if he just takes off?"

"We have an address for him. Anyway, he'll be a while cleaning up the boat. See if the scuba gear is a rental. We passed a dive shop right outside the marina."

A half-hour later, Mallory picked up Block outside the dive shop.

"What's up?" she asked as he got into the SUV.

"Like you said. The guy, Butts, he cleaned up and returned the scuba gear. You?"

"Would you believe she lives at the Wilmington Parish Retirement Home for Ladies."

"She didn't look like no senior to me."

"Yeah. And I'm wondering what she had in that metal case."

CHAPTER THIRTY-FOUR

A Question Of Genetics

"This one from Mrs. Conlon has some pretty weird stem cell configurations in his bloodstream," Dr. Weiss called over to Dr. Bowmeister who was across the table from him in the new wing's hematology main lab. His boss, the chief OB/GYN, was with hematology technician Leslie Shipp, whom he had brought on board after Nicole showed up with blood and tissue samples yesterday. "And they're not just *hematopoietic stem cells,* Jim, but all kinds of adult stem cells. You know, like we've only seen in bone marrow and tissue for organ and skeletal repair and regeneration. I'm not absolutely sure; there are even some that appear to be nerve building cells that we've only seen in brain tissue."

Dr. Bowmeister was looking at a computer screen that was showing the enhanced and magnified image of Julie Lobato's blood sample. "If you think that's strange, Leslie," Dr. Bowmeister called back, "come on over here and have a look at these red cells. They're large enough to carry five times the oxygen of human, or should I say Earth-humanoid, red corpuscles."

Nicole, who was sitting nearby, was amused by the reaction of the doctors to the samples she'd brought back on the *Butt-In.* At that moment, Dr. Ivan Altschuler, the geneticist, came rushing into the lab, carrying a computer printout.

"We have a problem, doctors!" he exclaimed excitedly. "I've never seen or even read about anything like this. In fact," he told them as they all gathered at Dr. Bowmeister's area, "I'd swear, under oath, that the gene and chromosome configurations of..." He turned to Nicole. "Where are these samples from?"

"You have the tissue from Freida Riggs' mate, Jinko," she answered. "But they all come from Marlino, Gimm and Roonio nine."

"All from the ladies' mates?"

"I believe they are," Nicole answered, no longer amused, but concerned. "That's what I was told, anyway."

"What's wrong, Ivan?" Dr. Bowmeister asked.

"Everything. Look." Dr. Altschuler took a flash drive from his lab coat pocket and slipped it into a USB port of the computer on the lab table. The image on the screen was a three-dimensional diagram of a colorful, DNA molecular helix structure that was turning and growing. The geneticist froze the image.

He pointed to a section of the helix. "That cell is missing fifteen chromosomes. But then again, it has thirty-three that I've never seen. I printed out the configuration of the DNA and RNA." Dr. Altschuler put the printout on the lab table, and then turned to Nicole. "I was told that you, and the pregnant ladies, said the mates were humanoid. What I'm looking at here is something beyond my understanding of that term. I mean, some of the missing chromosomes are the ones we've identified as disease carriers. With this DNA, these mates, and their offspring could live a very long time. Maybe indefinitely if their stem cell configurations are as functional as the DNA."

"They're more than that," Dr. Weiss interjected.

"And there are super-cells in the bloodstream," Dr. Bowmeister added.

"Built for far greater capacity than ours," hematology technician Shipp said.

Everyone in the room turned toward Nicole. "You once told us that there are some out there," Dr. Bowmeister said, "travelers you called them, like the Marlinons, who believe that all the known humanoid populations are derived from a common source."

"Yes. Many believe that."

"The samples you brought kind of support that, but the variations are troubling," Dr. Weiss told her. "The ladies' blood was particularly healthy, but, except for cell size, basically normal to our standards. The amniotic fluid had some indication of difference. Now we see large differences. Viability of the infants...actually our ability to sustain them after birth, could be a serious problem."

"The fathers," Ivan Altschuler muttered as aside to himself.

"What about the fathers?" Nicole asked.

"If they were here, and not light years away, we might be able to assure a more positive outcome for the children."

"Well," Nicole told the geneticist, "as we've told you, they live in atmospheres and gravity that are not compatible with ours."

"Exactly what compatibility problems are we looking at here?" Dr. Altschuler asked.

"We've been through all of this before," Nicole answered.

"Not with me," the geneticist told her. "I'd like to hear about it firsthand."

"All right. Rosie has a chip to allow her to breathe on Marlino. On Gimm, Julie can breathe the oxygen-rich air for long periods of time, but the gravity is much less. And Freida's home, Roonio nine, also has a fairly breathable atmosphere, but combined with an extremely hot and dry climate, and much stronger gravity, her adaptation was prolonged and difficult."

"Sounds to me like a good chemist and contractor might have created rooms with contained atmospheres and temperatures for the fathers."

"The Marlinons weren't sure that would be possible here. Their experience with most mixed matings is that blood and tissue samples usually suffice."

"That's too bad. We could really use those mates."

"Well, that impossible now, Ivan," Dr. Bowmeister said. "At least they had the good sense to send along the blood and tissue samples."

Ivan Altschuler, though recognized and well published in his field of expertise, was only thirty-two. His personality was aggressive, opinionated, and self-assured.

"I can't imagine they made the mother's home planet regulation without taking every precaution to insure the safety of the babies," he told Nicole.

"There is much about them that you could not imagine, doctor," Nicole said with a shrug, as if to say, that's the end of that. She picked up thoughts of acceptance from the three doctors and the female lab technician—all they were resigned work with the samples that she had provided.

But Nicole's thoughts were elsewhere with Alex Legum, Rosie's younger grandson from Maui. She had been attracted to him, and sensed it was mutual, but at the moment, it was the fact that he was a chemist that was driving her desire to see him as soon as possible.

CHAPTER THIRTY-FIVE
Secrets On The Beach

That evening, after dinner, Nicole asked Alex Legum if he'd like to take a walk. It was nearly the end of October. The night air was brisk, with a warmer breeze coming off the ocean. They made their way down to the beach. The moon, rising out of the rippling, outgoing tide, laid a sparkling, bright yellow-white line in the water.

"That's a harvest moon," she told the young chemist. "I haven't seen one in three years."

"No moons out there?"

"On Marlino, they have two moons. Remember we showed them the night you arrived? One is reddish and large; the other, silvery like ours, only smaller." Nicole slowed down a bit, and deliberately blocked off her ability to read some of his thoughts. She wanted to have a conversation on equal terms. But just before she did that, she felt the warmth of how he cared for her and let it linger for a moment.

"Where'd you grow up, Nicole?"

"Elkhorn, Nebraska. I'm what they call pioneer stock. They came west in the land rush of 1878. Farmers. But by the time I came to be, the farm was long gone."

"Brothers? Sisters?"

"No. Just me. My dad's an engineer. My mom's a teacher. High school biology."

"Wilmington's a long way from Nebraska."

"After high school I sort of thought I had a calling to do service. Well, not sort of, I did then. Now, I think that maybe I just wanted to get out of Nebraska. Anyway, I joined the Order of Servants of Mary. Their motherhouse, the Lady of Sorrows Convent, is in Omaha. And from there, I was sent here as a novitiate."

"And then you met my grandmother."

Nicole stopped and looked at Alex. "Your grandmother, who always seemed to be cheering everyone on, mischief and all, is in my book, a saint. You cannot imagine what...where...who we have seen."

"I saw the pictures..."

"Not like being there. Touching, smelling, feeling what it is to be part of something sooo much larger and, well, just absolutely grand."

Alex took her hand in his. "You're the most alive woman I've ever met. I think it's wonderful." Nicole took his other hand in hers. They stood facing each other, feeling something magical pass between them. It lasted for a long moment. And then, Nicole reached up and put her hand behind Alex's neck. She drew him to her lips. He did not resist, but rather embraced her as they kissed. And they kissed again and again, with hearts beating fast and adrenaline coursing through their entwined bodies.

At the same time, Drs. Bowmeister and Weiss, with the assistance of Nurse Allison Tracy, were doing individual examinations of the three ladies in their rooms at the Residence. Rosie's baby had grown a bit more. By touch, Dr. Bowmeister could tell the infant was still in that impossible position of having her long legs folded up against her body. This kept pressure off Rosie's spine and pelvis.

"You've got one smart little girl in there," Dr. Bowmeister told Rosie.

"Not so little by my standards," Nurse Tracy said, correcting him. The doctor smiled and nodded. He was used to her abrupt manner. It was a personality quirk that kept several prenatal problems from turning into serious situations, or worse.

Other than the baby's size, everything else was good.

"You're showing signs of being close to giving birth, Mrs. Conlon," he said as he finished the exam.

"I prefer Mrs. Cohestle, if you don't mind."

"Of course. Sorry. How are things going with your family being here?"

"It's really very nice. A comfort."

"I wish your mate could have made the trip."

"Me too. It would be wonderful to have him here. She'll be his first child."

Dr. Weiss was completing his exam of Julie in her room. Her baby was normal size with a strong heartbeat. Julie was in excellent physical shape. He saw no problems with the birth.

"I'd say you're due in about ten days. Two weeks, tops. Your little girl is looking good."

"She's not too big, is she? I mean, it can be a normal birth. Not a C-section."

"Vaginal, as far as I'm concerned. Why do you ask?"

"My mate, Yanar...he's six-foot-eight. His father is seven-foot-five. Yanar did say not to worry, like he knew she wouldn't be big, but I do."

"Well, he was right. She's a normal female baby." He hesitated for a moment, wondering if he should mention the genetic data they had for Yanar, but saw no reason to alarm an expectant mother. "I guess she's got your genes," he said. "She's lucky, and quite beautiful, I'm sure."

Both doctors, and Nurse Tracy, examined Freida last. In the last sonogram, the amniotic fluid was darker than normal, and they thought they saw shadows indicating a multiple birth.

Otherwise, Freida was as healthy as the others. Indications were for a normal birth within the next two weeks. Dr. Bowmeister gave Nurse Tracy a regimen for the three women and suggested that it might be best to move them to the hospital in a week or so.

Nicole and Alex sat on the cool sand, looking out to sea. She was in front of him, between his spread legs, with her back leaning on his chest. His arms enveloped her shoulders. He inhaled the scent of her hair and kissed her neck. She lifted his hand and kissed it.

"Can you come with me back to Maui?" he asked. They had been talking about how strongly they felt about one another. She knew the subject would come up and wasn't sure how to handle it.

"I don't know that I could be happy here, on Earth, after what I've... you know, being out there and seeing what I've seen." She looked up at the night sky. It was clear. The moonlight overpowered some of the fainter stars, but the bright swath of starlight that the Milky Way presented was visible.

"Then can I come with you?"

She turned her head and looked at him. "And never come back? Your mom? Your brother?"

"I've been thinking about that since I first saw you," he admitted. She knew that to be true because she had felt it. "If that's what has to be, then okay. I never thought I'd feel this way, but I do. I want to be with you."

She moved around, up onto her knees, and faced him. "I feel the same way, Alex. I guess it's possible."

"You're not sure?"

"I'm sure. Oh yes, I'm sure!" She kissed him, hard and long. "But there are circumstances. There are things that have to happen, and things that cannot happen."

"What are you worried about?"

"Your grandmother, Julie and Freida. They've found a place for them-selves. Their mates fawned over them. They were romanced." She smiled. "They found respect, and then love. A wonderful life ahead. Starting a new family. If they are discovered here, they could lose everything."

Alex took her hand. "Then we just have to make sure things go right, and they, and you, are not discovered."

She took a deep breath and held his hand against her breast. "Okay, Alex. Here it is. The doctors are worried...let me back up. I made a trip to the Marlinon spaceship yesterday. I brought back samples of their mate's blood and tissue. There might be problems with the births."

"What kind of problems?" Alex asked, concerned.

"They're not sure. But they said that if the fathers were actually here, they could know better what to expect."

"And they're not here?"

"They come from different atmospheres, temperatures and gravities. In order for them to be here, habitats would have had to be provided." Before Nicole could go any further, Alex got it.

"They are here, right?"

"Yes," she admitted. Alex sat up. His mind was going a mile a minute. She felt his surge of energy. It was stimulating. Emotional. Sexual.

"Tell me, exactly how different are these environments from ours?"

"I can't tell you exactly."

"Who can?"

"Dr. Cohestle. Your stepgrandfather." Alex burst out laughing. He hugged Nicole, held her face in his hands and kissed her.

"You're wonderful," he told her. "When can I see him?"

"Tomorrow. I have to call the charter captain."

"Does he know?"

"No. He thinks I'm a NOAA marine biologist checking the reef out there." She hesitated. "Wait. There is a problem."

"What? I dive all the time in Maui. I'm certified."

"The reef is fifty feet down. The Marlinon ship is down over four hundred."

"Four hundred? I couldn't... How do you get down to it?"

"I just can. The processing. Actually, I don't even need my scuba gear." Alex was amazed, and then disappointed.

"I'm still leaving with you, right?"

"Oh, yes. You can be processed then. Just not now."

"Okay. What if I gave you a list of what I need to know to build habitats in the hospital rooms? Specs, so their mates would be comfortable. Could you bring that to my step-grandpa? He's a chemist, Grandma said. He'd understand."

"I could do that," she said, smiling. "I could do that tomorrow." Alex got up off the sand quickly. He offered his hand and pulled Nicole up, close to him. He kissed her.

"Mmmmm... Now, let's get back to the Residence and plan all this out." They hurried back up the beach to the path to the Residence.

When they entered the front door, they took no notice of the black Subaru Forester parked right beyond the driveway.

Coast Guard Investigator Chris Block had just returned to the SUV after taking down Drs. Bowmeister's and Weiss's license plates.

"Got them. Both MDs," he reported to Annie Mallory. He began to put them into the computer to check registrations.

"The girl from the boat just came up from the beach with her boyfriend," she told Block.

"How'd you know it was her boyfriend?"

"They were holding hands and before they came into the light from the Residence, they kissed far too long to be anything but."

First thing in the morning, Nicole called Davis Butts and made a date to charter the *Butt-In* out to the reef that afternoon. Rosie, Julie, Freida, Nicole, Kate, Arthur, Herbie and Alex ate breakfast together at the same table the three ladies and their three friends had always used. Nurse Tracy sat nearby, ever vigilant and fussing over what her charges ate.

The ladies picked up some interesting energy coming from Alex's thoughts. Nicole, aware of what they heard, blushed. Freida and Julie smiled. Rosie winked at Nicole and threw her a thought—"Watch out, or you'll be calling me Grandma, and your mate might be my daughter's brother." Julie burst out laughing.

"You know there was once a popular song called, 'I'm My Own Grandpa'?" Freida said aloud. Knowing the lyrics, Julie and Rosie immediately laughed. Nicole tried to keep from smiling. Everyone else at the table had no idea what was happening.

"Private joke," Rosie told her family. "Something that happened on Gimm," she fibbed.

After breakfast, Nicole met privately with the ladies. She told them why it had become necessary to try to get their mates to the hospital wing. She explained the plan and that Alex said with the right information, he could design rooms for them in the hospital where they'd be comfortable and the doctors could get the information they needed.

"Is there something that the doctors aren't telling us?" Freida asked.

"Not really. They want as much information as they can get so they can anticipate and solve any problems that might occur."

"That's a whole lot of words that mean they're flying blind, dear," Julie told Nicole.

"I don't think that's accurate. They're only being as careful as they can."

"Speaking of being careful, Rosie, I've picked up some vibes from your daughter's boyfriend," Julie said.

"Kate's Arthur? What?"

"He was thinking about how our being here has great media potential and how he can make money from it."

"Really?" Rosie was disappointed. "He seems such a nice young man."

"Well, that nice young man has friends at CNN in Atlanta and he's thinking of calling them in on this, on us. He hopes it will get him a producer's job there."

"I'll talk to Kate," Rosie told her friends.

"No," Julie said quickly. "I'll take care of it."

"Remember, we're not supposed to use our new abilities to influence beings on other planets," Freida reminded Julie.

"The regulation also states, unless in danger. I consider this a danger to us, our babies and the Marlinons offshore," she told Freida. "I'll be discreet and kind. I'm sure he'll see it our way."

"So what's going on with you and my Alex?" Rosie asked Nicole.

"We like each other." The three ladies grinned and nodded. "And I know you were listening in on him at breakfast. That's not fair."

"Listening in? How could we not hear with his mind bubbling full of sweet thoughts about you?" Julie told her.

"I heard too," Freida agreed. "He's fallen for you."

"And me, him," Nicole admitted. "He's coming back to Marlino with us."

"He is! Does Kate know? Herbie?" Rosie asked.

"Alex will eventually tell them. Good grief! He's twenty-seven years old. He's a man. A smart man. I really like him. And he likes me. But right now, we're here on a mission to have your babies. Let's not get distracted."

"She's right," Rosie admitted. "First things first. What's the drill, Nicole?"

"You three hang in here. I'll tell Nurse Tracy and Father Bernard what's happening. Father's got to tell the bishop about getting rooms ready for your mates, and fast. I'll see Dr. Cohestle today and get the specs that Alex needs. Julia takes care of Arthur. Gently, Julia. Don't spook him. Okay?"

"I'll make him an offer he can't refuse," Julie said with a decent imitation of Marlon Brando from *The Godfather*.

When Nicole left the Residence in the van at noon, she was followed by CG Senior Investigator Annie Mallory in a black Honda Accord. CG Investigator Chris Block stayed parked in the Subaru at the Residence, keeping it under surveillance. He didn't have to wait long. A half-hour later, Dr. Bowmeister, whose license plate had been verified last night, drove in and picked up Father Bernard in front of the Residence. Block followed them to Saint Simeon's RC Church. As the two men went into the rectory, he parked at a distance and notified Investigator Mallory of his location. She was at the marina. The *Butt-In* was preparing to leave. She told Block she was calling in for a CG chopper to shadow the boat.

Father Bernard, Dr. Bowmeister and Bishop Draper met in the Rectory study. When he heard the news, the bishop was upset.

At that moment, Carol DePaulo, the bishop's housekeeper came into the study with a tray of coffee and cookies.

"If the story gets out, Jesus, Louis, we'll be between rocks."

"That's a rock and a hard place," Mrs. DePaulo corrected him as she set the tray down on the bishop's desk.

"What?"

"The expression you meant to use. It's between a rock and a hard place, not between rocks."

"Thank you, Mrs. DePaulo," the bishop said slightly exasperated. "Are you finished?"

"Not quite. Monsignor. Milk and sugar, doctor?"

"Just black, thanks, Carol. How've you been?"

"Feeling fine. Those hormones you gave me really worked." She poured the coffee and turned to the priest. "You just take milk, right, Father?"

"Yes. Thank you, Mrs. DePaulo." She fussed with the coffee and cookies, taking her sweet time, and making the bishop fidgety.

"Can't you leave that to us?" he asked, frustrated.

"No I can't, Monsignor. Now you gentlemen go on with your business. I'm invisible."

"The safety of the mothers and babies is paramount," the priest began, as though they were talking about a general subject.

"The, uh, special rooms are very important," Dr. Bowmeister said, watching Mrs. DePaulo gently place his coffee on the edge of the desk in front of him.

"We'll know the technical requirements later today," Father Bernard continued.

"Something in the new wing?" Mrs. DePaulo asked.

"What? What are you talking about?" the bishop asked her.

"The new hospital wing. It opens in January, right?"

"Yes. It isn't quite finished yet."

"And Mr. Carlson's company is still the contractor?"

"Yes. But it's almost all done. What is your point, Mrs. DePaulo?"

Bishop Draper said sharply. Carol DePaulo had been at the Rectory long before he came here. Her seniority was golden. "We're having a private meeting here."

"I know that. No need to snap. I'm only trying to help."

He realized his attitude was a mistake. "I'm sorry. Please... If you don't mind..."

"So, I was thinking," she began, interrupting and ignoring him, "that maybe Mr. Carlson would be the best way to get those rooms you're talking about in the new wing ready for you. He is your friend, Monsignor."

"Yes, yes... And?"

"Well then, they could be justified being in the hospital without anyone taking notice. You still have the wing sealed off, don't you?"

"She's right. Carlson and his men could have a good reason to be there. Maybe something he didn't finish," Father Bernard added.

"That's true," Dr. Bowmeister concurred. "We don't have to involve Father McDonough, and Carlson's men don't have to know why they're building the rooms. We can tell them it's a new kind of treatment facility."

Mrs. DePaulo nodded with satisfaction and then finished distributing the coffee cups.

"And how do we pay for this?" Bishop Draper asked. "The building fund is controlled by the Raleigh Diocese."

"Those uh, you know, the three rich ladies? I think they talked about having funds for an additional donation. Sort of a slush fund.

Mrs. DePaulo started for the door.

"How did you know that we were talking about the new wing, Mrs. DePaulo?" the bishop asked. She stopped and turned to face the three men.

"There's little that goes on in this Rectory that I don't know about, Monsignor."

"Yes. Of course. Thank you." She turned to leave. "I'll have to talk to Bubba Carlson," the bishop said in a whisper to the two men seated on the other side of his desk. "I think this plan might just turn the trick."

"Do the trick," Mrs. DePaulo said aloud over her shoulder as she opened the study door.

"Now what are you talking about?" Bishop Draper asked.

She turned to face the men again. "The expression you want is, do the trick. It's hookers who turn a trick, or tricks, Monsignor, depending on how busy they are. Lunch is at two." She gently closed the door behind her. Father Bernard and Dr. Bowmeister held their hands over their mouths to hold in their laughter. Frustrated, Bishop Draper held his head in his hands and slowly shook it back and forth. Then he started to laugh too.

"She's a gem," he said.

"And a bright one at that," Dr. Bowmeister added.

CG Investigator Block watched as Julia found Professor Arthur Baumgartner on the porch, reading the *Wilmington Star-News*. She pulled a wicker chair over and sat down next to him. It was little before lunchtime. He thought the woman looked a little young to be a resident, so Block assumed that they were a couple who were visiting, or worked there.

"Nice day, Professor Baumgartner," Julia said.

"Lovely. It's Arthur. Please call me Arthur." He put aside the paper.

"You're a journalist, right?"

"Media consultant."

"Yes. Media. No more press, or the fourth estate, as it was called in my day."

He smiled. "I suppose that's true. Things do change. Technology."

"You're right. Just look at me. I'm seventy-four and pregnant."

"Yes. That is amazing," he said as he wondered what it would be like to make love to a seventy-four-year-old woman.

"Terrific, I've been told. A strong, well-developed body, and the knowledge that comes with experience."

"What?" How did she know what he was thinking? He hadn't spoken a word.

"That's what you just thought about, isn't it?"

"How in the hell...?" She reached over and touched his arm. He felt a hot, uncomfortable sensation course through his body. He shuddered. "Jesus..."

"Not Jesus. Just me. I know that you're planning to call your friends in Atlanta and expose our being here. Expose the whole story."

Arthur felt his heart skip a few beats. His face flushed. "No. I didn't... how do you? Who told you?"

"You did the night we talked to the residents about our adventures, and showed images of where we'd been. Please don't deny it."

"You can read minds," he said, matter-of-factly.

"We can use much more of our brain capacity than Earth-humanoids do," Julie told him. "The question is, how much of yours will you use? We are here to have our babies and leave. What you were thinking of doing would turn this very private, wonderful event into a media circus, and a government zoo."

"Not necessarily. Things can be controlled. The secret could be kept until after you leave."

"Really?! An international media organization keeping a secret? Not these days, Professor Baumgartner. It's all twenty-four/seven. And mostly speculation, at that. We don't want CNN, or anyone else, here."

"But the world has to know."

"Know what?"

"What you've shown us. What you know about the universe. That we are not alone."

"Why?"

"Why? It's information. News. Important News."

"It's not important to us. And to Rosie, Kate, Herbie and Alex. Do you want to destroy that family?" Julie sensed that he really cared for Kate. He was weighing the question. She heard his honest answer before he spoke it.

"No. I'm sorry. I didn't think it through."

"Look, Arthur. Scientists and astronomers on Earth already have identified systems with planets like ours. In some cases, they are correct. More than they imagine. Mathematicians have calculated the odds that are completely in favor of life elsewhere. But actual proof will disrupt and confound the deniers, the religions and the arrogant fools who think they are the top of the food chain. What was that great Jack Nicholson line from *A Few Good Men*? 'You can't handle the truth!'"

"Yes. I understand. You're right, Julie."

"Okay. Look. I'll make you a deal. You have a camera in your smart phone?"

"Yes."

"We can set it up so that you can take some pictures. Stills. No video. No sound. You can have the exclusive story to use, or not use, however you see fit, after we have our babies and leave. You make the call, but remember there are still people who believe we never landed on the moon in nineteen sixty-nine. You'll be called a fraud and charlatan. So watch out. How does that sound?"

"That sounds fair. Thank you."

"We're not going to listen to your thoughts. We can do that. Turn it off. It means we trust you. Can we trust you?"

"Absolutely."

"Good. Let's shake on that." Julie took his hand. "Thank you." Arthur felt a comfortable sensation course through his body. It was much gentler and welcoming than the heat he'd experienced earlier.

Hidden behind the trees near the entrance to the Residence driveway, CG Investigator Block watched the handshake.

"They're no couple, shaking hands like that," he muttered to himself. *Two visitors on a porch. Employees?* he wrote in his log book under his earlier entry—*Doc B's car PU's priest. 1130 hours.* He noted the time and settled back to continue surveillance.

CHAPTER THIRTY-SEVEN

Outward And Inward Pressure

Two hours later, the United States Geological Survey marked another mild, but now familiar underwater disturbance off the North Carolina coast, near Wilmington. They notified the Blossom Point Naval Station for Space Technology who marked it, and in turn, notified the Southeastern office of the U.S. Coast Guard Command Center in Washington, D.C. They immediately patched into their Intelligence and Criminal Investigations Section chief who had already received a report from the Wilmington CG station that their chopper had tracked the *Butt-In* to the same location. No coincidence now. All of this activity occurred as Nicole started to swim up to the reef from the Marlinon spacecraft buried in the sea floor in deep water.

As she headed for the surface, Captain Butts became aware of an approaching helicopter. As it drew close, he recognized the markings on the fuselage identifying it as a U.S. Coast Guard Rescue aircraft.

In the cockpit, the pilot was on the radio to Wilmington Base.

"Charlie Golf Roger one-one. Over."

"Copy Charlie Golf Roger one-one. Over."

"We're on the coordinates. That sport-fisher, *Butt-In*, out of Wilmington, is anchored here. Over."

"Copy. *Butt-In*. Wilmington. Proceed to visual. Over."

"Roger. Going close for a look-see. Over and out."

As the chopper dropped down and swung over toward the *Butt-In*,

Nicole broke the surface at the stern. Butts helped her aboard. No metal case this time, just the same sealed, black plastic folder she had taken with her when she went over the stern forty-five minutes ago. Nicole removed her mask and swung her harness and scuba tank onto the deck. "We've got visitors," Butts said. She glanced up at the approaching chopper. "Who's that?"

Butts was suspicious. Thirty years in submarines made him savvy regarding naval and CG operations. Coast Guard Rescue is rarely used for surveillance. Something wasn't right.

"Coast Guard. Any reason you know why they're snooping around?"

"No," Nicole assured him. "I mean, they know who I am and what I'm doing here on the reef." Butts looked up at the chopper, now hovering overhead. He looked back at Nicole. She was getting out of her wet suit.

"Are you people okay?" the pilot asked over his PA system. Butts waved back a thumbs-up. Nicole looked up, smiled and waved. The pilot held in place for another moment, and then peeled away and up, heading back toward the coast.

"Okay now, Miss," Butts said with a serious tone of voice. "You wanna tell me what's really goin' on or am I gonna lose my license in total ignorance?" Nicole kept to her NOAA reef study story, but imagined that soon it might be necessary to add Captain Dave Butts to their growing team.

The case officer at the U.S. Coast Guard Intelligence and Criminal Investigations Section was not satisfied with the report from the CG Wilmington Base, or the current observations of their investigators, Mallory and Block. He ordered continued surveillance, and then requested a naval vessel be sent to the area for another undersea scan and probe.

That night, after dinner, Alex and Nicole met for another walk on the beach. Rosie had mentioned that she suspected the two were attracted to one another to Herbie and Kate. Kate was not happy about it. Herbie was ambivalent. He had other things on his mind. He told his mother and grandmother that he had to head back to L.A. Work was piling up, and his fiancée, Mara, was up for a good part in a new cable series. Some of it could be shot in the Atacama Desert in Chile, the driest, non-polar desert on Earth. It might mess up their marriage plans. He had to get back quickly, but promised to return as soon as Rosie went into labor.

It was a chilly night. November was only three days away. Nicole and Alex dressed warmly and walked with their arms around each other's waist. Alex was surprised that Nicole's grip was as strong as his.

"You work out up there on Marlino?" he asked as they settled down behind a small dune, blocking the light breeze from the west. The ocean water temperature was still near seventy degrees, making it warmer to face the ocean.

"I keep busy. The processing didn't make me younger, like the ladies, but I'm sure it made me stronger."

"Well, it feels good."

"What?"

"The way you held onto me."

"You, too. I think we're a good fit." She bent toward him and kissed him on the cheek. "Now, tell me, did you look at the specs that Dr. Cohestle gave me?"

"Oh, yeah. Where did he learn his English?"

"From Rosie, and the Internet. They always try to pick those kinds of things when they plan to visit a planet."

"Well, Grandma taught him well. The information was precise and complete."

"And can you do it?"

"I think so. There are some things, gasses mostly, that I'll need to locate. The alteration of three rooms shouldn't be a problem. That's mostly a matter of height. One room will need refrigeration."

"Dr. Cohestle's, I assume."

"Yes. And one dry heat for Freida's mate. Julie's guy's environment is pretty close to tropical Earth. Maybe a bit more oxygen. That can easily be adjusted."

"Any idea where you'll get the gasses?"

"I've been working on it. I can design the plumbing for mixing them myself. But we don't know how long the mates have to be here, or when the women and babies will be able to travel. So the problem is quality and quantity. I don't know how much I'll need. To be safe, I have to find a good source close by, and someone to install the plumbing to make."

"But it can be done."

"Oh, yeah! I can do it. In fact, I called an old friend at Monsanto and gave him the problem." Nicole was alarmed.

"You told him about us?" He laughed.

"You really think I'd do that?" She was embarrassed.

"No. Sorry." She put her hand on his thigh and stroked it. He put his hand over hers.

"Mmmm...that feels good. Okay. You're forgiven. Anyway, he knows a chemistry professor at the Georgia Tech School of Chemical and Bimolecular Engineering in Atlanta. I called the guy before diner. Name's Myron Gelgeiser. Nice guy. My friend at Monsanto told him I was with the company and doing some work down here. Said it was a new type of hyperbaric chamber installation at the Hanover Regional Medical Center. Gelgeiser knew about the new wing...how it was state of the art and all that. All I have to do is fax him the types of gasses and the cubic feet required and he said he'd be able to ship it down overnight. He orders all of those gasses for the school locally. He asked about the billing. I said I'd work it out and get back to him.

What do we do about that?" Nicole thought for a moment, then smiled. "What?" he asked. "I can see you've got something cooking in that devious mind of yours."

"Not devious. Brilliant. I'll check with your brother and Bishop Draper."

"About what?"

"One of our ladies is about to make a hefty contribution to the hospital's building fund through the Wilmington diocese."

About 1:15 a.m., Rosie began tossing and turning in her sleep. Then, a sharp pain woke her up. She was sweating. The bed cover had been thrown off and was on the floor. Her swollen belly was surging and rippling. She could not move.

In the next room, Julie was sleeping peacefully. Her swollen belly grew slightly under the cover. Then it shrank, and swelled again. The third time it happened, Julie was awakened. She sat up in bed, alert. An urge, that she didn't understand, drove her out of bed and toward the door. When she opened the door, she found Freida, wide awake, standing in the hallway.

"Rosie," was all Freida said. The two women held hands and rushed to Rosie's room. The door was closed. Julie opened it. Rosie was naked; her belly undulating wildly. Both women ran to the bed and got on either side of Rosie. They pulled off their nightgowns and instinctively lay down, pressing their bellies and bodies against Rosie, embracing her. The undulation immediately stopped. The three ladies remained in place, holding on to one another and laughing.

Awakened by the noise, Nurse Allison Tracy rushed into Rosie's room to witness a sight she had never seen in her twenty-five years of nursing—three naked, pregnant women, embracing one another on a bed, and laughing joyfully.

"What in God's name are you doing?" she asked.

"It's our babies," Freida told her. "They wanted to meet one another."

CHAPTER THIRTY-EIGHT

Two More On Board

Two days later, events began to move quickly. Perhaps too quickly as far as Nicole, Father Bernard, Bishop Draper and Dr. Bowmeister were concerned. But nature has its own schedule, and marches to its own drumbeat.

The pressing items were: one, the three ladies were approaching term; two, they had to be moved to the hospital wing very soon, and three, their mates had to somehow be brought there as well to ensure that the births be as safe as possible, under the circumstances.

To accomplish the latter, the prime contractor who built the new wing, Bubba Carlson, had to be brought in to do the work. Bishop Draper had approved the financing of it using funds that were "donated" from Freida's and Julie's bank accounts and investment portfolios. But first, an estimate and immediate commitment from Bubba Carlson was required. The conversation with Bubba would be difficult. Bishop Draper argued that he didn't have to know about the ladies, or the Marlinons and their spaceship.

"He's a pretty feisty and smart guy," the bishop argued.

"You know the man. I don't," Alex said. "But I think it's dangerous not to be up front with him. What happens if something goes wrong and we need an adjustment or repair while the fathers are here?" Nicole concurred, as did Father Bernard.

"Perhaps we just tell him, but not any of his workers. That's only adding one more to the team," Dr. Bowmeister suggested.

"There'll be two," Nicole told the group.

"And who might that be?" the bishop asked.

"Dave Butts. The charter captain who's been taking me out to the ship."

"Why him?" Father Bernard asked.

"Alex and I have a plan for how to bring the mates here. But it means that the Marlinon ship has to come to the shoreline near the Residence and they think their previous undersea movements have been detected by the Navy and Coast Guard."

Dr. Bowmeister was worried. "Oh boy! Really?"

"A Coast Guard helicopter came by the last time I dove down to the ship. The Marlinons monitored their radio. They seemed to be suspicious of something under the water. We have to be careful."

"That throws a monkey into things," Bishop Draper said.

"Wrench," Alex corrected him.

"What?"

"A monkey wrench is the expression."

"Have you been talking to my housekeeper, Mrs. DePaulo?"

"No. Why?" Alex asked, confused by the question.

"Never mind. Okay. So, Nicole, while you talk to this Captain Butts, Alex and I will talk to Bubba Carlson."

"What about a plumber, Monsignor?"

"Carlson uses his brother-in-law and his two sons. Mexican guy. Jorge Jackalman. I don't think they need to know."

"Doesn't sound like a Mexican name," Alex commented.

"It was Chakal. Means Jackal. He changed it to sound more American. But he's aptly named. At times during construction he seemed to have the personality of a jackal."

Dave Butts was working on the *Butt-In*, cleaning and oiling the teak inlay that ran along under the rails on the sides of the boat. Nicole, who borrowed Father Bernard's car, was followed by CG Investigator Chris Block. She parked in the South Harbor Marina lot and walked down to the *Butt-In*'s slip. On the way, she passed close enough to Block's Honda Accord to pick up a faint thought coming from the CG Investigator. She glanced over and saw the middle-aged black man as he brought a radio microphone up to his mouth. "The young lady just drove over to see that guy Butts at the marina," she heard. That confirmed the Marlinon's suspicions. *Time to be very careful*, Nicole told herself.

Butt's acceptance of Nicole's story was easier than she imagined it might be. Being in submarine service all those years gave him a basis to believe she was telling the truth.

"I think we picked them up many times, especially on our longer cruises that took us under the Arctic ice pack," he told Nicole. "They also liked to travel real deep down through places we couldn't readily go like the Mariana Trench and valleys of the Mid-Atlantic Rift. We reported them as whales or anomalies. Some of them had excellent stealth capabilities. They seemed to be able to use storms, rough seas and fog to come and go and move about. Always seemed to know where our spy satellites were too. I remember one CO, Captain Dixie Oheler, we called him Dix...anyway, he was an amateur astronomer. Had a neat telescope he'd bring up on the conning tower when we surfaced. On dark nights he claimed he could see the whole damned universe. At officer's mess he used to talk about it, how there had to be life out there. But he never reported those undersea hits as space visitors, although I know he often thought about it."

Nicole explained how they were going to bring the fathers up, out and to the hospital wing. Butts was going to play an important part in the scheme.

The bishop, Alex, Dr. Bowmeister and Father Bernard, had a difficult time bringing Bubba Carlson on board. They met on the third floor of the new wing. The doctor explained that there were some new treatment facilities, state-of-the-art as he put it, that had to be ready and tested by January for the grand opening. The adaptation of a few of the patient rooms had to be done in the next few days and it included some plumbing. Carlson still had some painters and one carpenter on the first floor and lobby doing touch-up. Alex showed him the rooms they had to convert. The group then went to the hematology lab to go over the specs.

"This all looks kinda weird," Bubba told them. "I mean, makin' the doorways that big and super-coolin' one room and super-heatin' another. And the third, makin' it like a sauna. That's pretty far-out."

"These are all new techniques, Mr. Carlson," Dr. Bowmeister explained. "All quite necessary. There's equipment that's large and cumbersome to get into the rooms as they now stand."

"Well, I can get the carpentry, doors and walls prepared in a few days. Removing and sealing off the windows too. But I don't know about all this cooling and heating equipment. And those gas tanks? Where do you suppose I'm gonna find them so fast? You understand those things aren't somethin' you can pick up in some junkyard, or on the Internet."

"I've already looked into that," Alex said. "I've been in touch with a friend. Dr. Myron Gelgeiser. He's a Professor of Chemistry at Georgia Tech School of Chemical and Bimolecular Engineering in Atlanta. He's got the tanks and the gasses that we need. They can be delivered overnight, as we need them."

"All you have to do is get things prepared to hook them up, Bubba," the bishop said.

"No offense, Monsignor, but has Father Malone signed off on all this? I mean, he's the administrator and none of this stuff is in my contract. I mean, the cost, well, it isn't..."

"He knows, and it's covered," the bishop interrupted. "We have a special donation pledged to pay for it. Just give me the estimate and I'll take care of it."

"It's gonna be several thousand. Maybe more. But I can be reasonable if you guys wanna tell me what this is really all about."

"We told you, Mr. Carlson," Father Bernard said, feigning innocence.

"Excuse me, Father. What you told me was a story. I've been in this business thirty-five years. I know how hospitals and churches work. This isn't normal. Far from it. It'll go easier, and a lot faster, if I know what's going on, and if it's legal."

Alex, Father Bernard and Dr. Bowmeister looked at the bishop. They had discussed this possibility. The bishop nodded, letting them know that he would take it from here.

"Okay, Bubba," Bishop Draper began, "you want to hear it? I'm going to tell you the real story. When I'm done, I don't want you to say two things. One, 'I don't believe you,' because that would be calling me a liar and that would mean I broke my sacred vows. And two, 'I'm not going to do this,' because that would give me no choice but to excommunicate you." Bubba Carlson smiled.

"Deal. Shoot, Monsignor. I'm all ears."

Bubba did not say the two things that Bishop Draper mentioned. But he had some questions. First to Alex.

"The molecular structures of these gases are quite exotic. These mates, they're not strange, are they?"

"I've not seen them. What do you mean by strange?"

"You know...I mean we got enough trouble in this country with foreign people and all..."

"They're not staying."

"Okay. Now, no offense, but I don't believe in mixing."

"You have a problem with the choice my grandmother and the others made?" Alex asked.

"Hey no," Bubba said, looking at Bishop Draper. "I say live and let live. Personally, I think we should all keep to our own kind. The church says that, right, Bishop?"

"Not anymore, Bubba. That kind of prejudice is wrong."

"But what if they're out to invade us? I mean, they must be way more advanced than we are, having spaceships and all. All the movies show they're kinda, you know, dangerous."

"Those are movies, Bubba," the bishop said.

"Yeah, but this isn't. You want me to believe they came in a spaceship, then I've got to believe they're more advanced."

"So they are. So what?" Dr. Bowmeister asked.

"So maybe this is a plot to begin some kind of invasion. I was in the Army. Still serve in the National Guard. We train for..." Father Bernard had heard enough. He stood up.

"Mr. Carlson, did it ever occur to you that this planet is no bargain? We've got mass starvation, pollution, systematic extinction of species, megalomaniacs, slavery, exploitation, acid rain and disease. Oh yeah. And war. Maybe these invaders, as you call them, have a better place where they live." Bubba thought for a moment, nodded and smiled.

"Point well taken, Father." He nodded a few times, took a deep breath, and turned back to the plans. "So, let's see how much plumbing we actually need. That'll have to be done before I seal up the walls." He paused. "Question. Do my brother-in-law, the jackal, and his sons? Do they have to know what's really going on?"

"Do they, Bubba?" Bishop Draper asked.

"Not if I can help it. He'd hold this over my head forever."

"Then don't tell him, and we won't either. Now, as to cost. The donation is going to the building fund so please be as accurate as you can."

"You got it." Bubba Carlson took the plans to another lab table and began to calculate.

Later that afternoon, before he left for L.A. to deal with his job at CBS, and his fiancée's film career, Herbie Legum used his power of attorney and arranged for the transfer of the necessary funds to the Hanover Regional Medical Center's building fund as a donation from Freida's and Julie's accounts.

At the same time, Bishop Draper and Father Bernard met with Father Colm Malone in the hospital administrator's office to advise him of the donation and to tell him that a few of Bubba Carlson's people would be working in the wing over the next few days.

"I'm glad you understand why we met with Mr. Carlson. We appreciate your cooperation, Colm," the bishop told the priest.

"I'm just following orders, Monsignor," he said curtly.

"You sound like a misunderstood Nazi at the Nuremberg Trials," Father Bernard said. "In any case, now I'd like to have those files so Dr. Weiss and Dr. Bowmeister can peruse them."

"You won't tell me what you're really doing in my hospital. You won't allow me into the new wing. Strangers come and go. Now you want these files. What do you expect?"

"I expect you to have faith. I expect you to trust me," the bishop answered.

"Well, with all due respect, Monsignor, I expect the same from you."

"When the time comes, Colm. When the time comes. Now, for the last time, the Pediatric and Obstetric staff files, please, Father?"

CHAPTER THIRTY-NINE
Unexpected Movement

The work at the hospital wing went well. Alex had been able to get Professor Gelgeiser to mix the gasses to Dr. Cohestle's specs, and load the tanks at the Georgia Tech School before trucking them overnight to Wilmington. By the third day of construction, three weeks' worth of mixed gasses in two separate tanks had arrived—one for the Marlinon atmosphere, and the other for the Roonio 9 atmosphere. Bubba's men had opened the walls and enlarged the doorways of the rooms. But George (Jorge) Jackalman, and his sons, Carlos and Emilio, were behind schedule on the plumbing installation. The heating unit, for what would be Freida's mate Jinko's room, was installed. The cooling unit, for Dr. Cohestle's room had yet to be connected and tested. And the pipes, filters, controls and ducts for the gasses to those rooms were not yet connected behind the open walls. The hope was still that the mates could be brought into the wing before the ladies needed to arrive so that tests on them could get the complete attention of the current medical staff before more people were added. Also, the hope was that once the tests were done, the mates could be returned to their spaceship before labor began, thus avoiding all contact with the obstetric and pediatric people. But Dr. Bowmeister was not so hopeful. He had been to see the ladies that morning. All their temperatures were up, and they were feeling slightly uncomfortable.

The famous line from the Robert Burns' poem "To a Mouse," "The best-laid plans of mice and men often go awry," was about to come true.

On the night of that third day, about a half-hour after dinner, the three ladies, Kate, Arthur, Alex, Nicole and Nurse Tracy were still at their table, having a second cup of coffee while listening to Nicole talk about a trip she had taken to a planet called Kunk, near the red star Rigel. The humanoids there, Finogels, have a society that encourages what Earth-humans would call dark or sick humor. It keeps things in perspective, since it is a planet where life and survival can, at times, be an awesome struggle against harsh elements. Much of their humor consists of physical pranks. Kate mentioned that it sounded like her mother would fit right in. Rosie, feigning insult, started to respond when something stopped her. She stood up abruptly. It was more like a jump up.

"Whoa," she said, holding her belly. "That was a jolt!"

Immediately after that, Freida suddenly began to perspire profusely. A moment later, Julie felt a contraction. Nurse Tracy was up and alert.

"Okay, everybody. Here we go!" She turned to Kate and Arthur. "You two go downstairs and get their travel bags. They're behind my ladies doors, already packed. Alex, find Sammy and Bogdon and tell them to get the laundry truck." She took out her cell phone, punched in a number and handed it to Nicole. "That'll be Dr. Bowmeister. Tell him we're all coming to the hospital."

Nicole took the phone and walked away toward the dining room's sliding glass doors to get a better signal. Nurse Tracy turned to the ladies.

"Okay, dears, sit down. I want you to take deep, even breaths like we rehearsed, and relax as best you can. I'm here. Everything's going to be fine. This is just a beginning. Maybe even a false alarm." Her voice was calm and reassuring, but after the first episode in Rosie's room a few days ago, when she was told the babies were greeting each other, she was fairly certain that labor was close. She had come to believe that these babies were capable of choosing their own time to be born.

Alex, fascinated by that was happening, was still standing near the table, watching Nurse Tracy and the ladies.

"Alex!" Nurse Tracy shouted. "Go!" Her call startled him.

"Uh, oh, right. Yes. Sorry. It's just that I..."

"Put a cork in it! Get Sammy and Bogdon. Get the truck. Go! Now!"

"Okay. Okay. I'm on it." He ran off to the kitchen.

"He's young," Rosie said.

"Not my problem," Nurse Tracy told her. Freida winced a little. "Another contraction, Freida?"

"A little one. Smaller than the last."

"Okay. That's good. It's all going to be fine." Tracy moved from woman to woman, taking pulses and feeling brows. They were all warm. "Your rooms at the hospital are ready. By the time we get there, the doctors and staff will be waiting."

Everything switched into high gear. Dr. Bowmeister took the call from Nicole on the second ring. He then called Judy Lennard, his office nurse, and told her to gather Dr. Weiss, Dr. Altschuler and Harold Watanabe.

"Tell them to meet me at the hospital. You get there too. I'm going to stop by the Residence to be sure everything's okay. If you all get to the hospital before me, prep the ladies' rooms and set up for monitoring labor. Bring in the staff in and the new ones that we picked. Prep the incubators, pediatric ICU, labs and nursery." He rushed off to his car, and as he drove to the Residence, he called Bubba Carlson at home.

Within a few minutes, Bubba called his crew, and the plumbers. He told them to prepare to work a twenty-four-hour shift to complete the job on the mates' rooms. His brother-in-law started to complain and then demanded overtime for the work.

"If you ever want to work for me again, George, drop it now. There's no negotiation. Finish the job by tomorrow night and then it'll be between you and me. Hold me up now, and like I said, that's the last time you ever get a check from Carlson Contracting, or for that matter, anyone else in North Carolina." Bubba had never talked to his brother-in-law that way. For a moment, George thought to challenge him, but something in Bubba's voice told him he'd better not. He seemed a man possessed.

A half-hour later, Bogdon slowly backed the laundry truck toward the rear kitchen door of the Residence. It was a clear, chilly November night, with a bright half-moon directly overhead.

Father Bernard and Sister Mary Francis waited inside, near the kitchen door. The three ladies waited behind them, being supported. Freida had another mild contraction. Nurse Tracy had her arm in Freida's and held her close, comforting her. Kate held one of Rosie's arms, while Arthur held the other. Nicole held one of Julie's arms, while Alex held the other.

Dr. Bowmeister had already come by and examined the ladies. Satisfied that there was no need to rush, he had every confidence that Nurse Tracy and the others could manage to get them to the hospital safely. He left to prepare the third floor to receive them.

The activity at the rear of the Residence had CG Investigators Mallory and Block on alert. They were on a tag team surveillance schedule, with each taking eight-hour shifts. Block had just arrived in the Accord to relieve his boss who had parked the Forester outside the Residence grounds.

"That doctor...the car with the MD plates? He came in the front, and then left a few minutes ago," Block told Mallory. "And a laundry truck just pulled around back."

"Could be on a house call. But it's kinda late to be delivering or picking up laundry, Chris," Mallory commented.

"Ya think?"

"Leave the Honda here. Hop in and let's have a look. We can scope the back of the place from the end of the road."

Father Bernard stepped out from the kitchen door as Bogdon brought the truck closer. Sammy was guiding him.

"Easy. Easy does it there, Chef Polski." Bogdon stuck his head out of the driver's side window.

"Keep it up, busboy, and you'll feel this Polski boot up your Korean butt."

"Not now, you guys," Father Bernard told them. "We've got three ladies who need a ride to the hospital." Bogdon stopped the truck and turned off the motor. Sammy opened the rear doors. Father Bernard turned back to the kitchen door. "Okay, Sister, let's go."

One at a time, the ladies came out, aided as they made the fifteen-foot walk from the kitchen door to the rear of the truck. Mallory and Block were parked behind thick bushes at the end of the road. Mallory had her binoculars dialed on night vision.

"Jesus!" she said. "Look at this, Chris." Block took the binoculars and watched the three very pregnant ladies being helped into the rear of the laundry truck.

"They're pregnant," he said. "Hey, that's the girl from the boat with them."

"Yeah. Sneaking around in the night. Loading pregnant women into a laundry truck. What does that tell you?"

"You don't think... But that's a Catholic Residence."

"And?

"Young unwed mothers?"

"Those 'mothers' ain't young. I'm thinking we've got us a baby ring here. Gimme the binocs." Block handed the binoculars back to Mallory. She got out of the Subaru and moved closer to the bushes, peering through them. Block joined her. "They're in. The Asian guy is closing the doors. The nun and that girl are staying behind with some guy. Maybe they've got more women inside. Let's get back to the SUV and wait out on the road. Leave the Honda where it is."

Rosie, Julie, Freida, Nurse Tracy, Kate, Arthur and Father Bernard were settled in the truck among bags filled with clean laundry to be delivered tomorrow morning. Sammy finished closing the rear doors. He walked to the passenger door and got in.

"Good to go, Bogdon."

"We are like smugglers with valuable cargo."

"Drive carefully. I don't want to be smuggler in jail."

"Not to worry, little man. I am expert driver."

"I hope better than cook."

"Not cook. Chef!"

"Okay, Chef. Drive!" Bogdon slowly pulled away and headed for the road.

Sister Mary went back through the kitchen door, hoping that none of the residents had seen what happened.

Nicole and Alex went around to the parking lot and got into Father Bernard's car.

The truck pulled out onto the road and turned right toward the Wrightsville Beach Bridge.

The two investigators in the Subaru pulled out from their shadowy hiding place on the road and followed the truck.

"I can't believe what we just saw," Block told Mallory. "I mean, for God's sake, a baby selling ring in a Catholic Retirement Home. And a priest and nun doing it!"

Mallory noticed a pair of headlights coming out of the Residence behind them.

"Maybe they were just dressed like a priest and nun, boss."

"What makes you say that?"

"We've got a tail."

Two days passed quickly. The three ladies were settled in their rooms, and their labor pains had ceased. Dr. Bowmeister was convinced it was a false alarm, but Nurse Tracy wasn't so sure. She reminded the doctor about the scene she came upon in Rosie's room where the three women were huddled together, belly to belly to belly and she was told that the babies wanted to talk to each other. Dr. Bowmeister imagined that was only a mother-to-be fantasy. Nurse Tracy suggested that these babies might be "special," perhaps able to choose when they wanted to be born.

"To what end?" he had asked.

"I'm not sure. I asked the mothers about it yesterday, but they didn't seem aware of any more communication beyond what had happened that night. Julie thought they might be waiting for their fathers."

The nursing and lab staff had grown by four people. They had been told that the three expecting women were volunteer patients of Dr. Bowmeister, being used as a sort of shakedown for the third-floor facilities and staff.

The construction on the mates' rooms, down at the end of the hallway from the ladies' rooms was completed. The debris from the existing walls and doors had been removed. The plumbing was done. The gas tanks, heating and cooling systems were in place and functioning. When asked about toilet and shower facilities, the ladies laughed and gave a version of what was now becoming a familiar answer.

"They are humanoid. Surely the biology you studied in school covered those subjects. Yes. They wash, they eat, they eliminate. One of them even shaves. We won't say who or how."

Dr. Cohestle's room was kept at a steady thirty-eight degrees Fahrenheit. The atmosphere was completely Marlinon. A bank of ultraviolet lights had been installed on the ceiling to simulate the Marlinon sunlight. Nicole confirmed that Dr. Cohestle would bring a breathing device with him so that he could visit with Rosie and his daughter.

Yanar's room was easily set up to simulate the tropical conditions on Gimm. Julie, and her daughter, would be able to spend time with him in there. The temperature was kept at eighty-six degrees Fahrenheit with humidity at sixty-nine percent. Several tropical plants had been brought in to make the room feel homier for the Gimmian navigator.

Keeping Jinko's room hot and dry to match the environment of Roonio 9's surface was the biggest problem. The heating unit ran on propane. It had a fairly sophisticated thermostat control. But the dehumidifier that kept the air dry tended to reduce the oxygen level in the room when it kicked on. Getting a balance took some fine-tuning. There was no time, or available technical expert to install a computerized system. Bubba Carlson wasn't sure the environment could be reliably maintained for more than a week or two at best. The doctors agreed that would most likely be enough. Dr. Weiss was concerned it might not be the best situation for Freida or her baby to be in there, but for now, Bubba said he could keep it, as specified, for Jinko.

After their scheduled morning meeting, the doctors and staff set out to see to the patients, do blood tests, check dilation, check and double check the surgical facilities, incubators and pediatric ICU.

Dr. Weiss did a Triple Test—a Multiple Marker Screening that checks a specific protein produced by the fetus, a specific hormone produced within the placenta, and an estrogen that was produced by both. The results were within normal range, but he requested a final ultrasound anyway. Those were scheduled to be done later that evening.

Meals presented a problem. At first, the plan was to bring food in from the Residence for the ladies, Nicole and Nurse Tracy. The doctors and staff could use the main hospital cafeteria; likewise Kate, Arthur and Alex, who had moved from the Residence to a nearby motel. Herbie was in L.A. Bubba Carlson was on call, but not required to be in the wing. But Dr. Bowmeister was not comfortable with the arrangement. The possibility that they might all be working long hours, or in emergency situations, bothered him. And there was also the need to feed the fathers. It was decided that a makeshift kitchen be set up in an area that was designed to be a waiting room. Bubba brought in an electric stove and refrigerator. Plumber George Jackalman, and his sons, adapted the room's water fountain plumbing and installed a small sink. Dishes would be washed back at the Residence.

With that in place, if necessary, Bogdon and Sammy could be recruited to prepare simple meals. Being humanoids, the father's diets were basically proteins and carbohydrates. Rosie, Julie and Freida gave Bogdon lists of what Earth foods they thought might be acceptable.

The ultrasounds were done before dinner that evening. Specifically, Drs. Bowmeister, Weiss and Altschuler were looking for fetal presentation, fetal movements and any undiscovered uterine and pelvic abnormalities that might have developed since the last ultrasound two weeks ago. Nothing had changed. But on close examination, the shadows in Freida's womb that made them suspect a possible multiple birth, were now more pronounced, making that possibility even stronger. The nurses responsible for the incubators were told to prepare six instead of the three originally scheduled. In addition, they were to prepare six more as backup.

PA Harold Watanabe questioned the possibility that the babies might require atmospheres and environments other than what the incubators or nursery had. Installing anything like that was beyond Bubba Carlson's scope. The solution came from Nurse Allison Tracy.

"The fathers," she said at the first morning staff meeting.

"What about the fathers?" Dr. Bowmeister asked.

"If the babies need their father's environment, then we move them there. We have oxygen and masks, so the mothers can be in their mates' rooms. I have a fur coat I can lend to Rosie so she can nurse her daughter in that icebox you built for Dr. Cohestle."

While all this was happening, CG Investigators Mallory and Block kept their distance and watched the comings and goings of various people and equipment through the loading dock of the new wing. Each investigator sat in their own car. Each took photographs, checked license plates and kept copious logs.

Block discovered the motel where Kate, Arthur and Alex had moved. They were commuting to the hospital with a Chevy that Arthur had rented at the Wilmington Airport Avis. He checked the contract, got Arthur Baumgartner's ID, address in Cambridge, and place of work, Harvard. With nothing specific to report, they kept their suspicions about a baby ring to themselves, building a case, piece by piece. When they felt it was solid, they planned to organize a Coast Guard raid, keeping the publicity and kudos, rather than sharing them with the local police, Navy or FBI. Their commander agreed, ordering them to keep him in the loop directly.

CHAPTER FORTY-ONE

Up from The Deep

That evening, just after dusk, Alex came to the new wing's loading dock and picked up Nicole. Mallory recorded that on infrared film. She radioed Block to follow them. They led him to the South Harbor Marina where Dave Butts was waiting on the Butt-In. There was a brief conversation.

Nicole and Alex left.

Butts pushed away from his slip and headed out to sea. Block notified Mallory.

Mallory called the CG Commander, who was home. He ordered a CG patrol boat to shadow Butts. He also put a CG helicopter and crew on standby. Then he asked her to come in and bring him up to date. She said she wanted to wait a half-hour and see if there was any more activity at the new hospital wing.

It didn't take long for the action to begin.

Butts made directly for the reef. The patrol boat kept its distance. Butts saw it on his radar screen. He then turned south, away from the reef and began to run southwest toward Myrtle Beach. The CG patrol boat reported in and followed. It was nearly dark—a clear, chilly, moonless November night.

Father Bernard and Sister Mary Francis gathered all of the residents into the day room. They had rented a DVD of the movie Cocoon—a favorite of the senior audience.

Nicole and Alex arrived at the Residence and parked in the rear, near the kitchen door. They walked down to the beach, holding hands, on the path they had often used. Block, who had discreetly followed them from the hospital to the South Harbor Marina, had followed them back to the Residence and kept hidden. Having observed these two walk down to the beach before, hand-in-hand, he assumed it was young lovers' time again. He called it in to Mallory, who was still at the hospital. She told him to sit tight and wait. Nothing was happening at the hospital. She was going back to headquarters to check in with their commander.

What Block had not seen was that Bogdon and Sammy had earlier driven the laundry truck down onto the beach.

Nicole and Alex met up with them. Alex then tuned to a prearranged channel, number 29, and keyed the handheld marine radio's mike.

"Okay, Dave. We're in place."

"Roger," was all Butts answered. He glanced at his radar screen and then gunned his twin Yamaha engines up.

The seaman operating the radar on board the CG patrol boat sang out. "Bearing one-nine-fiver, Captain. Speed just bumped up to thirty knots."

"Okay. Helm, take us up to thirty, bearing one-nine-five. Kill the running lights. Let's keep this clown in range." He then radioed the news into the CG commander who had gone to his office. He ordered the chopper up and told the pilot to moved toward the patrol boat's position. Mallory had not yet arrived at headquarters.

It took a moment, and Butts saw the blip from the Coast Guard boat pick up speed to match his. Then, in his best impersonation of The Wicked Witch of the East, he said aloud, "Ah-Ha. There you are my pretties." He then pushed his throttle up all the way, adding another ten knots to his speed on the calm sea. At the same time, he switched to the voice of the Olympics announcer, and above the roar of his engines, added, "And let the games begin!"

Ten miles to the northwest, the Marlinon spaceship slid up and out of its sandy, ocean bottom covering. It kept as close to the bottom as possible and accelerated underwater, around the reef and directly toward the beach below the Residence—a distance of six miles. Aware that they had been observed in the past, the Marlinon pilots activated a reflective shield, similar to what Earth-human engineers attempt with stealth aircraft and surface ships. However, the Marlinons used electronic masking to effectively match surroundings, like a chameleon. The result was that the Blossom Point Naval Station for Space Technology's satellite saw nothing out of the ordinary.

Sammy was on the roof of the laundry truck, watching the dark, hardly discernable horizon. The ocean was fairly calm—a mild, on-shore breeze. The breakers lapping the shore were no more than two feet.

"You see anything, Sammy," Father Bernard asked.

"No. Very dark."

"They're close," Nicole said. "Wait. There!" she shouted, pointing slightly offshore to the north.

The Marlinon spacecraft rose up from the sea floor, remaining a few feet under the surface like a mammoth stingray, and moved toward shore, causing a slight ripple.

"Okay!" Sammy shouted, jumping down off the truck. Let's get the lead out, Chef."

"Lead?" Bogdon asked. "Where we have lead?" Sammy got into the truck and started the engine.

"It's idiomatic. Get in," he told Bogdon.

"You don't call me idiot!" the Chef said angrily as he got into the truck's cab.

"Lighten up, greenhorn. We're about to make history."

"You make fun because I don't know all things American."

"Not true. I make fun because I like you, my friend." Bogdon could not hold back a broad grin.

"I like you too, busboy. Drive." Sammy put the truck in low gear and drove slowly over the sand toward the shoreline. Nicole, Alex and Father Bernard trotted close behind.

A portion of the Marlinon ship slid out of the phosphorescent water onto the beach. In the dark, it looked like the shell of a giant, metallic, horseshoe crab. Ninety-five percent of the craft was still offshore, underwater.

"Oh, my dear God, it's huge," Father Bernard said when he imagined the actual size of the spaceship.

"Back the truck down as close to it as you can," Nicole called to Sammy, "and open the rear doors. Bogdon, Father, come with us." She headed for the ship with Alex. Bogdon got out and the two men followed. Sammy began to turn the truck around and carefully back down toward the shoreline. He got stuck in the sand for a moment. He gunned the engine and moved on.

Above the beach, CG Investigator Chris Block had his car window rolled down. He heard Sammy rev the truck's motor and someone shouting. He got out of the car and walked to where he had a better view of the beach below. He saw the truck and four people running toward what looked like the nose of a submarine stuck in the sand at the shoreline. He trotted back to the car and called into Mallory, who was then on her way to headquarters. She radioed Block's news to her commander who ordered the CG chopper to turn around and head toward the Residence. She then continued on to headquarters.

The Marlinons picked up the CG commander's orders. A few seconds later, a thick fog appeared out of nowhere, enveloping the Marlinon ship and the beach.

As the four people on shore approached, a doorway opened in the spaceship. A rainbow of lights flickered out from it diffusing in the surf spray and fog. A very tall, thin, gangly figure appeared in the doorway. He wore a mask over his mouth and nose, but it was clear from his body shape and limbs that he was humanoid.

The sound of the CG chopper's rotors was heard approaching in the distance. The pilot turned on its strong spotlight, but it was unable to penetrate the fog as it came closer. Alex was concerned. He hesitated.

"That's probably the Coast Guard. Maybe they didn't buy Butts going out."

"Don't worry, Alex," she assured him. "The Marlinons have it under control. Come on," Nicole told the three men. "Our guests are here."

The tall figure, wearing a mask, dressed in a silvery jumpsuit with black trim, and a hat, moved out of the ship's doorway. His large feet fought the strong gravity that he was not used to. Nicole greeted him with an upraised palm.

"This is Dr. Cohestle," she told the others. They raised their palms as she had done. The doctor responded in kind. "Father, will you help him to the truck? He's not used to our gravity, so go slowly."

Father Bernard stepped forward and extended his left hand. Dr. Cohestle took it. His fingers, three times longer than the priest's, enveloped his hand. But the grip was gentle and warm. Father Bernard felt a surge of friendship flow through him as they started slowly toward the waiting truck.

An even taller, stockier figure appeared in the doorway, dressed the same way as the first. He wore no breathing mask. His mouth was wide; his eyes, nose and ears, large as well. He had a shock of dark, thick hair, down to his shoulders. Even in the fog, and backlit, he was handsome by Earth-human standards. He too raised his palm. Nicole, Alex and Bogdon responded.

"This is Julie's mate, Yan-Ar-Betch. Yanar the Navigator. Bogdon, please help him. He will have an even harder time with our gravity. And be careful he doesn't step on any seashells. He does not wear shoes."

Bogdon took Yanar's massive hand in his. He too felt the warmth of greeting and friendship from the six-foot-eight, two hundred ninety-pound Gimmian. They slowly made their way to the truck.

Chris Block had returned to his perch above the beach. To his surprise, he could see nothing below. The thick shroud of fog hid everything. He could see the CG copper circling above; its powerful spotlight unable to pierce the fog. He stood mesmerized, wondering if he should report to Mallory now and go down to the beach, or wait until she got there or the fog cleared. He decided to wait.

Down on the beach, Father Bernard had reached the truck with Dr. Cohestle. Carefully, Sammy and he helped the Marlinon into the back of the truck using the tailgate lift.

A third figure appeared in the spaceship doorway. He was tiny, compared to the previous two males. But his shape, though short and bulky, was definitely humanoid—head, torso, arms, legs, hands, feet... and a deep baritone voice.

"Greeting, my Earth-human friends," he said. "I am Jinko of the Chertack people and mate of Freida Riggs, my only love." He stepped out of the doorway and bounded onto the beach. Being from Roonio nine, whose gravity was three times that of Earth, his next step brought him up into the air and over Nicole and Alex, landing onto the sand behind them. He, too, was dressed in the same type jumpsuit, but no hat. His head was bald. Alex went to Jinko and helped him to his feet.

"You could win the Olympics with that jump, Mr. Jinko," Alex joked. "Let's be careful." Nicole took Jinko's other hand. Despite his diminutive size, the Roonionan was heavy and muscular. Carefully, they made their way to the truck, getting there just as the lift delivered Yanar to the rear of the truck. Sammy brought it back to the sand and Jinko got on. Alex stayed with him; acting as an anchor to be sure he didn't bounce off.

That accomplished, the three visitors settled down on the soft packages of laundry. Alex came down off the truck. Nicole hopped on board. The CG chopper was still circling overhead. Its spotlight glow was visible from below, but unable to illuminate anything on the beach.

"They'll keep the fog until we get to the road. I'll see you at the hospital. Well done, guys." Nicole blew Alex a kiss. Bogdon closed the rear doors and then headed for the cab with Sammy.

The door of the Marlinon spaceship closed. It slipped back under the sea and out of sight, invisible to detection. The fog remained. Sammy drove slowly, back up to the road. Alex walked up the path with Father Bernard, hidden by the fog as well. Once on the road, Sammy turned toward the Wrightsville Beach Bridge to Wilmington. At that point, the fog cleared. The spaceship was gone. The chopper scanned an empty beach.

Above, as the fog cleared, Chris Block saw Alex shake hands with the priest and head for the rental car. He trotted to his Accord and waited for Alex to drive down to the road and pass him. He then pulled out and followed. He concentrated on driving and didn't think to call Mallory to let her know he was on the move.

When Alex got to the bridge, the truck was already over it and out of sight. He had seen headlights pull out behind him past the Residence. Suspicious, he kept driving straight past the bridge. The car, a black Honda that he suspected was following him, continued to do so. Then he was sure he was being followed. He would not go back to the hospital now. Instead, he made a tour of Wrightsville Beach, eventually stopping at a popular bar for an hour. He called Nicole. She had arrived at the hospital. He told her he was followed.

"Well, no one followed us," she assured him. "We arrived, safe and sound. Dr. Cohestle said they had picked up radio conversations from the Navy and Coast Guard. We have to be more careful. I'll let everyone here know."

"Okay. I'll give Father Bernard a heads-up tomorrow."

"Good. Are you coming here?"

"No. I'll hang here a while and then drive around again until I'm sure I'm not being followed anymore. What's the drill tomorrow?"

"Tests on the fathers. More prep. After the fathers went to their rooms, there was some more indication of labor. Dr. Bowmeister thinks we're close."

"Good. The sooner the better."

"But then we'll be leaving," Nicole said wistfully.

"We'll talk about that later. You were great tonight."

"You too, my dear Alex. See you tomorrow."

Block had parked in the bar's lot and called in to Mallory. She was annoyed that he did not call when he'd left the Residence.

"Stick with him. When I finish with the boss, I'll check out the Residence. If he goes to the marina or hospital, let me know."

When Alex came out of the bar, he noted that the Honda was still in the parking lot. He drove around for a while and then he went back to the motel where he related the evening's events to his mother and Arthur. Not to alarm them, he said nothing about being followed. When Block saw where Alex went, he called Mallory and went home to get some sleep. She took her shift at the hospital. By then, the laundry truck was gone. Nothing seemed out of the ordinary.

Earlier, as they were told that the truck had arrived, the three ladies eagerly waiting at the third-floor service elevator door. They had not seen their mates for a long time. The elevator door opened. Their mates were standing at the front of the car.

Dr. Cohestle, who towered over Rosie, embraced her close to his tall, thin body. He held her head against his chest, stroking her hair as he made a soft, humming sound. They rocked back and forth and side-to-side in what Rosie would later describe as a Marlinon deep expression of love.

Yanar the Navigator, as Julie said he liked to be addressed, was taller and far more muscular than Dr. Cohestle. Julie was taller than Rosie. Yanar embraced her. Then he bent over and slipped one arm behind her back and the other behind her knees. In one swift and powerful motion, he picked her up and cradled her in his arms. He kissed her lips, and then kissed her belly. He said something to her in a language only she and Nicole understood. She began to cry tears of joy as she wrapped her arms around his thick neck and buried her face in it.

Freida and Jinko had their own special way to unite. By now, the Roonionan had adapted somehow to the Earth's gravity. He hesitated for a moment and then took two tentative steps. But Freida did not hesitate. She rushed to him and knelt so that her face was at the height of his barrel chest. He looked down at her and, although he had a deep baritone voice, he now let out a soft, high-pitched sound that was undoubtedly a song. A love song. His powerful arms embraced her neck and shoulders, taking care not to press on her extended belly. He then kissed her, sliding his thick lips across hers rapidly while increasing the pitch and volume of his song.

While Alex was leading CG Investigator Block on a merry goose chase, the full staff was enthralled by the sight of the reunion. There was no doubt that these three couples loved each other, and that the women were, and always would be, safe in their mates' embraces.

After the initial reunion at the elevator, and some private time with their mates, the fathers were settled in their rooms. In each, the environments had to be adjusted. Dr. Bowmeister, Bubba Carlson and Dr. Weiss were there to accomplish what was needed. Nicole went along to translate if necessary.

Yanar the Navigator requested, through Nicole, that the temperature in his room be increased. It was at seventy-eight degrees Fahrenheit. He was comfortable at ninety. He also asked, in simple, broken English, that the oxygen level be raised to fifty percent. When he was understood, Nicole praised him. Julie had done a good job teaching him.

"Thank you," he told Dr. Bowmeister in his soft, guttural voice. "This plants and flowers are friend to me. And small trees with nice branches." He stretched out his six-foot-eight frame on the oversized bed. "Nice too. Softly. Here I can rest now."

"If you don't mind, before you rest, we have some tests we must do," Dr. Bowmeister told him. Nicole translated.

"I know this. My Juliette Lobato tells me."

"Dr. Weiss will take you now, Yanar the Navigator." The Gimmian sat up and smiled, revealing a mouthful of large, gleaming teeth that had the texture and color of animal bones bleached in the desert sun. The doctor also noted he had two sets of incisors, top and bottom. Dr. Weiss gestured for Yanar to come with him.

Jinko's room was next. The Roonionan was with Nicole and Judy Lennard, Dr. Bowmeister's nurse. The temperature had been set at a hundred degrees Fahrenheit. The humidity was at twenty-five percent. When Dr. Bowmeister and Bubba Carlson came into the room the blast of hot, dry air hit them in the face. Nicole, who knew what the Roonio 9 environment was like, had taken off the warm clothing she'd worn to the beach and was in shorts and a light T-shirt. Nurse Lennard was wearing her whites. She was obviously uncomfortable. So was Jinko.

"Breathe is a hard," he said in stilted, Hollywood-type Italian-English. He pointed to his throat. His normal voice was a deep baritone. Now it was pitched higher—almost like a choking squeal.

"It's the CO_2, argon and helium mix," Bubba said. "Hear his voice? Too much Helium. And the irritation? Argon. I can adjust that." He went to a small door in the wall and opened it, revealing a black metal panel with gauges and knobs. "How's this feel, Mr. Jinko?" Bubba said as he turned two of the knobs. "Give it a sec."

"What's a sec?" Jinko asked.

"Short time."

"My Freida calls a-me shortee. Is that like a short time?"

"No, Mr. Jinko. Short time is like one-two-three-four... So, how do you feel now?"

"No more a-hurt," Jinko said, pointing to his throat. His voice was deeper too. "You a good engineer. Work in a mine?"

"No. I build this," Bubba said, gesturing to the walls and ceiling.

"Good. Can make a-more dry?"

"More dry?" Dr. Bowmeister asked.

"More dry."

"No problem," Bubba said. He went back to the wall and adjusted another knob. The air quickly became noticeably dryer, and it felt much warmer.

"Good-a to me," Jinko said. His voice was deep again. He jumped up onto the bed, nearly hitting the ceiling in the process.

"You have to be careful, Jinko. Your gravity is much stronger than here on Earth," Nicole warned.

"Careful. Yes. But a-fun to do for me. And more. I thank-a for the music. I do music. Freida Riggs tell-a you?"

"Yes. She told us that you play the flute," Dr. Bowmeister said, pointing to a wooden one that had been placed on the night table.

"Yes. Thank. A-nice. I do-a to a violin. She teach."

"Can we get to the testing, doctor?" Nurse Lennard asked quietly. "This dry heat is drying my throat and baking my bones."

"Of course. Sorry. Mr. Jinko, Nurse Lennard will take you to do some tests. If you need to come back to warm up, or to catch your breath, please let her know. Do you understand, or would you like Nicole to translate for you?"

"I know what-a your words say. Freida has-a my childs. She-a rests. I am good." He did a controlled bounce off the bed, over Nurse Lennard's head, landing at the door. "Careful, yes?"

"Yes," Dr. Bowmeister told him. Nurse Lennard opened the door and took Jinko by the hand.

"Come along with me, my shortee young man in the flying trapeze," she said with a friendly smile. They quickly disappeared down the hall in the direction of the labs.

Nicole went to Dr. Cohestle's room with Bubba and Dr. Bowmeister. Dr. Ivan Altschuler, the Geneticist, was waiting outside the room wearing a sweater and jacket.

"He seems okay," Dr. Altschuler told them. "I poked my head in for a moment. Rosie is in there. She's okay. She's activated her breathing chip implant. It seems to work fine."

Dr. Bowmeister knocked on the door. Rosie opened it a crack. She was wearing a mink coat borrowed from her friend Lynn Milsop at the Residence.

"Hi, guys," she greeted them.

"How is he doing?" Dr. Bowmeister asked.

"Fine. Just fine. He says the temp could come down a bit, but otherwise, he's impressed with my Alex's and Mr. Carlson's work." Bubba puffed up with pride.

"Glad to hear that, ma'am," Bubba said, peering beyond her, into the room. Dr. Cohestle had his back to the door. He had taken off the top of his uniform. His thin body showed more than twenty ribs. It had a definite blue tint to it. Tufts of fine white hair were visible down the length of his straight spine. The vertebrae were twice the size of an Earth-human's, indicating that although he was thin, the Marlinon chemist was strong.

"I figured there might be adjustments so I put the controls out here," Bubba said. He opened a small door in the wall, similar to the one in Jinko's room. "Colder, you say?"

"He said about fifteen degrees colder than now."

"That'll take it below freezing, Ma'am."

"Yes. We know that. But freezing to us is quite different than freezing on Marlino, to a Marlinon, that is."

"That's part of what I saw in my genetic workup," Dr. Altschuler said. "And the blood work showed a tendency to that tolerance also."

Bubba made the adjustment. "It'll take about a minute," he told Rosie.

"Can you ask Dr. Cohestle if he's ready to do some tests now?"

"He is," she answered immediately. "We discussed it."

"Great. If he can put on his breathing apparatus and go with Dr. Altschuler, we can get started. Tell him we have made the lab as cold as we can. Also, there's a bank of ultraviolet lights installed there. But if he feels any discomfort, he's to speak up, and we'll get him back here immediately."

"I'll tell him," Rosie said. "He knows some English. He downloaded several medical textbooks from the Internet while waiting for us. He said that if you need any help with the lab work, he'd be happy to oblige. He's a chemist, you know."

CHAPTER FORTY-THREE

Exams And Plans

The tests on the fathers were the subject of the morning staff meeting. They were all eager to see the results. Fresh blood samples gave a little more insight into the genetics of Yanar and Dr. Cohestle since Yanar's mother was a Marlinon. Dr. Weiss noted a suppression of the growth hormone in Julia's fetus that coincided with the Gimmian half of Yanar's genes.

Geneticist Dr. Ivan Altschuler was fairly certain that the growth gene was dormant at the moment, accounting for the normal Earth-human size of her baby. Dr. Weiss put up videos of the MRI full body and bone scans he had done on all three fathers.

"This is Roseanne Conlon's hus...uh, mate, Dr. Cohestle," Dr. Weiss said as a bone scan video was displayed. "Note his long skeletal structure is extended with multiple joints, much like that of the fetus. The fact that the fetus has adjusted itself to Mrs. Conlon...or Cohestle...to her uterus in a safe, compact position, is quite remarkable."

"But of course a vaginal delivery is out of the question," Dr. Bowmeister interjected.

"C-section. Absolutely," Dr. Weiss concurred.

"With a much larger than normal incision, I'm afraid," Dr. Bowmeister added. "Also, after examining Dr. Cohestle, we are going to construct a much larger incubator. My PA, Harold Watanabe, and Dr. Weiss, have figured out a way to do this using two of the incubators, removing the non-access sides, and sealing them together. That system should be ready to test tonight. Last night we drew blood from the three males, and more from the mothers. Yanar and Jinko were able to give two pints. But Dr. Cohestle has difficulty with his blood loss. So we have only one pint of his."

"Blood won't be the problem with his daughter. It's her size that worries me," Dr. Altschuler commented.

"Tall men marry short women," Nurse Tracy suggested. She had made it clear on a few occasions that she didn't care much for the Geneticist's bedside manner. He acted aloof toward her three pregnant charges, dismissing their questions about his specialty as "too complicated."

"Not six-foot-three blue men with fur and a body temp of sixty-three degrees Fahrenheit," he remarked.

"Maybe," she shot back, "but I'll bet he's a lot smarter than anyone is this room. And kinder than a few I could name."

"Okay. Enough of that," Dr. Bowmeister said, raising his hands toward the two antagonists. "Let's be sure we have stored the blood well and have it ready in the operating room. That's about it for Mrs. Cohestle. Dr. Weiss will fill you in on Mrs. Lobato's situation."

Dr. Weiss put up a video of Yanar's blood slide.

"The man from Gimm poses no great problem. In fact, he's got just about the healthiest blood I've ever seen. These Gimmian blood cells, red and white, are large. Hemoglobin's excellent. I believe it's due to the rich oxygen content of their atmosphere, and a largely protein diet. The MRI, PET and bone scans showed remarkable similarity to us in terms of organ location and function, circulatory and nervous systems, and musculature. Brain size is in proportion to his body."

"One source," Nicole commented.

"Say what?" Dr. Altschuler asked.

"The theory among many of the travelers." She looked around the table at the newcomers to the group. "After the year I spent on Marlino, I met many humanoids on my galactic journeys—humanoids who travel within our galaxy, and some who travel to other galaxies. Eva, Gina and Bonnie are out there, in other galaxies, right now. These travelers have encountered many humanoids who have adapted to their unique environments, but have maintained similar physical attributes and DNA. The theory is that all humanoids have a common ancestor; a common beginning, if you will."

"From where?" Leslie Shipp, the hematology technician, asked.

"There's the big question," Nicole answered. "I suppose it might be likened to how we believe, scientifically, that we are all derived from Lucy."

"Who?" one of the surgical nurses asked.

"That's what scientists called the fairly complete female skeleton discovered in nineteen-seventy-four in Ethiopia," Dr. Altschuler said, answering the nurse's question. "Its name came from the Beatles' song, 'Lucy in the Sky with Diamonds.' It was carbon dated back to around three-point-two million years ago. A family of thirteen was found nearby. It's believed that all of us are descended from those folks. Some even older humanoid bones have been found since Lucy. Maybe four million years old. Maybe more. Evolution is..."

"Yes," Nicole interrupted. "It is. Anyway, the travelers think that the first travelers may have discovered secrets of speeding up or shaping evolution so that it was possible for them to, in effect, plant the seed of humanoid DNA on planets they believed could sustain carbon-based life that might evolve to humanoid."

"Have you brought this up with Bishop Draper and Father Bernard?" Dr. Altschuler asked. His tone in asking the question was mischievous. Nicole was about to answer, but Dr. Bowmeister interrupted.

"Okay. That's enough about lessons in evolution." His tone of his voice brought silence to the meeting. "Listen up, people. We have some babies on the way, and some really extraordinary visitors to care for. I want us to concentrate on that mission. When it's over, we can turn to philosophy or religion or science or whatever. Okay?" They all nodded their agreement. "Good. Now what about Freida's mate, Jinko?"

"I'm betting that those shadows we saw on Mrs. Riggs, or what's her husband's name?" Dr. Weiss said.

"He is her mate, and his name is Jinko," Nicole said. "If it's confusing to you, why not just call her Freida? Call them all by their first names—Freida, Rosie and Julie."

"Good idea. Thank you, Nicole. I will. Okay," he continued. "Those shadows are, in my opinion, more fetuses. Smaller, and somehow hidden by an amniotic fluid that has grown darker. It also seems to deflect the oscillating ultrasound waves. Maybe a protective element we have not developed on Earth. They are more than one or maybe two babies there," Dr. Weiss concluded.

"Do you have any idea of cause?" Dr. Bowmeister asked.

"Gravity. Jinko told me that his people, the Chertack, have mated with humanoid females from other planets. Planets with less gravity than Roonio nine. They have all had multiple births. It's why he wanted an off-planet mate."

"What about the gravity?" Bubba Carlson asked. He had been sitting in on the morning meetings to see if his services might be needed. He was a smart, curious, self-taught man with only a high school education. This adventure had tweaked his curiosity as never before.

"The Marlinon processing reactivated Freida's ovaries. They sprang into action simultaneously. Roonio-nine has a force of gravity three times more than Earth's. I believe it caused several eggs to be released."

"But Freida told me that births are rare on Roonio-nine," Nicole said.

"The effect may work against ovulation in Roonionan females," Dr. Bowmeister told her, "but not off planet humanoids from lower gravities."

"There's this too," Dr. Altschuler said. "He put up a slide of two genetic charts. One, a human chart from Freida, showed twenty-four sets of chromosomes. The other, from Jinko, showed thirty-six chromosomes. "It's a mind bender. These are Freida's and Jinko's individual chromosome charts. She has twenty-four. That's normal. Jinko has thirty-six. Not normal."

"Not normal for Earth, you mean," Nicole said.

"But how did they procreate?" Nurse Judy Lennard asked.

"Selectivity is my guess," Dr. Altschuler answered. "We've done genetic splicing, first with bacteria and now, well, we've got people messing with all kinds of stuff."

"Frankenstein," Nurse Tracy commented.

Dr. Altschuler shrugged and chuckled. "Call it what you will. The new creations, when combined with a normal population, show selectivity. They reproduce only where other cells from the same original stock are prevalent. There's some kind of genetic memory, common to the DNA that we share with all living matter."

"So that goes back to what Nicole said that the travelers believe. We share a commonality with these humanoid people from distant planets."

"And so," Nicole said, "who's to say what our true origins really are?"

An awesome silence prevailed in the room for a long moment as they all studied the genetic charts, contemplating their place in the Universe. The concept of so much life beyond Earth was mind-numbing, and at the same time, liberating. Many of them, much like the other women at the Residence, felt that they had become part of something more than they had ever imagined. It felt wonderful.

"Multiple births for Freida Riggs," Dr. Bowmeister said, breaking the mood. "Let's all be prepared."

CHAPTER FORTY-FOUR
Snoops

A little before midnight, Chris Block watched the young man he followed from the Residence and, now knew as Alex Legum from Hawaii, leave through the front entrance of the Hanover Regional Medical Center. He called Annie Mallory.

"The guy from the motel is gone. The lights are low. Looks to me like they shut down for the night on the third floor of the new wing."

"Okay. I'll be there as quickly as I can."

Twenty minutes later, Mallory and Block entered the front lobby of the hospital. They flashed their IDs to the security guard at the front desk and explained they were picking up some blood samples from the lab. They made their way to the third floor and found the footbridge that connected the main building to the new wing. The entrance to it was blocked off with yellow tape and a large "Do Not Enter—Construction" sign.

"You sure this is the right way?" Mallory asked.

"Yeah. Third floor. The lights from the new wing line up with this bridge." He slipped under the tape and tried the door. It was locked. "Must open from the inside only," he told Mallory. "What do you want to do?" Mallory mulled over the fact that they did not have a warrant. She let it pass.

"We know they go in from the loading dock," she said. "This must be the way they come out. So it must be unlocked from the other side. Open it."

He took out a small leather case and unzipped it. It held a set of lock picks. He chose two, slipped them into the keyhole, and the lock opened.

The bridge to the new wing was about forty feet long, with windows on both sides. Ambient light from the parking lot and roadway below was strong enough to see the other end.

"That'll be locked from this direction too," Mallory told her partner. When they got to the door leading to the new wing's third floor, Block picked that lock too. They entered and found themselves at the end of a long hall. There was a door on their right. A bluish light, emanating from along the door jamb and saddle, was visible in the dark hallway.

"Let's start here," Mallory whispered. Block put his hand on the doorknob and slowly turned it. The door gave a little but did not open.

"It's stuck."

"So push." He pushed hard. Too hard. The door flew open and, off balance, he stumbled into the room, and fell on the floor. The blue light was intense, blinding him for a moment. He was aware that it was also very cold in there. Chris Block steadied himself and, as he got up, he looked up. Dr. Cohestle loomed above him. The doctor had seen Earth-humanoids before. But this was Chris Block's first Marlinon, or for that matter, any off-planet being. Stunned by the sight of a tall, thin, bluish figure, covered with tufts of white hair, Block froze in place. A scream of fright and surprise gagged in his throat. He fell backward, into Annie Mallory, knocking her down. He didn't stop to help her. He panicked and ran back out the door to the bridge, leaving his boss lying in front of Dr. Cohestle, who had come to the doorway.

Unlike her partner, Annie Mallory was mesmerized by the apparition who stepped closer and offered his hand to help her up. She took it and immediately felt the warmth of welcome through his cold blue skin. Any fear she might have had dissipated. The Marlinon chemist stepped back into the cold, blue room while Mallory remained in the hallway. He put on his breathing mask and came back out, into the hallway. He then raised his hand in greeting. Mallory, sensing this was a peaceful greeting, raised her hand in return.

"I am Dr. Cohestle," he said through the translator in his mask. "Marlinon. Hello." Condensation came from the mask as he spoke. He extended his thin blue hand. Mallory shook it, enjoying the calming warmth is exuded.

"Annie Mallory. U.S. Coast Guard. American. Hi."

On the bridge, Block calmed himself, feeling ashamed that he panicked and left his boss with the creature. He gathered up his courage and picked the lock again. When the door opened into the hallway, he saw Mallory holding hands with the tall, blue creature.

"You okay?" he called out.

"Fine. Calm down."

The door across the hallway opened and Jinko, Freida's mate, poked his head out.

"Who you?" he asked, in a loud, deep voice. It startled Block. Fear grew again. He stared at the little man who stepped out into the hallway. "Strangers here, Cohestle?"

"Visitors," the Marlinon answered.

"Who...what the hell are you people?" Block asked loudly. "The circus?"

"Chill, Chris," Mallory ordered. "They're okay."

"Okay? Jesus, Annie. Look at them. You call that okay? I don't call that okay. What's okay about it?" She realized he was losing it.

"Calm down, Chris. They're friendly."

At that moment, Nurse Tracy came out of the room beyond Jinko's — Yanar the Navigator's room. Freida had been feeling some contractions and Nurse Tracy had been taking her vitals.

"Who in the hell are you people?" Nurse Tracy demanded. Relieved to see a human being, Block struggled to frame an answer as Yanar stepped out into the hallway behind her. The huge Gimmian, wearing only a pair of briefs, had Schwarzenegger's body, Shaq's height and Brad Pitt's looks. He brandished a large knife. The blade was a huge, tapered emerald. The handle was studded with diamonds. Block again froze in place.

Yanar, whose skin was copper in tone, changed his color, like a chameleon, to match the hallway décor. He then assumed a defensive posture. His body seemed to expand. His eye color morphed from black to yellow-orange.

"Holy Mother of God!" was all Block said before he passed out.

With Investigator Mallory's permission, Investigator Block was sedated by Nurse Tracy. They put him in a hospital room near the ladies' rooms. His weapon and clothes had been removed. He was in his underwear and a hospital gown. As a precaution, his left wrist had been handcuffed to the bed. He was asleep; expected to be out until mid-morning. But Nurse Tracy kept an eye on him anyway. She was going to be up all night regardless, concerned about Freida whose contractions had stopped.

Once apprised of the two Coast Guard inspectors' presence, Bishop Draper, Father Bernard and Dr. Bowmeister got to the hospital as quickly as they could. In the meantime, Dr. Weiss, who was on duty that night, took Annie Mallory, whom Nurse Tracy had formally introduced to the fathers, and took her to meet the expectant mothers, all of whom had been awakened by the ruckus in the hallway.

It was nearly three-thirty in the morning when the bishop, the priest and Dr. Bowmeister met with Nicole and Annie Mallory. What was happening in the new wing was in jeopardy of being exposed unless the CG Investigators could be convinced it had to be kept secret. After explaining everything that had happened, the bishop put the question to Mallory. Would she keep quiet, and would Block do likewise?

"I sympathize, Monsignor," Mallory told him, "but I can't be a party to kidnapping. That's a federal crime. A Class-A felony."

"You came in uninvited," Bishop Draper responded. "And without a warrant. That, too, is a crime."

"Kidnapping trumps that."

"Then is there no way you can keep this secret?"

"Even if I would, I can't speak for my partner. We're both sworn to protect, uphold and defend the Constitution. He takes that very seriously." Sensing that Annie Mallory might be willing to join them in protecting the situation, Father Bernard pressed the issue. "Perhaps you might persuade Mr. Block to hold off for a little while. Perhaps he would remain here of his own free will."

"I know him, Father. He's a good man and dedicated to the service. But like some people, he may be too afraid of what he doesn't understand. You saw how he reacted to the visitors. The mates. He could never keep quiet about all this."

"And you? Could you, Ms. Mallory?" Dr. Bowmeister asked.

"To be honest, doctor, I'm fascinated. I'd really like to help. But I can't compromise my Coast Guard officer's oath."

"Does that oath have to do with your current assignment?" the bishop asked, trying another approach.

"Yes."

"And what is that assignment?"

"My current assignment is to investigate the disturbances off our coast that were detected by the Navy. That led us to Mr. Butts and this young lady," she said, smiling at Nicole.

"Aside from what you have learned tonight," Bishop Draper asked, "how was your investigation going?" Mallory smiled and shook her head.

"I had nothing on the disturbances, Monsignor. But Block and I caught sight of the pregnant ladies being moved here and thought we were onto a baby smuggling ring. Seeing a priest and nun involved made us, well, a little gun shy to report it. So we decided to pursue the matter before making any accusations."

"And where are you with it now?"

"Now I know what the disturbances were. You also told me that the uh, Marlinon spacecraft was it?"

"Yes. Marlinon."

"Well, as you told me, the Marlinons are onto the Navy now and they can mask their ship. So if I report an alien spacecraft, and no one can detect it, I'm going to be, at best, the laughingstock up in Washington, and worse, given a desk to drive down here."

"So, unless you turn us in, am I correct in surmising that you have no investigation to report on?" the bishop asked. Mallory hesitated, digesting the bishop's logic. She realized where he was going with it.

"That's right," she said with a smile and a nod.

"So?" was all he said, and waited.

"So, I guess I'm still investigating."

"And what if your superiors find out?"

"Honestly? I believe that if my commander knew, he'd be, well, you might be able to talk to him. He might look the other way for a bit, but not too long. Probably not long enough, because if it got out, he'd catch hell. If Washington knew about this, they'd jump all over it and ruin everything for you and the ladies...and God knows what they'd try to do with those mates of theirs. And there are always leaks, so you could count on the media finding out. Then it's Katy bar the door. Forget about it."

"All true," Father Bernard said. "Okay. So you're investigating. Thank you. That's wonderful. What do we do about Mr. Block?"

"I guess you, we, keep him under wraps here, but not too long. He's a bachelor. No kin nearby. But no more sedation. I'll talk to him. With your permission, I'll tell him the truth. He might come around when he knows that you folks aren't selling babies. That's what got him all fired up. Me too."

"But, keeping him under wraps...doesn't that make you an accessory to kidnapping?" Nicole asked.

"Kidnapping?" Annie Mallory answered with a frown. "What kidnapping?"

By dawn, Block was awake and sitting up. Mallory sat in a chair at the side of his bed. He was still handcuffed. Sammy had brought him a breakfast tray with orange juice, scrambled eggs, bacon, toast and coffee.

"I think it's best that you hang in until I find out exactly what's happening here," Mallory told him. "How's the food?"

"Good. Listen, boss. Whatever they're up to here, someone has to report this. I mean, did you see those...those freaks?"

"What freaks?"

"What freaks? The skinny blue one. The little Sumo wrestler. And the hulk with the knife. Christ, he changed the color of his skin. Not to mention that scary nurse. There's something real funny goin' on here. Why am I handcuffed? Where are my clothes and my weapon?" He saw she still had her Glock sidearm. His expression changed. His eyes narrowed. "I see you're still packin'. You wanna tell me what's really goin' on here?"

Mallory knew that she wouldn't be able to stall her partner. *She had warned the bishop that she might have to tell Block the truth. Everyone at the meeting had agreed that if Mallory believed that it was absolutely necessary to try to convince Block, then she could do it.* She got very serious.

"Listen to me carefully, Chris. We've stumbled onto the happening of the century...maybe in the whole existence of mankind. I'm going to level with you, but it's got to be kept secret. You've got to swear that to me."

"Swear to what?" he asked.

"What I'm going to tell you?"

"Jesus, boss. We're partners. You can trust me."

She told him the truth—the whole amazing story. But when she was done, she wasn't quite sure he believed her.

The rest of the day was reasonably quiet in the wing. Julie's contractions ceased. As a precaution, Block's room was kept locked from the outside. Dr. Bowmeister arranged for Mallory to have a key to the bridge from the main hospital to the wing. She went back to Coast Guard HQ and told her commander that her investigation was now centered on the Residence. She reported that she had confronted Dave Butts about his activities near the reef and his trip south two nights ago.

"He said the young woman was a charter. Took her out only twice. She told him that she was a marine biologist checking for reef damage from some disease called Atlantic White Pox. Said it affects Elk Horn Coral 'cause of higher water temps. She was getting samples. That checked out. The other night, Butts confirmed he was heading down to Myrtle Beach for supplies. Said he gets a better price down there on tackle. And the sales tax is lower."

"You know the chopper couldn't see that section of Wrightsville Beach that Block told you about. Thick fog came in out of the blue."

"Yeah. He told me. By the way, Block called me early this morning. He's got a brother in Richmond. Family emergency."

"Did he go?"

"I told him to do what he needs to do. I'll cut him emergency leave paper."

"You want someone on the case with you?"

"Not necessary. With Butts out of the way...I mean, he's no drug smuggler, for sure, I'll zero in on that Catholic Residence for a few days. I don't think it has anything to do with the Navy's request about offshore. My guess is seismic activity. Lately there's been activity up and down the East Coast." Knowing her commander was a very conservative Republican, she added, "The administration in D.C. will probably blame it on global warming or fracking." The commander laughed heartily.

"Of course. Okay. Check in and let me know when you want to close the file. I won't say anything to Washington until then."

Later that morning, after being sure he wasn't followed, Alex brought Kate and Arthur to the wing. They went to Rosie's room. Nicole then brought Dr. Cohestle there. He wore his breathing mask and the clothes he had worn when he came ashore two nights ago. Although Alex had prepared Kate and Arthur, when the tall, bluish Marlinon came into the room, they were stunned. He raised his hand, palm out, in greeting.

"He's saying hello," Nicole informed them.

"Hello," Arthur said, raising his hand.

Kate was speechless. Dr. Cohestle felt her surprise and fear. Or was it disgust? Disbelief? Rosie felt it too. Kate stared at his body, his long, thin arms and tapered fingers.

"This is my mate," Rosie told her daughter. "Your stepfather." The Marlinon chemist came forward a few steps, took a deep breath and removed his mask. Kate gazed at his sensitive face; his almond-shaped eyes and thin lips around a tiny mouth—a Modigliani painting. Kate stared and said nothing.

"I am so pleased to meet you, daughter," Dr. Cohestle said, one deliberate word at a time as he exhaled. He then replaced the mask.

"Kate," Rosie said sharply, "I said this is my husband." Dr. Cohestle sent Rosie a silent message to please be calm. Nicole heard it and agreed. *Let her absorb it, dear Rosie. She could not be prepared for a being like me. She must absorb and adjust.*

Dr. Cohestle then extended his hand to Kate. She took it cautiously, keeping her eyes glued to his. He sent a warm, calming feeling to her. A sincere greeting. She felt it and relaxed.

Later that afternoon, Nicole and Alex took a walk along the water's edge. The surf was up, roiling and churning as it ground into the fine sand of the beach. The sky was gray and threatening—a sure sign that winter was approaching. Gulls and terns were circling one-hundred yards off shore, diving for pieces of bunker that a school of bluefish were devouring underwater. The birds were screaming with excitement.

"The rooms you designed for the mates are wonderful," Nicole told Alex. She unclasped his hand and pulled the collar of her jacket up around her neck.

"You're cold. Let's go back," he said.

"No. I'm fine. I've been in much colder places, believe me. Marlino's surface is always below freezing." Alex tried to picture that and shivered from the thought. "Dr. Cohestle said you're a fine chemist."

"Well, I can tell you, he's brilliant." She stopped and faced him. The bluefish school moved away to the south. The feasting birds followed.

"So, Alex? Have you decided?"

"About what?"

"You know what. The ladies are getting close to their time. When that is done, we will be leaving."

"I can't go. And you?"

"I will go with them." A surge of disappointment knotted Alex's gut. He didn't want to lose her. She sensed his desperation, but kept it to herself. The traveler's regulation she knew well: "Never, unless absolutely necessary to life, interfere or attempt to control beings on planets visited."

"What about your vows?" Alex asked.

"I was only a novitiate. I took no final vows."

"I really like you. I want you to stay. With me."

"First you want me to be a nun. Then you want me to stay. For what?" She felt his pain at her response. "I'm sorry. I do care for you too. But out there..." She gestured to the sky. "...out there, my God, you can't imagine how wonderful it is. How much there is to see and learn. I am forever part of that. You can be too." Alex was captured by her excitement and eagerness.

"But how? I mean, my mother...brother...life here."

"Well, only you can decide that. It's like Rosie said when we were confronted with staying or leaving three years ago. 'There comes a time when you have to live your own life.'" She looked up, into his eyes, his heart, his soul, but sent no emotions. And then she felt his emotions swell until they burst forth. He took her in his arms and kissed her lips, her face, her neck and then back to her lips where he lingered and loved her. She sent him her love, and he gasped with delight.

At that same time, Kate and Rosie were alone in her hospital room. Rosie, who was in bed, per Dr. Bowmeister's orders, had sent Arthur to find the temporary kitchen. She told him to look in the freezer of the fridge where there was some butter pecan Häagen-Dazs ice cream that she craved.

"No matter how much I eat," Rosie said, as Arthur left the room, "I don't gain weight. Just the baby grows." When the door closed, Kate came to her bedside.

"Mom. Listen. I can't deal with this. I thought I could, but meeting him... It's not a prejudice thing. I mean he seems like a nice, uh, man, but..." She looked down at the floor and paused.

"But what?"

"You're my mother! And you're seventy-six and...God help me, this is just too weird. You're having a baby! Jesus! A baby!"

"She's going to be your sister. There's nothing weird about that."

"You're kidding! She's a...she's from space! God! It's a dream. A nightmare. It's insane!" She began to cry. Rosie got off the bed and embraced her sobbing daughter.

"No, my dear Katie. It's not like that. Not insane. Not at all." Kate pulled away. She was trembling.

"Oh, Mom. For God sake! He's seven feet tall and blue with white hair and cold and...and you have to wear fur coats to see him and breathe through a chip in your...in that thing in your neck...and..."

"What are you talking about?!" Rosie yelled, cutting her off. "Get a grip! I love him. He loves me. We have...We have a life!" Kate pulled away, got up, and backed off the bed. She put her hands up as if to hold her mother at bay.

"I don't know who you are anymore. You're as alien as he is to me."

"I know you did once, sweetheart," Rosie said calmly. "The question is, how do you really see me now, my dearest Kate? What do you mean by alien? The universe is teeming with life that is not exactly like us. But it is life! If they are alien, then so are we. I mean that if, after meeting my husband, my mate, the male whose child I bear...if he is unacceptable to you then it is you who are alien to us, and to the rest of all life. If, as you say, you don't know me anymore, my question is, do you ever want to know me and the rest of my family as we are now?"

The morning staff meeting covered yesterday's events. There were questions about why the CG Investigators were snooping around. Why one was being held, and for how long. Where the other one went and whether she would report what she saw—namely the mates. A few of the newly added staff were nervous about being involved in what one of them called, "holding a federal officer against his will," but came short of calling it kidnapping.

Dr. Bowmeister, Father Bernard and Bishop Draper had discussed the matter earlier that morning by phone. The doctor and the priest felt that CG Senior Investigator Mallory understood the situation and would keep her word to respect their secrecy for the time being. She also promised to look after her partner, Chris Block.

"This is not against his will," Father Bernard assured everyone at the meeting. "His superior was here and spoke to him. He was a bit shaken by the event and is resting here, under observation." That answer wasn't completely satisfying to a few of the surgical and pediatric staff, but they accepted it.

"Okay, that's settled," Dr. Bowmeister said. "Now, let's get down to our work. Julie has been having more contractions. She is slightly dilated. I suspect we're all going to be quite busy very soon." He turned his attention to Nurse Tracy. "Allison, I'd like you to do an hourly work-up on her, starting after the meeting. And let's get delivery room number one prepped and the incubators fired up. Judy," he said to his office nurse, "I'd like you to keep a close watch on Freida and Rosie. Hourly, please, as well. Dr. Weiss and I will be around twenty-four/seven with surgical team one. The rest of you are on call, round the clock, until we deliver, and all is well. This is the home stretch, people. You've done a great job in preparing and keeping this all hush-hush. You are part of an incredible and historic event. On behalf of the ladies and their mates, thank you."

The humidity and temperature in Yanar's room was bearable for Julie, although uncomfortable after a while because of her pregnancy. She stayed with her mate during the day, but Dr. Bowmeister insisted that she be in her own cooler, and drier, room at night.

It was just after one p.m. Nurse Lennard had examined Julie and Sammy had brought a steak sandwich lunch to the Gimmian Navigator's room. They sat among the green, leafy plants that Alex had provided for atmosphere, and as a natural supplementary oxygen source. They spoke a mixture of Gimmian and English. Yanar was far more proficient in English than Julie was in his native tongue. This was because as a navigator, Yanar had to know several languages and dialects. He was a linguistic expert.

"What is this animal?" Yanar asked, pulling a piece of steak from the sandwich. He didn't care for the roll, Dijon mustard, tomato and lettuce.

"It's called a steer."

"Are they difficult to hunt?"

"They are not hunted. They are grown."

"I understand. That is why it has a weak taste and is soft. Animal protein that is wild is strong and healthy."

Julie was about to explain that Earth had a much larger population than Gimm, and that feeding everyone was a serious problem. But as she framed her response in his language, she was interrupted by a sharp contraction. Her body stiffened.

"Oh!" she exclaimed. "That was no false alarm. Our daughter is coming!"

Yanar jumped to his feet. He began to tear leaves from the plants and make a bed of them on the floor next to Julie. His body color changed to match them. His facial tones became red and blue, like a Mandrill Baboon.

"Here, my Julie. I have prepared the place." Julie saw that he had formed the leaves into a nest. She was about to say something when another contraction surged through her body.

"Yanar, my love. Go and get the doctors. Hurry!" she said in a loud and urgent voice.

"But this is the birthing place," he told her.

"No, my sweet. On Earth we do it differently. It's called medication!"

"But on Gimm..." Another contraction.

"We are not on Gimm. For God's sake, Yanar! Please! Call the doctors! Now!"

Yanar changed back to his copper color, ran to the door and stepped out into the hallway. "My child comes! My child comes!" he bellowed loud enough so that everyone on the floor heard him.

Twenty minutes later, there was no sound in the operating room except Julie's breathing and ethereal, classical music in counterpoint to the tension as the first interplanetary Earth-human baby was about to be born, according to intergalactic regulations, on her mother's home planet.

A mass of equipment surrounded the central table. The delivery staff was dressed in green gowns; the pediatric staff in blue. Julie was giving birth, naturally. Yanar, dressed in a blue surgical gown, had changed his skin tone to match it. But his facial tones were again deep red and brilliant blue like a mandrill. He towered over everyone. His dark eyes, like black, polished ebony, were filled with primitive awe, and male pride, as the baby's head began to crown. Dr. Bowmeister and Nurse Tracy gently urged Julie to push. Yanar held his mate's hand and encouraged her with soft, loving, Gimmian words.

Dr. Weiss and the other nurses busily attended to their assigned tasks. And then, rather quickly and easily, in a moment of joy, a baby girl was born—healthy, a little larger than the average female human baby. The head nurse wiped off her face. Her features were perfect. Her eyes were open. She was stunningly beautiful.

As Dr. Bowmeister and the delivery nurse prepared to cut the cord, Yanar gently pushed them aside and lifted the infant with his large hands. He cradled her in his massive arms. The baby turned blue, not from lack of oxygen, but to match her father's coloring. He performed the act of separating the baby from the umbilical cord in a ritual manner, using the emerald and diamond hunting knife that he had strapped to his leg. Once cut, he placed the tip of the knife on the small piece of the cord that was still attached to the baby. It disappeared, leaving a naval that was perfectly formed and healed. Yanar then took a towel, offered instinctively by Nurse Tracy. He cleaned the blood, mucus and fluid from the baby's body. He put his mouth to hers and blew one breath, in and out. The baby coughed once, and then cried.

Satisfied, Yanar placed the baby at Julie's swollen breast. The baby's flesh color turned from blue to match Julie's; her lips to the darker shade of her mother's nipple and areola. Julie's eyes filled with tears of joy as she supported her baby's head. It immediately found the nipple and began to busily suck at her breast. Julie smiled and cried and laughed. Yanar knelt next to his mate and child and kissed them both on their foreheads. He, too, had tears of joy. The proud parents then accepted applause and congratulations from everyone. Yanar named their daughter then, and there, proclaiming it in a deep, resonant voice as though he was speaking to those in the room and others light years beyond that place.

"She is Joc-Yan-Betch. Her mother is Julie of Celia. Her father is Yan-Ar of Betch." Celia was Julie's mother. Betch was Yanar's father.

It was determined that Joc-Yan-Betch did not need an incubator, or any time in the pediatric ICU. Before the baby left the operating room for the nursery, she had grown an inch. By the time she had her next feeding, she had grown another inch. As Dr. Baumgartner had predicted, the growth gene that had been dormant came alive and went to work. Jocyan, as her parents lovingly called her, would be tall. And her hair would be as white and fine as that of her grandmother from Marlino.

CHAPTER FORTY-SEVEN
A Convenient Distraction

Early that evening, Julie, Yanar and little Jocyan, who was obviously not as little as when she was born several hours ago, settled into Julie's room. Julie's recovery astonished Dr. Bowmeister and Nurse Tracy to the point that they understood their attention was not required. The rejuvenation that her body had gone through from the deep space travel processing had obviously enhanced her immune system and cellular healing capability.

But after a while in Julie's room, the baby seemed to grow listless. She was not interested in nursing. Dr. Weiss, who had taken over their care, wrote it off to a normal reaction of a newborn.

"But she doesn't change her color the way she did in the operating room," Julie told Weiss.

"Her colors are not bright or true," Yanar added. That chameleon-like attribute, obviously inherited from Yanar, was beyond Dr. Weiss's knowledge. Harold Watanabe, who was assisting Dr. Weiss, placed a bright green leaf next to the baby who was sleeping in her pink infant's cradle. Her skin tone turned from light pink to a very pale green.

"Maybe there's something missing in this room. Temperature? Humidity?" the PA mused softly to himself.

"What was that? You say something is missing?" Weiss asked. Watanabe hesitated. "No time to be shy, Harold. Spit it out. What do you think?"

"I don't know exactly. But look at Yanar. He's still wearing the hospital blues. But I'm sure his skin isn't bright blue the way it was earlier in the delivery room." Dr. Weiss looked at Yanar.

"You're right. His skin is dull. Do me a favor, Harold. Put that leaf next to Yanar's arm." Watanabe did as asked. Yanar's arm turned green, but the tone of the color was as pale as Jocyan's skin.

"That should be brighter," Julie said, with some alarm.

"Okay," Dr. Weiss said. "Relax. Yanar? Take a walk back to your room with Mr. Watanabe. Harold, see if his coloring is any brighter in there."

Fifteen minutes later, they all moved to Yanar's room. The temperature, humidity and oxygen levels made Jocyan more alert and comfortable. Her skin change ability, and Yanar's, improved dramatically. The baby nursed, slept and grew a little more.

An hour later, Sister Mary Francis, who had yet to meet the fathers and was anxious to see the new baby, was picked up by Alex and Nicole and brought to the hospital wing. She arrived as Sammy and Bogdon were on their way to pick up dinner dishes from Dr. Cohestle, Jinko, Yanar and Julie and Block. She went with them, and stayed behind in Yanar's room after Sammy and Bogdon left. She was in there, visiting, for about twenty minutes when she became flushed and began to sweat profusely. She had worn her black habit to show the fathers her calling. But the heavy wool was far too warm for Yanar's environment. Sister Mary excused herself and stepped out into the hallway to cool down and catch her breath.

Three rooms away, Chris Block was reviewing his plan to escape. Meals had been brought to him by a slim Korean and a burly guy with a heavy European accent. *Probably Russian*, Block thought. He knew, basically, the timeframe when they came and went to bring the meals, and again to pick up the dishes. The two men had picked up his dinner dishes ten minutes ago.

Earlier that afternoon, his partner and boss, Senior CG Investigator Annie Mallory, had visited him. She was glad to see he had apparently accepted the situation. "The commandeer thinks you're away on family business," she told him truthfully.

"But that's a lie. When he finds out, he's gonna bust me, or order a court martial, for sure. Maybe if I talk to him now...maybe he'll understand. Whaddya think?"

"I already explained why you can't leave, Chris. We've got to give these folks a chance for some peace and quiet to have their kids."

"They've got you all twisted up, Annie. They're playing you. You saw these so-called mates. They're not human..." Mallory saw that her partner really wasn't convinced. In fact, he was scared. There was no use reasoning with him.

"I'm sorry, Chris. This is too big a deal to mess with. When it's over, you'll see...we'll be famous."

"I don't wanna be famous. I simply want out of here."

"Not yet."

"Well, can I at least have my clothes back? This hospital gown is a pain." She agreed and got them, but kept his weapon and phone. She apologized again, and locked the door to his room behind her.

"I'll show you famous," he said softly, after he heard the clicking of her heels fade away as she walked down the hallway. He eagerly felt for the small, secret pocket he had in the inside lining of his jacket. He smiled when he found it had been undiscovered. His fingers grasped the Velcro flap that sealed it, and pulled it open. Once inside, his fingers grasped the small leather case that held the tools he used to jimmy open locks. First the cuffs, and then the door.

Dressed and ready to escape, Block knew he had to wait for the right moment. He listened, following the activity outside the door. After he heard the two men roll the cart with the dinner dishes away, he let ten more minutes pass. Then he slowly turned the knob and opened the door a crack. All was quiet. He peered out and looked down the hallway to the right. Deserted. Cautiously, he opened the door and stepped out a bit, looking to the left. He froze, shocked to see a nun standing outside of the room two doors down. She was fanning her face with a white handkerchief. Beyond her was the door that led to the bridge over to the third floor of the main hospital, and freedom. He contemplated just walking past her and smiling, as though he worked there. He looked to the right one more time. The hallway was still empty.

Okay, he thought. *I'll do it. The worst thing that can happen is that she knows who I am and says something. I can run to the bridge door. I know it's open on this side. So is the door leading to the main hospital? Even if she calls out, before anyone gets here, I'm gone.*

But just as he opened the door and stepped out of his room, the door across the hallway, Freida's room, flew open. Jinko, the sturdy, dark, diminutive Chertak miner from Roonio 9, came rushing out.

"Nurse-a! Doctor! Help-a!" he bellowed. His deep voice had a much higher, panicked pitch. More like a squeal. As though Jinko's voice had physical substance, Block stopped and fell backward, into his room. In moments, all hell broke loose in the hallway. He had presence of mind to close the door.

Sister Mary Francis, startled, screamed. She had not seen Jinko before.

Nurse Tracy popped out of her nearby room and ran toward the ruckus.

Yanar came out of his room. Not sure what was happening, his color blended with the dark hallway. He pushed Sister Mary into his room and closed the door. Brandishing his knife, he crouched in a defensive stance.

Dr. Weiss and Harold Watanabe came rushing down the hallway with a gurney. Dr. Cohestle, who had been with Rosie in her room, followed, wearing his breathing mask and space uniform.

Jinko continued to squeal, run back and forth, and jump up and down, disregarding the difference in gravity between Earth and Roonio 9. He bounced higher and higher until his head hammered into the soft, foam ceiling tiles, dislodging several. He reached out into the air in an attempt to stabilize himself. This action only caused him to bounce off the wall and then across the hall to the opposite wall, like a ping-pong ball.

As help arrived, Freida came out of the room. She was obviously in distress, holding her belly. When she saw her mate bouncing from pillar to post, she let out a squeal to match his. Together, their sounds harmonized. The result was that they comforted one another.

As she usually did, Nurse Tracy immediately sized up the situation and took charge.

"Freida is in labor," she called to Dr. Weiss as he approached. "Bring the gurney here. Yanar. There is no danger. Will you help us get hold of Mr. Jinko?"

Yanar sheathed his knife and went after Jinko who, in his attempt to reach Freida, was actually bouncing away from his room. He grabbed Jinko's leg and brought him to down to the floor.

"Thank you, Yanar," Nurse Tracy said. "Okay, people, let's head for operating room two."

Chris Block listened intently from behind his closed door. There was the sound of many feet moving about; moans of pain from Freida, and deeper, more comforting sounds from Jinko. The contractions were coming faster. Then the sound of the wheels of the gurney being rolled along the hallway floor and the shuffle of people moved away. He heard the door to Yanar's room close. Then there was silence. Block waited ten more minutes and peeked out again. The dark hallway was clear. He stealthily moved along the wall to the door to the bridge. He opened quickly. and ran to the main hospital building. He was free.

Operating room two had been set aside for Freida after the doctor agreed that a multiple birth was a possibility. Aside from the normal equipment, three incubators, a transfusing unit and a resuscitator had been moved into the room. Freida was prepped and mildly sedated. The contractions were coming often, and were longer. Effacement was one hundred percent, and her cervix was at nine centimeters—almost fully dilated. This transition period was normally when the contractions were most intense, but Freida was smiling, seeming oddly comfortable as she bore down.

As with Jocyan's birth, Drs. Weiss and Bowmeister were in attendance, as well as the surgical and pediatric nurses, PA Watanabe and technicians. But this time so was Sister Mary Francis. She had traded her woolen habit for a surgical gown, and now that she was in the air-conditioned operating room, she was chilled. But she was excited to be there and said nothing about it. This was her first time witnessing birth. Freida and she had been close friends before the ladies left the Residence on their great adventure three years ago, which made this more exciting and personal.

Jinko stood next to his mate, holding her hand and soothing her with a deep, humming sound that was barely within Earth-human audible range. Freida responded in harmony. Their duet relaxed her during the contractions and bearing down. The Chertack miner had ten-pound weights that Harold Watanabe had hurriedly collected from the hospital rehab center, wrapped around his ankles. It kept him, as Freida joked, "Down to Earth."

The doctors were delighted at how smoothly things were going so far. Then, just as Nicole came into the room, a baby's head began to crown. But instead of pausing and waiting for the shoulders to come out, which is when the nurse normally has time to suction the baby's mouth and nose, the shoulders followed immediately and the baby turned, rotated and the rest of the body slipped out, faster than the doctors had ever witnessed. It was as though the baby, a smallish boy, was in a hurry to make his appearance.

He looked very much like a miniature of his father. Jinko made a joyful, purring sound, akin to "Yippie!" and kissed Freida's hand. The surgical nurse clamped the umbilical cord in two places. Dr. Bowmeister offered the scalpel to Jinko to cut between the two clamps. The Roonio 9 Chertack reached for it, but was interrupted.

"There's another one coming, Jim," Dr. Weiss exclaimed as another head crown.

"Sorry, Jinko," Dr. Bowmeister said as he quickly cut the cord himself. "No time." Jinko nodded, understanding.

The ends of the cord were tied off and the senior pediatric nurse wrapped the baby boy in a blanket and took him to a nearby table to be cleaned and tested for heart rate, breathing, muscle tone, reflex response, and color.

"Two-a Chertack babies-a good!" Jinko exclaimed. This time he kissed Freida on the forehead. She was remarkably calm as though having babies, one after the other, was a piece of cake. Like the first boy, the second came quickly, only he was smaller. He, too, had a torso like his father, but his facial features were like Freida's.

The senior surgical nurse suctioned the little one. Dr. Bowmeister did the cord. Then, he was wrapped in a warm towel and handed to the other pediatric nurse who took him to another table. A moment later, the nurse at that table with the newborn, signaled for Dr. Weiss to come to her.

"He seems in respiratory distress," she said quietly.

Dr. Weiss did a quick check. His breathing was shallow and his flesh tone pallid. He recalled the conditions on Roonio 9.

"Suction him again," he ordered. She did. The boy was not responding. He was pale. "Get another warm towel. Bring me the breathing mask." Dr. Weiss worked over the little boy and told Nurse Lennard to have another incubator prepared.

Back at the delivery table, Freida asked for her babies.

"They're being cleaned, warmed and tested," Dr. Bowmeister assured her. At that point, the senior pediatric nurse had completed her work on the first born and brought her to Freida. She laid the baby on his mother's chest. "Here we are," Dr. Bowmeister said. "He's beautiful."

Jinko kissed his first son, but was aware that Dr. Weiss was working on the second boy at the nearby table.

"Doctor!" the surgical nursed called out. "Another one." Dr. Bowmeister picked up the boy from Freida's chest and handed him to the senior pediatric nurse. "First incubator. Setting as discussed." She took the baby and went into the pediatric ICU. When Jinko saw the first boy being taken to the ICU, he frowned and looked questioningly at the doctor. "They're fine," he assured Jinko.

A third head had fully crowned. There was no doubt it looked like Freida. Once again, the shoulders came out fast, turned, and the baby slid out. By now, the team had the drill down pat. The second surgical nurse suctioned.

"It's a girl, Freida," Nicole called out as Dr. Bowmeister clamped and cut the cord. The nurse wrapped the baby, and took her to the first table that had been cleaned off and prepared. PA Watanabe helped her. This baby was the spitting image of Freida—light coffee and cream skin, full lips, broad nose and jet-black hair. She was also smaller than the first boy. She responded to the cleaning and warm blankets and was breathing well on her own, with good color and awareness.

After the second boy had been suctioned for a third time, he began to respond. But his breathing was shallow. His heart rate was slow, and he was still slightly pale. The nurse wrapped him in a new, warm blanket.

"Incubator," Dr. Weiss ordered. "Heat it up to one hundred. Dehumidify. Turn up oxygen to forty percent. Stat! Then draw some cord blood and check type. Stay with him and let me know how he's doing every five minutes." He then turned to the sound of crying as the third baby, the girl, let everyone know she had clear, strong, and working lungs. "Now that's what I like to hear," he called out to the room. "Let's get her cleaned up and give her to her mother."

At that moment, Geneticist Dr. Ivan Altschuler came into the room wearing a hospital gown over a tuxedo. Active in the state Republican Party, he had been at a fundraising event.

"I hear we have triplets," he said, approaching the delivery table. The chief surgical nurse stepped in his way.

"That's close enough, doctor. I see you haven't scrubbed. We're trying to hold this as a sterile area." Altschuler frowned, but didn't object.

"I'm going to have a look at the two in the ICU," he said, and left the room as the pediatric nurse brought Freida's daughter to her, removed the baby's blanket, and laid her on her mother's bare chest.

"Your body will warm her better than the blanket. And you girls can do a little bonding. She's a feisty one. She may even want to have a little meal."

The first boy was breathing evenly in the incubator when Dr. Altschuler got to him. His eyes were open, and he seemed aware.

"Hey, little guy," Altschuler said, bending over the glass incubator. "You look just like your daddy." He turned to the pediatric nurse who was close by. "You have this one's blood from the cord?" She picked up one of the two vials she had filled, and handed it to him. He took it and then had a look at the second boy whose color was better and breathing even and steady. "I'll be in the hematology lab," he told the nurse who was watching the baby for Dr. Weiss, and left the room.

Back in the OR, Jinko and Freida were falling in love with their little girl. Her body shape, coloring and features were all Freida. "She is definitely your daughter," Sister Mary told Freida. But before Freida could respond, she felt a sharp contraction, and then another. The senior surgical nurse, who was standing at the foot of the delivery table waiting for the afterbirth, looked and saw another head crowning.

"Doctor!" she called out, stopping both Dr. Bowmeister and Dr. Weiss, who were halfway to the ICU to check on the two boys, in their tracks. "We have another. It's coming even faster than the last," the nurse insisted. She then turned back just in time to catch a small baby girl who slid out completely, in one smooth motion, like toothpaste out of a tube. "We have another girl!" she cried with excitement as the doctors arrived at her side.

The senior pediatric nurse rushed over, took the first girl off Freida's chest, wrapped her in a blanket and handed her to the closest person, Sister Mary Francis.

"Can you hold her for a minute, Sister?"

"Why, yes. Of course." She was delighted and at the same time concerned. *Four babies,* she thought. *Oh, my dear Freida, you will have your hands full.*

The nurse then grabbed another warm blanket while the senior surgical nurse suctioned and cradled the new girl in her arms as the doctors prepared to clamp and cut the cord. This girl looked like her first two brothers—Chertack through and through. The senior pediatric nurse arrived with the warm blanket. When the cord was cut the baby began to take breaths. Her brown skin took on a reddish glow, and then she began to gasp for breath.

"That's the oxygen toxicity again," Dr. Weiss said. "Get her into an incubator, stat. You can clean her and do the testing in there."

The senior pediatric nurse took the infant and headed for the ICU where the incubators had been positioned. Two were in use.

"Increase the CO-2 until her color normalizes, like before," Dr. Weiss called after her. "Give her point-five milligrams of Vitamin E and Selenium in solution." The nurse didn't acknowledge that she had heard him. "Never mind," he called out. "I'll do it." He followed after the nurse. That left Nurse Lennard alone at the delivery table with Jinko.

"Uh-oh," was all Freida said when there was another major contraction. Dr. Bowmeister turned back to the delivery table to see Nurse Lennard reaching in between Freida's open legs.

"We have another boy!" she cried out.

Jinko let out a joyful sound.

Sister Mary, who was still holding the first girl, cradled her in one arm and crossed herself with her other hand. "Praise God," she said aloud. "Quintuplets! A miracle!"

Dr. Bowmeister rushed to the table. The second pediatric nurse had run into the OR from the ICU, sent by Dr. Weiss to help, when he heard Nurse Lennard's cry. She began suctioning the fifth baby. Nurse Lennard held him while Dr. Bowmeister clamped and cut the cord. He looked like his first sister, like Freida, only smaller. Dr. Weiss trotted back into the OR. Both doctors stared at each other.

"He's smaller than the others," Dr. Weiss said, concerned. They both had the same thought. *There was only one more incubator set up in the ICU.*

"You'd better fire the last one up, Les," Dr. Bowmeister said.

Dr. Weiss took off for the ICU. The baby coughed, then gasped and finally cried and breathed.

"That's my boy." Dr. Bowmeister handed the baby to the pediatric nurse. She took him to the table, cleaned him off, wrapped him in a fresh warm blanket and took him to a newborn's cradle crib. That meant there were three babies in incubators and two in cradle cribs being watched by the two pediatric nurses and Dr. Weiss.

Freida closed her eyes, exhausted. Jinko was beside himself with joy. Sister Mary sat down in a chair. The surgical nurses relaxed. One of them wiped Freida's face, neck and chest. Dr. Bowmeister came over to Freida.

"You did really great," he told her. She opened her eyes.

"Five is it?"

"Five beautiful children. Three boys. Two girls. All healthy and doing well." He reached across the table and shook Jinko's hand. "Well done, Daddy."

"I have-a big-a family now-a. My-a Freida she-a wonderful!" Standing, held down by his ankle weights, Jinko's head was even with Freida's on the table. He kissed her lovingly and stroked her hair, damp from perspiration. She smiled. Dr. Weiss came back into the OR.

"Okay, people. The three boys are stabilized and breathing on their own. The first girl is good too. And the last girl is settled in her incubator, and her color is normal. That was quite a performance everyone, especially yours, Freida. I have no doubt that the gravity on Roonio nine had a lot to do with bringing this gang into the world."

"Into the Universe, Les," Dr. Bowmeister corrected him.

"How will she nurse all of them?" Sister Mary asked.

"I'll have Nurse Tracy get some formula together," Dr. Bowmeister said. "Did we get all the bloods and tests done?" he asked the head pediatric nurse.

"Yes, sir. Done, labeled, and on the way to the lab."

Dr. Weiss sat down for the first time in two hours. "All right," he said. "We did it! Now there's just Rosie to go."

Suddenly, Freida's eyes opened and she grimaced, and then she grunted. Jinko was startled. Freida slid her legs up and apart. The head surgical nursed was closest to the end of the delivery table.

"Good God! I don't believe it. There's another one crowning!" She moved toward Freida's parted legs as the two doctors hurried to join her. By the time they got there, the nurse had another boy in her hands. He was small, like the last girl. When he was suctioned and cleaned, he looked like none of the others—a bit of Jinko, a bit of Freida, but with a light complexion and fine, fair hair. Nurse Lennard brought him to Freida and laid him on her chest. He found a nipple and began to suckle.

"And who are you?" Freida asked. "All fair and... Wait." She looked at Jinko who said something to her in the Chertack language. She answered back in Chertack. He laughed and nodded. Nicole, also laughing, came to the delivery table.

"Did I hear that right?" she asked Freida.

"Yes," Freida answered. "Something, huh?"

"May I ask what?" Dr. Bowmeister said.

"Of course," Freida told him. "My great-great-grandmother, way back...well, her mother was a slave in Virginia. Story was, she served in George Washington's kitchen. Mount Vernon. Seems one of his colonels took a liking to her. She bore three daughters by him. I guess genes have a way of hanging around."

"Maybe he'll grow up to be the father of a planet one day," Nicole joked.

Suddenly, the little boy stopped nursing and began to gasp and cough. He turned red.

"Oxygen toxicity again," Dr. Weiss said. "And no incubator is ready."

"Out of incubators?" Nicole asked. "How can that be?"

"It isn't," Dr. Weiss answered her. "I mean, we're not out of them. It'll take ten minutes to get one going."

"Do we have ten minutes?" she asked. There was a moment of silence in the room.

"I'm not sure," Dr. Weiss said. He looked at the baby who was getting redder and struggling for breath.

"The girl," PA Watanabe cried out. "Put him with the second girl."

"Exactly right, Harold. You're a genius," Dr. Bowmeister said, plucking the baby from Freida's chest and handing him to Dr. Weiss. "Take Harold with you, Les, and make some room in that last incubator. Same deal as the girl. When his color normalizes, Harold, give him the Vitamin E and Selenium."

Dr. Weiss and PA Watanabe headed for the ICU with the boy. Dr. Bowmeister turned to the concerned parents. "He's going to be fine. We're getting pretty good at this. So, Freida, are you done, or are there more surprises?"

"I think I'm done, doctor."

"You're sure? Other than the afterbirths which I'm sure our Dr. Altschuler can't wait to get his hands on."

Freida thought for a moment. She was exhausted, but felt strangely calm as though she was completely satisfied and at peace.

"Yes. I am sure." But then she grimaced again and moaned.

Everyone stiffened and stood up. She held her expression for a moment longer and then relaxed and laughed heartily. "Gotcha!"

CHAPTER FORTY-NINE
A Time To Move

Chris Block wasn't sure what to do. After crossing over the bridge into the main hospital, he took the stairs down to the lobby and left through the main front door. The SUV that Annie Mallory had been driving was gone. But his Honda Accord was still in the parking lot. His cell phone was missing, but he had a set of car keys in his secret jacket pocket. His first instinct was to go to CG headquarters and report to the base commander.

But then he remembered that Mallory had told their base commander that he had gone to Virginia on urgent family business and might be away for several days. Also, reporting what he knew could get her a court martial, or worse. He couldn't bring himself to do that to his partner. On the other hand, he didn't buy the story that those weird characters he saw were from outer space. They must be some of the people he had read about once in a Human Freaks and Circus Oddities *magazine. Besides, the baby ring that he observed, run by people from the Catholic Residence in the hospital's new wing, were matters for the civil authorities. If Mallory had bought the space creature thing, that was her problem. He made his decision.*

While Freida was delivering her sextuplets, Block presented his ID at the new Hanover County sheriff's office to Elissa Westbrook, the deputy on duty.

"I'm tellin' you, they're breeding freak babies in there."

"You mean the freak Catholic babies that your partner told you were from outer space?" she said sarcastically. "So, have you been drinking, or did someone put you up to this? Maybe my boss is having a little joke?" This was her second month on the job.

"I'm not drunk and this isn't your boss's joke. My partner wanted me to stay locked up. Keep it a secret, she said. I'm thinkin' maybe they drugged or brainwashed her or something."

"Uh-huh. And what's your partner's name?" the deputy, who was taking careful notes, asked.

"Mallory. Chief Investigator Annie Mallory. Buy we don't have to drag her into this now."

"Look, Mr. Block, did you ever consider that maybe your partner was telling you the truth about the space people?"

"Truth? Sure. And I'm the Easter Bunny. Let's get on it. And that's CG Investigator Block to you, deputy," Block told her, inferring he outranked her. Deputy Westbrook kept her outward calm but inside was getting pretty ticked off.

"Okay, Investigator Block. I'll write up a report and leave it for the sheriff in the morning. How's that sound?"

Block became agitated. He stood up. "That's no damn good. Listen to me. You've got to go there...to the hospital. Now! And arrest those people!"

"Calm down, and sit down!" Deputy Westbrook said firmly.

"Look here, deputy. I'm tellin' you that something very weird is happenin' in your jurisdiction. If you won't deal with it, I need to talk to someone who will. Call your boss!" Block insisted, still standing. "In fact, I demand you call your boss. This can't wait until tomorrow."

The deputy set aside her notepad, stood up, and calmly drew her semi-automatic Ruger SR40 pistol.

"Turn around. Put your hands behind your back."

"Whoa. Look. I'm just upset. I'm sorry...I didn't mean to demand... to raise my voice."

"Behind your back!" Deputy Westbrook said firmly. "I'm the one demanding now."

Reluctantly, Chris Block put his hands behind his back. The deputy cuffed him and put him in a holding cell.

The next morning, before she went off duty, the deputy called Sheriff Grinnell at home and told him about her visitor last night.

"His ID check out?"

"Yes. Seems okay. Said he was on some kind of temporary leave. If you ask me, I think he's lost it. Space creatures and Catholic baby rings."

"I hear that. Okay. Leave him be. I'll deal with it when I get in."

In the hospital wing, Freida and Jinko were back in Jinko's atmospheric controlled room. She was nursing the two babies who were stabilized without an incubator. The other four were still in incubators in the pediatric ICU under the watchful eyes of Dr. Weiss and the two pediatric nurses. Those babies were all growing stronger by the hour. According to their vitals, in spite of their diminutive size compared to Earth-human babies, Dr. Weiss concluded that they would be viable, without their incubators, by evening.

Rosie, Kate and Arthur were having breakfast together in Rosie's room. Her enormous belly had obliterated her lap, making it impossible for her to feed herself in bed, so Kate was standing and feeding her from a tray that Sammy had placed on an adjustable hospital table next to the bed.

"We heard about Freida's delivery last night," Arthur said. He was sitting in a chair devouring a blueberry muffin, five strips of bacon, and coffee. "Nicole took us to see all the babies this morning."

"I hear they are quite wonderful," Rosie said.

"A sight to see," he told her. "So, Roseanne, are you nervous about having yours?" Rosie smiled and shook her head.

"No, Arthur. I had your girlfriend here, without any problems. I feel just about ready, and I have every confidence in Dr. Bowmeister and the staff. If they can deliver six in an hour, one should be a piece of cake. No, I'm not nervous. Just very anxious to see my new daughter."

"Mine wasn't a cesarean birth, Mom," Kate noted as she slid a spoonful of Grape Nuts Flakes with raisins into Rosie's mouth.

"No matter, dear," Rosie said as she crunched the crispy flakes. "All I know is how wonderful it is to bring a life into the world. You know that, too."

"You told me Dad cried when he saw me."

"Yes, he did. You were so beautiful."

Kate put down the spoon and took her mother's hand. "I want to tell you... No. I mean I want to ask you to please forgive me."

"Forgive you for what, sweetheart?

"For being distant. For staying away after Dad died. I should have had you come and live with us."

"Don't be silly. You had the boys. You were in the midst of a divorce."

"A lame excuse. And afterward, being alone."

"It was okay."

"No. I was selfish and stupid. And I am so very sorry." Tears filled her eyes. Rosie reached over and took Kate's hand.

"We were both foolish."

"I don't want you to leave me again. It's what I meant...about all this."

"To be honest, leaving here the last time? I admit the decision was kind of easy. I didn't feel I had much here. I mean, of course you and the boys? That was certainly the hard part. But I did it. And now I have a new husband, a mate, a new life, and very soon, we'll all have a new member of the family. Where I live isn't the point, my darling. How I live, is." She pulled Kate's hand to her breast.

"The things I said the other day," Kate told her, "about not being able to deal with all this and your husband...what I said about his appearance and being an alien? I didn't mean it that way. It was all just too overwhelming."

"Of course. I understood, sweetheart. It's okay."

"No. No, it isn't. Please. Let me say this, Mom. Before coming to see you this morning, Alex and Nicole took us to see Julie and Freida. We saw their babies. And mates. Mothers and fathers. They are families. Like us. Like I have Alex and Herbie and his fiancée, Mara. They're coming later today. Our whole family will be here."

"That's wonderful."

"And Dr. Cohestle is our family too. And my new sister, when she comes. I love them all."

Rosie gave Kate a broad smile and opened her arms to embrace her.

"Yes," Rosie said softly. "We are a family." The embrace lasted a few long moments until Rosie felt her baby turn slightly as if to say, "That's all very nice. Now remember me?"

While Rosie and Kate were reconciling, Larry Grinnell, Sheriff of Hanover County for fifteen years, and up for reelection next year, had Chris Block brought up to his office from the holding cell in the basement of the county office building. The sheriff was a smart, weathered man, in his mid-sixties. Block, some twenty years his junior, had been given breakfast, but accepted a cup of fresh coffee as he sat down in front of the sheriff's desk. Grinnell had Deputy Westbrook's report in front of him.

"I see you spun quite the tale to my deputy last night, Mr. Block."

"CG Investigator Block. I told her the truth. I gather you think I'm making this up too."

"No, son. I just need to understand it all before we go off half-cocked and stir up a hornet's nest. I mean, the last thing we want to do is go a-rushin' in and arrest a bunch of nuns, priests, doctors, nurses and parents. Not to mention little babies. See I have no facilities here for little babies." He smiled and put his elbows on the desk, leaning forward, closer to Block. "I'm runnin' for reelection next year, if you take my meanin'." He pointed to the deputy's report. "So what you're sayin' is we have three alien spacemen beins' used to breed in that Catholic Residence with human women by nuns and priests and rogue doctors, and now they're in this unfinished wing of the Hanover Regional Medical Center? Is that about it?"

"You make it sound like a fantasy. They held me hostage. My partner seemed to be involved in some way."

"That'd be Ms. Annie Mallory?"

"She's a Senior CG Investigator. Yes. But I'm sure they've duped her."

"And just how'd they do that?"

"I don't know. I only know what I saw. They stripped me and put me in a hospital gown. Then they took my ID, wallet, weapon and car keys. She told me to sit tight. She gave me back most things, but not my weapon."

"I think maybe you should have taken this problem to your boss last night. Not here to my office."

"My partner told the base commander I was on temporary leave — out of town on family business. I don't want to get her into trouble."

"Right. She's been brainwashed by the aliens."

"Look, Sheriff. There's no time to argue. They could leave at any moment. Take the babies. Do something to the mothers. I mean, I don't know what..."

"That'd be in their spaceship, right? Okay. Now tell me, Investigator Block, you actually seen this spaceship?"

"No. But I did see something happening on the beach at that Catholic Ladies' Residence."

"Which was?"

"A fog came in. I couldn't see clearly."

The Sheriff closed the report and got up. "No," he said. "I imagine you couldn't. Billy Joe," he called out. A deputy came into the office. "Kindly take our guest, Coast Guard Investigator Chris Block here, back downstairs while I straighten this matter out." Billy Joe unhooked his handcuffs from the rear of his belt. "That's not necessary, is it, Chris?"

"No."

"Good."

Billy Joe led Block out of the office, closing the door behind him. Sheriff Grinnell sat down and punched a button on his desk console. "Gale, honey? See if you can get me the Wilmington Coast Guard Base Commander on the horn."

Late that afternoon, there was a gathering, called by Dr. Bowmeister, in Rosie's room. Kate and Arthur had left with Alex to pick up Herbie and his fiancée, Mara, at the airport. Freida and Jinko brought their two adjusted, and as of yet, unnamed babies. Julie and Yanar brought their daughter, Jocyan, who had grown three more inches, and gained a like number of pounds. Dr. Cohestle, wearing his breathing mask, was there, as was Nicole and Nurse Tracy. Nicole was also there. The purpose of the meeting was to discuss the ramifications of CG Investigator Block's escape.

"Investigator Mallory is trying to track him down, but she's had no luck yet," Dr. Bowmeister began. "The good news is that he hasn't contacted his base. Yet, that is. Nevertheless, we have to assume he will, so we've got to move things along here quickly for safety's sake. Nicole and I have discussed the situation with Bishop Draper and Father Bernard. We are in agreement that as many of you as possible, and by that I mean everyone except Rosie, must move to the Residence tonight."

"What about the incubators?" Freida asked.

"My PA Watanabe, and Nurse Lennard, along with one of the pediatric nurses are setting up a room in the Residence for them now. Dr. Weiss and the other pediatric nurse are preparing the incubators to travel. Mr. Carlson has provided battery packs for the trip over. Sammy and Bogdon will help with the move in the laundry truck. That's about it. Any questions?"

"Yes," Julie said immediately. "What about Rosie?"

"Rosie is definitely at term. Her C-section will be done tonight. As soon as she and the baby are ready to travel, they will join you at the Residence. Nicole has alerted the, uh, the Marlinon spacecraft, your transportation home. They will await her signal to come and get all of you."

"I do not go from my mate," Dr. Cohestle said firmly.

"We've been extremely fortunate that so far our presence has been kept secret," Nurse Tracy said, "considering all the people here in the wing, and at the Residence, who know about it."

"She's right, doctor," Dr. Bowmeister added. "At this point, being so close to success, why risk being discovered?"

"I do not go from my mate," Dr. Cohestle repeated, standing up to his full height.

"I stay to protect," Yanar said, also standing.

"And I-a go protect mates-a and-a babies," Jinko announced.

Everyone in the room knew, except Dr. Bowmeister and Nurse Tracy, that this had been silently decided.

"They must stay," Nicole said, "if for no other reason that Alex told me he cannot duplicate their atmospheric and temperature condition at the Residence." Dr. Bowmeister and Nurse Tracy were familiar enough with the visitors to know there was to be no more discussion.

After Sheriff Grinnell's phone conversation with the Wilmington Coast Guard Base Commander, Annie Mallory was contacted on her cell phone and told to report to the Coast Guard Headquarters immediately. She had been out looking for Block.

"I just didn't want to get Chris in trouble," she told her commander after he related the sheriff's concerns. "I'm sorry," she said, sitting across from her boss at his desk. "He's a good man."

"I admire your loyalty, Annie, but he's made a nuisance of himself and embarrassed me and the Wilmington Coast Guard."

"His brother-in-law messed up. Drugs. His sister put a lot of pressure on Chris. He had a big argument with her," she lied. "I didn't know that he'd come back so fast and start to drink. I was able to get him home. I thought he'd sleep it off. My bad."

"I thought he had the drinking thing licked."

"Me, too. He stopped going to AA nearly two years ago. I think this family business just knocked him for a loop. His sister has four kids. It's the only family Chris has. I didn't see this coming."

The commander was an officer who liked to keep his station's problems contained. With Wilmington being in the path of hurricanes, the Coast Guard here was under a media microscope from time to time.

"The sheriff understands. He agreed to keep this under wraps. You go over there and take Chris home. I'll let the sheriff know you're coming. Straighten Block out and tell him he's on probation. He gets clean and as far as I'm concerned, this business never happened."

"Yes, Sir. Thank you, Sir," Mallory said. She got up, saluted, did an about-face and headed for the office door.

"One more thing, Mallory," he called after her. She turned around. "Yes, Sir?"

"Go have a talk with those folks at that Catholic Home. Block said he saw something going on down at their beach and our chopper couldn't confirm anything because of fog. See what they know."

Thirty minutes later, Chris Block was in the Subaru with his partner. After they were clear of the County Offices, she pulled over.

"You were right," she said. "I was wrong about those people. They sold me a bill of goods, and I'm pissed off. Let's go back there, just you and me, and clean house."

"Now you're talkin', partner. You have my weapon?"

"It's still there. I'll make like I caught you and have brought you back. The gun's always been in that room. I didn't want it floating around so I stashed it under the mattress."

CHAPTER FIFTY

Last One Out Turn Off The Lights

As planned, by eight o'clock, all the Earth-humans not involved with Rosie's C-section had gathered and loaded what was needed to move to the Residence. The monsignor had come to see the babies, and to thank and bless the staff that had been so helpful in the births and for keeping the secret.

CG Agent Mallory brought her partner to the wing in handcuffs. When she met up with the doctors and staff about to leave, she told them she had captured Block and was going to lock him up securely this time. She brought Block to his room but didn't take off the handcuffs. Dr. Weiss went with her.

"I'm sorry about this, Chris," she told him. "I asked you to trust me. You're going to have to stay here for a while. When these people are gone, I'll let you out."

"You're a traitor to your country," he told her.

"Quite the contrary," Dr. Weiss said. "She's protecting the mothers, the fathers, and the newborns from what could very well be a miserable life here on earth."

"Think what you want," Mallory told him. "You'll be free to turn me in, or whatever. I'm doing what I think is right. Just remember that there are a whole bunch of people here who are witnesses of this amazing event. It will change the world. I think the last thing decent America family people would want to do is to turn it into a criminal matter, or a media circus." She took off the cuffs, and had him give her his jacket, wallet, keys, shoes and belt. Then she locked the door from the outside and had Dr. Weiss seal it by hammering a steel wedge into the jamb. Block looked under the mattress. His gun wasn't there.

When they passed the fathers' rooms, heading back to help with Rosie's C-section, Dr. Ivan Altschuler trotted up the hallway behind them.

"Just a minute," he called out. Mallory and Dr. Weiss stopped and waited for the geneticist. He was agitated.

"I've completed the initial blood and placenta studies," he told Dr. Weiss. "There are remarkable genetic indicators. I saw the incubators and the babies being loaded into that laundry truck." He was excited, speaking rapidly. "You can't do this. What these kids have to offer our gene pool could change the entire health matrix of the human race."

"We can talk about this later, Ivan," Dr. Weiss told him. "This is neither the time nor the place."

"Oh, no you don't," Dr. Altschuler quickly responded. "I know they're leaving tonight. I can't allow that."

"You can't allow what?" Agent Mallory asked.

"I'm an American and a doctor. My discoveries about the children, and the parents, must not be kept secret. They are too important to our country. To the world!"

"We've been over this, Ivan," Dr. Weiss told him. "We promised them secrecy. These people are not of our world. They deserve to leave in peace."

"I disagree."

"Would you have them arrested?" Agent Mallory asked.

"Whatever is necessary. As a federal law enforcement officer, your duty to your country is clear. If you don't end this secrecy, I will. All it takes is one phone call." He took out his cell phone.

CG Investigator Mallory took out her Ruger.

"That's not necessary," Dr. Weiss told her. "I'm sure Dr. Altschuler will listen to reason."

"No, I think he won't do anything of the kind," she said. Dr. Weiss paused and looked at Dr. Altschuler. He realized that Agent Mallory was right.

"The question is, where can we put him now?" he asked.

"There's room for him with my partner," Mallory said, taking her handcuffs from her belt. "Two obstructive peas in a pod."

At nine o'clock, Rosie was still in her room, Alex, Nicole, Kate, Arthur, Herbie and Mara wished her good luck and left for the Residence. Rosie, lightly sedated, was wheeled to operating room number one. Dr. Cohestle, with his breathing mask on, walked beside, holding her hand. Nurse Tracy pushed the gurney. Annie Mallory stayed behind and kept an eye on the locked room that Chris Block and Dr. Ivan Altschuler now shared.

Drs. Bowmeister and Weiss, and the two remaining surgical and pediatric nurses, were scrubbed and ready. The other nurses were with the babies and mothers at the Residence. PA Watanabe, Bogdon, Sammy and Bubba Carlson were finishing the final cleanup, loading all traces of the ladies and their mates into the laundry truck. Nurse Lennard was gathering the bedding and towels for the laundry truck too. Jinko and Yanar were in their rooms, ready to help as needed.

The operating room was prepped. Due to the baby's estimated size, a second double-size incubator had been put together and a battery pack attached for transport to the Residence. Rosie was wheeled in. A gown was draped over her mate's narrow shoulders. He held onto Rosie's hand as she was transferred to the delivery table and given an epidural injection.

The surgery was quick and uneventful. The final cut of the amniotic sac exposed the baby. She was in the folded position she had taken weeks ago to protect her mother. Dr. Bowmeister carefully cradled her head and Dr. Weiss her butt and folded legs and lifted. Once free of the womb, the large female baby unfolded her arms and legs, stretching out to nearly an incredible four feet. She had bright blue skin and a beautiful Earth-human face that left no doubt Rosie was her mother. Dr. Cohestle saw her and let out a joyful, whistling sound through his tiny mouth.

The surgical nurse helped Dr. Bowmeister to clamp and cut the cord. Then the pediatric nurse and Dr. Weiss hurried her to the receiving table to be suctioned and dried her. As they worked on her, white, downy hair became visible over most of her body. But the baby was not breathing. A warm blanket was wrapped around her, and she was suctioned again. But still there was no breath.

"Aspirator!" Dr. Weiss called out. The pediatric nurse rushed to get it.

"Is something wrong?" Rosie cried out.

"She's fine," Dr. Bowmeister assured her. Dr. Cohestle left Rosie's side and went to see what was wrong with his daughter. Dr. Weiss squeezed the aspirator bulb several times, but without effect.

"I can't get her to draw breath," Dr. Weiss said. Dr. Cohestle bent over the baby, inches from her face. He removed his mask and breathed in deeply. He then put his mask back on and pulled the warm blanket off the placid infant. He slipped his long fingers and hands underneath her body and lifted her off the table. Dr. Weiss reached to take the baby from him.

"No. We'll try the incubator," he told the Marlinon chemist. But Dr. Cohestle refused to give up his daughter who remained limp in her father's arms.

"We're losing her," Dr. Weiss called over to Dr. Bowmeister, who, with the surgical nurse, was in the process of closing Rosie's abdomen.

"I can't stop now," he called to Dr. Weiss. Dr. Weiss reached for the baby again. He touched her limp body. It was hot. "She's burning up!" he shouted.

Suddenly, Dr. Cohestle gathered the baby close to him and ran toward the door of the operating room. Before Dr. Weiss or the pediatric nurse could stop him he was out the door and running down the hall.

"Get after him!" Dr. Bowmeister shouted.

"What's wrong?" Rosie cried out. "What's happening to my baby?"

Dr. Weiss and the nurse ran after Dr. Cohestle, shouting for him to stop. The Marlinon was heading for the hallway that led to his room.

Agent Mallory, who had stationed herself near the bridge, heard the shouting and drew her gun, thinking the worst had happened and they had somehow been discovered. Her two charges were still safely locked away. Then she saw the tall, blue Marlinon coming toward her, carrying the baby.

"Door," he called to her through his mask. "Open door!"

She went to the door of his room and opened it. Dr. Cohestle's long legs had adapted to Earth's gravity. He was quickly there, and pushed past into the room. At that point, Dr. Weiss and the nurse came toward Mallory shouting, "Stop him!"

Mallory went into the freezing room. Dr. Cohestle was in the middle of the room, holding his naked daughter up against the ultraviolet lights, next to the main vent of the cooling unit. He then pulled her away and blew cold air into her mouth. Dr. Weiss and the nurse arrived at the doorway. They knew better than to go into the room. Its atmosphere and temperature would quickly overcome them.

"She has fever. He'll kill her!" Dr. Weiss exclaimed.

"For God's sake, Agent Mallory, stop him!" Dr. Cohestle glared at him and again held his daughter up close to the light and vent. Mallory was confused. The caustic atmosphere and cold was getting to her. Her head was pounding. She backed away toward the doorway.

"Look!" the nurse shouted.

The baby's fingers began to move. She gasped for breath. Dr. Cohestle ripped off his mask and spoke to her in Marlinon. He urged her. He kissed her. She took a deep breath and then let out a cry so loud that they heard it in the operating room. Dr. Cohestle matched her cry. The baby put her long, thin arms around her father's neck. He held her close and made a sound that was surely laughter.

Two hours later, with Rosie's incision already showing remarkable healing, and the baby sharing her father's breathing device, everyone was packed up and ready to leave. Bogdon and Sammy had the laundry truck and parked it at the loading dock. At Dr. Bowmeister's instructions, they had emptied all the ice from the Residence's commercial freezer and two refrigerators into plastic leaf bags, and put those inside the large laundry bags, making one corner of the truck a cold place for father and daughter. Bubba Carlson had rigged a bank of portable ultraviolet lights that used the truck's battery. Dr. Bowmeister got into the truck with Rosie, her mate, the baby and the surgical nurse and it headed for the Residence. Dr. Weiss, the pediatric nurse and Annie Mallory stayed behind to clean up and secure the operating room and pediatric ICU as best they could. They left an hour and a half later.

Around midnight, Annie Mallory double-checked to see that the door of the room where her partner and Dr. Altschuler were stashed was secure.

"I'll be back for you guys later," she told them.

Dr. Altschuler hurled a string of curses at her. Block said nothing. She turned out the main hallway circuit breaker, leaving them in the dark.

By one a.m., they were all settled in at the Residence. Dr. Weiss and PA Watanabe stayed on duty, along with Nurse Lennard and one pediatric nurse. Nurse Tracy was set up to look after the ladies' needs, should any arise. The surgical nurses were dismissed with the thanks of all. They promised that the secret was safe with them.

Dr. Bowmeister and Bishop Draper went to the Rectory for a nightcap, and to formalize their story, should word get out before the visitors left. They also discussed afterward, when they were fairly certain that someone, more than likely Dr. Altschuler, CG Agent Block or the hospital administrator, Father McDonough, or all of them, would let the cat out of the bag.

Mrs. DePaulo, whose room was on the second floor of the Rectory, heard them come in and go into the bishop's study. She put on a robe and went down to the kitchen to make coffee. Fifteen minutes later, after listening outside the study door that was slightly ajar, she shuffled into the room with a tray that held two cups of steaming black coffee, some heavy cream, and a half-full bottle of Jameson Irish Whiskey, surprising the two men who were deep in conversation.

"Mrs. DePaulo!" the bishop exclaimed. "Did we wake you?"

"No, Monsignor," she said, placing the tray on his desk. "I was up polishing off the first half this bottle...like I do every night." Dr. Bowmeister broke out laughing—partially at her sarcasm, and also as

relief from the night's pressures. The bishop shook his head, as he did often when his housekeeper answered questions in her own, inimitable way.

"Oh, lighten up, for God's sake, Monsignor," she chided him. "You guys have pulled off the miracle of the year."

"And what might you be talking about?" the bishop asked innocently.

"Oh please... Do you think I miss anything that happens in this Rectory? You two have been pussyfooting around and whispering about these ladies from space for weeks. Take my advice, fellas. Don't ever become spies. Now I'm going back to bed, so please keep your voices down." She started for the door. The doctor and the bishop watched her with amazement. Then she stopped and turned back. "If it means anything, I think you've done the right thing, you two. Actually, you've done a purely wonderful thing."

"Thank you, Mrs. DePaulo," they both said in unison.

"Just one more thing..." The bishop nodded. This was not an unfamiliar moment. There was usually a 'just one more thing' with Mrs. DePaulo. "If possible, I'd like to see those folks and their babies before they leave."

Morning brought great activity to the Residence. Rosie was almost healed. Nicole offered her opinion that it was due to their deep space travel processing. Dr. Cohestle spent the night with his daughter in the kitchen's walk-in refrigerator, next to the portable bank of ultraviolet lights that Bubba Carlson had constructed. The two successfully shared the Marlinon breathing device, but its efficiency was beginning to wane.

Extra oxygen, brought from the hospital wing, was available for Jinko and his brood. The two who did not require an incubator, and three of the four who did, were now able to breathe in Freida's well-heated, dry room. The extra oxygen, taken from tanks in the hospital, was being pumped in. The one baby still in her incubator was in a room in the basement being watched over by the pediatric nurse.

Julie, Yanar and their daughter, Jocyan, were settled in Julie's room where the thermostat had the heat and humidity supplied by a large pot of boiling water on an electric plate. Extra oxygen available, as needed.

Debra Dix, the resident from Tennessee, had a brainstorm when she learned that Rosie's baby had to be kept cold and under the bank of ultraviolet lights. She took a full-length, faux fur coat that she hardly wore and cut holes in it so that Rosie could nurse her daughter comfortably in the frigid room.

After the feeding, Rosie's family and Arthur, all wearing borrowed heavy coats, met their stepfather and new sister. It was an emotional and joyful event, colored with a tinge of melancholy because they knew that Rosie would soon be leaving with her mate and the baby. While the family was there, Dr. Cohestle and Rosie named their daughter Jaime Kala. Jaime for Rosie's late husband, James, and Kala for Dr. Cohestle's mother, Zekala.

Mara Walkley, Herbie's fiancée, had something to say that tempered the sadness of eminent parting, and lifted spirits. "Growing up, I imagined many things about coming into a new family and, one day, having a family of my own. But I never dreamt of having such a special, amazing niece, grandma and grandpa. Now, to think of how wonderful it will be when our children meet someday. Where, when or how, who knows? But I feel we will all be together, as happy as we all are now, and in a very special place. I already so look forward to that day."

After lunch, Dr. Bowmeister came by the Residence and examined the ladies, while Dr. Weiss did a thorough physical check of the infants. He happily certified that the last of Freida's and Jinko's brood could be removed from his incubator and join his siblings.

When the doctors were done, Sister Mary Francis gathered the residents in small groups so they might spend time with the ladies and their new families.

Nicole, Alex and Father Bernard, along with the doctors, finalized the logistics of getting everyone down to the beach and onto the Marlinon spacecraft, safely and undetected. They all knew that the danger of being discovered was acute. Too many people knew the secret. Time was running out. It had to happen this very night.

After sunset, as he was about to leave for home, Sheriff Grinnell got a call from the Coast Guard Base Commander. He was inquiring for confirmation that CG Agent Mallory had picked up her partner.

"Yes, sir. She did," the sheriff said. "About thirty minutes after we spoke yesterday. Is there a problem?"

"Don't know. She's out on a case. I tried to call her and raise her on her car radio and cell phone. No response. And Agent Block doesn't seem to be picking up his phone."

"Maybe they're together."

"Yeah. Could be. We'll track them down. Thanks for your cooperation."

The call stimulated the sheriff to once more look over his deputy's report about the claims Block made two nights ago. It was fantasy, to be sure. But that sudden fog over the Catholic Women's Home bothered him. That kind of thing rarely, if ever, happened there. And the way that Agent Block kept ranting about the new hospital wing made no sense. Talking about tall blue men, little Sumo wrestlers that bounced off walls and ceilings and a giant with a huge knife made out of diamonds and emeralds. But he must have been there doing something. Maybe he was drunk and visiting a patient. Maybe he had a hallucinogenic episode. Acid flashback? DTs? On a whim, he called the young deputy into his office.

"You remember that Coast Guard Agent two nights ago?"

"I'll never forget him. Loony tunes."

"Something about it bothers me. Not the weird people he was ranting about, but that baby ring thing."

"He was really upset about that. Fact is, he nearly had me convinced until he started talking about the weird people."

"Yeah. Me too. I know it's late, but grab your stuff and bring a car around front. Let's you and me take a ride over to the Hanover Regional Medical Center and have a look-see at that new wing."

CHAPTER FIFTY-TWO

Into The Night

After dark, the Marlinon spaceship, in full stealth mode, rose up from the depths and slowly began its approach to the North Carolina coastline and Wrightsville Beach. Once reaching the reef, it traveled close to the sandy bottom, honing in on the signal that Dr. Cohestle was silently sending.

At the same time, Sheriff Grinnell and Deputy Westbrook approached the third floor bridge that led to the new wing of the Hanover Regional Medical Center. They were reluctantly accompanied by administrator, Father Colm McDonough, who was aware that Dr. Bowmeister and his people had completed their use of the third floor. But he was nervous that some evidence of their presence had been left behind. The savvy sheriff noted the priest was uneasy.

"Everything okay, Father?"

"Yes. Of course. Why do you ask?"

"You seem, well, sort of distracted."

"Of course I am. You interrupt my dinner with a suspicion that something might be wrong here. Maybe something criminal. This facility is my responsibility. As far as I know, nothing's wrong. This is all just a bit disconcerting."

"Sorry about that." They arrived at the door to the bridge.

"Well, Sheriff, here we are." As he inserted his key and opened the door, Father McDonough silently prayed to himself that all was well on the other side of the bridge.

At the same time that night, a unique event was developing on the moonlit beach below the Residence.

Near the shoreline, Dr. Bowmeister, Alex, Nicole, Kate, Arthur, Herbie, Mara and Rosie, who seemed to be getting stronger by the moment, was in a wheelchair, being watched over by Nurse Tracy.

All of the residents had come down to the beach earlier. They were gathered in groups with Father Bernard, Sister Mary Francis, Bishop Draper and his housekeeper, Mrs. Carol DePaulo.

Annie Mallory, Bubba Carlson and Dave Butts stood aside. Every fifteen seconds, one of them would peer out to sea in expectation of the appearance of the Marlinon spaceship. They had no idea it was already submerged, one hundred yards offshore, awaiting the signal from Dr. Cohestle to take on passengers.

Above the beach, at the rear of the Residence, Sammy and Bogdon, along with PA Watanabe, Nurse Lennard, Dr. Weiss and the pediatric nurse, helped load the Chertack-Earth human sextuplets along with Freida and Jinko, followed by Julie and Yanar, who carried their daughter, Jocyan, into the truck. All of the infants were in carriers, wrapped in blankets and wearing skull caps that several of the residents had knitted. Dr. Cohestle and Jamie Kala were the last to get into the truck. The Marlinon-Earth human baby was nestled in her father's arms. A large, black, plastic leaf bag, filled with ice, acted as her cradle. The portable ultraviolet lamps bathed them with comforting rays, while the Marlinon chemist waited for a signal from Nicole to drive them all down to the beach.

The hallway of the new wing, leading away from the bridge, was dark.

"You two wait here," Father McDonough told the sheriff and deputy. "The main switch is located at the end of this hall. I have the key to the electrical closet." The echo of his footsteps faded as he disappeared down the hallway, into the darkness.

"I should have brought a flashlight," Sheriff Grinnell grumbled. He was a man who didn't like to rely on others when he was into an investigation. He liked to work at his own pace.

"Who knew this place would be so shut down? I mean it's supposed to be open soon, right?" Westbrook asked.

"Just after New Year's, I think."

Chris Block had heard the priest walk by in the hallway. The locked room was the fourth door down from the bridge.

"You hear that?" he asked Dr. Altschuler.

"Hear what?"

"Someone's out there."

"Maybe your so-called partner came back for us."

"Whoever it was, he just passed down the hall." Dr. Altschuler rushed to the door and began to bang on it.

"Hey! Hey out there! Open the door!"

Deputy Westbrook peered into the darkness. "You hear that, Sheriff?"

"Yeah. Knocking." He took a few steps. "It's down the hall a-ways." He felt for the wall. Block and Dr. Altschuler continued to bang on the door together and shouted for help.

"Down there. On the right," the deputy said. They both kept one hand on the wall and carefully groped their way toward the ruckus. It got louder. They reached the door.

"Who's that?!" the sheriff shouted.

"Open the door," Chris Block called out. "I'm Coast Guard Investigator Chris Block." The hallway lights suddenly came on. Grinnell and Westbrook looked at each other. Grinnell was frowning. West-brook's jaw dropped in surprised.

"Father McDonough." The sheriff looked down the hallway, and saw the priest coming toward them. "You got a key to this room?!" he shouted.

When they saw the laundry truck drive onto the beach, a wave of excitement rippled through everyone gathered there. Alex and Nicole, holding flashlights, went to guide Bogdon and Sammy where to park the truck. Rosie got up out of her wheelchair. She gestured for Kate, Arthur, Herbie and Mara to gather around her.

"It's nearly time. I don't want to make a big thing about leaving. I never liked long goodbyes. Give me a hug and let's say that we will all meet again soon. I want Jamie Kala to know her family. And as Mara said, we will all be together, as happy as we all are now, and in a very special place. I know we will." They each hugged Rosie singly, and then embraced as a group. "I'm going to my mate and daughter now. I love you all dearly." She turned, and with Dr. Bowmeister and Nurse Tracy helping, she slowly walked toward the water's edge where the truck was being parked. She did not look back.

With Nicole in front, and Alex in the rear, Bogdon turned the truck around and slowly backed down, closer to the water's edge. Nicole signaled for him to stop. Sammy jumped out of the cab and went to open the rear doors. Alex and he aided Dr. Weiss and PA Watanabe as they jumped down onto the sand first. They all then helped Freida, Jinko, Julie, Yanar the Navigator and Nurse Tracy to get down. The two other nurses remained in the truck. Nurse Lennard first passed Jocyan to Yanar. Then she, and the pediatric nurse, began to pass the sextuplets, one each, to Freida, Jinko, Nurse Tracy, Sammy and Bogdon. Then Nurse Lennard got off the truck and took the remaining sixth baby from the pediatric nurse who remained on the truck with Dr. Cohestle and Jaime Kala. Rosie arrived there and was lifted up to join her mate and daughter, protected by the ice and UV lamp, so that they could wait together for the spaceship to arrive. Dr. Bowmeister checked on the infants. They were all fine.

Chris Block and Dr. Ivan Altschuler rattled off what had happened to them as they, the sheriff, deputy and Father McDonough rushed across the bridge and down to the hospital lobby where Sheriff Grinnell tried to get the CG Base Commander on the phone. He was not on the base. A young civilian woman was on the switchboard. She wasn't sure who to contact.

"I'll have to check with the officer of the day. Please hold on." By the time they got to the sheriff's car, the officer of the day was on the phone.

"The base commander is not available. How may I help you?" Sheriff Grinnell understood that he was about to get immersed in military protocol.

"Hold on a minute," he told the officer. He handed his phone to Block. "See if you can make this guy understand the situation." The deputy, who had driven to the hospital, got behind the wheel. Sheriff Grinnell got in the front passenger seat. The other three men jammed into the rear seat. Block and Dr. Altschuler were large men. Both were over six feet tall, each weighing more than two hundred pounds. Father McDonough tried to squeeze in between them, making the back seat look like a circus clown car. All the while, Chris Block was trying to get the officer of the day to launch the chopper and rescue boat. The officer knew Block, and had heard, by the rumor grapevine, that the investigator had a drinking problem and was given time off.

"I cannot execute that level of order," he told Block. "I have the number you are calling from. Let me try to locate the commander and I'll get back to you, or have him call you."

"There's no time for that. This is an emergency!"

"I'll get right on it." He hung up. Block related that to Grinnell.

"The hell with that," the sheriff said. "Let's go, Elissa. Wrightsville Island. The Catholic Residence. Step on it." He switched on the siren and the red and blue flashing lights on top of the car.

Nicole informed Dr. Cohestle that everyone was in place and ready to depart. The Marlinon chemist signaled the spaceship. Within thirty seconds, the horseshoe crab looking entrance appendage of the spacecraft slid silently out of the water and up onto the beach. The outline of the huge submerged ship was slightly visible in the moonlight of the chilly November night. The enormity of it brought gasps and exclamations of awe from those who had not seen it the last time when it delivered the ladies' mates.

Alex and Nicole helped Dr. Cohestle, Rosie and Jaime Kala, still sharing her father's breathing mask, down from the truck. They were joined by Julia, Yanar, Freida, Jinko and the Earth-humans carrying their infants; Nurse Tracy, Sammy, Bogdon and Nurse Lennard. There was anticipation and excitement on the beach as the group made their way toward the vessel's entrance.

The residents lined up, forming a pathway to the ship's portal. At the end of the double line, closest to the portal, were most of those who had played an important role in helping the visitors—Father Bernard, Sister Mary Francis, Bishop Draper, Mrs. DePaulo, Dr. Bowmeister, Dr. Weiss, PA Watanabe, Bubba Carlson, Dave Butts and CG Senior Investigator Annie Mallory.

Nicole and Alex found Kate, Arthur, Herbie and Mara standing off to the side.

"We have something to tell you," Alex said. He was holding Nicole's hand. "I'm sorry to wait until the last minute, but it was a difficult decision for me. Now I've made it." He put his arm around Nicole and held her close.

"You're going with them," Kate said as a fact.

"Yes, Mom. We're in love. It was something just sort of..."

"No need to explain, sweetheart. I've been watching you two. All I wondered was if Nicole would stay, or you would go."

"Well, you're right. I'm going, Mom."

"Of course you are." Kate sighed, as she stepped forward and kissed Alex on the cheek. "Finding my mother alive, getting a new sister, father-in-law and Mara, a new daughter-in-law, has been overwhelming and wonderful." Arthur put his arm around Kate. Herbie and Mara moved next to her.

"Make that two daughters-in-law, Mom," Nicole said, embracing Kate. "We will stay in touch. There are ways we can do that. And, as Mara predicted, I too believe that we will meet in the not too distant future." Hugs, kisses, tears and good wishes followed. Then Nicole and Alex made their way to join the others who were leaving.

The portal of the spaceship slid open. The rainbow of lights flickered out from it, illuminating the beach all the way back to the path leading down from the Residence. Three tall, thin Marlinons appeared in the doorway. They wore breathing masks. Dr. Cohestle stepped forward to greet them, then turned and raised his long arms, gesturing for all those leaving to come on board.

Goodbyes and thanks were done with touches, gestures, kisses and embraces. It went too quickly for those remaining behind. The last to enter the ship were Nicole and Alex. Bishop Draper blessed them. Everyone on the beach began to applaud. The portal slowly closed. Then the rainbow light was gone. The entry portal slipped back into the sea.

There was silence on the beach as everyone gazed out at the final ripple made by the Marlinon spaceship as it moved away to deep water.

The majesty and wonder of the moment was broken by the distant wail of the sheriff's siren as his car approached the driveway to the Residence above the beach.

Too late.

The Marlinon spacecraft, using its stealth capability, traveled due east until it reached the Mid-Atlantic ridge. There it dove to a depth of twenty-five thousand feet, in a valley, and settled on the ocean floor. It remained there for seventeen hours and thirty-six minutes while the Marlinon medical specialists on board did a thorough check of the infants and mothers. Alex and the infants were then processed for deep space travel. Once that was complete, the ship rose up above the Mid-Atlantic Ridge Mountains and slid east along the ocean floor. As they approached night, they were ten nautical miles east of the Azores Islands, an autonomous region of Portugal, but over one thousand miles from the European continent.

Yanar the Navigator marked their position, depth and angle of ascent as the crew and passengers prepared for departure. The outer skin of the spacecraft began to glow with a ripple of rainbow colors. The stealth protection was shut off. The underwater propulsion units engaged. The surface above roiled and hurricane force winds presented the appearance of a severe tropical depression forming. When the ship reached the dark surface of the ocean it was traveling over three times the speed of sound, presenting what would appear to be an enormous, tornado-like water spout, rising into the stormy, cloudy, ink-black night. It accelerated, leaving behind the signature of a massive electrical disturbance that mimicked severe lightning activity.

It reached the far side of the moon in seven minutes, and then kept that body between it and Earth until it attained the speed at which it could not be detected by any Earth-human capability. Next stop, Marlino.

On a spring evening, sixteen months and three days after the departure, Father Louis Bernard and Sister Mary Francis sat in the kitchen reviewing food purchases for the upcoming week. The Residence was filled to capacity. Sammy and Bogdon were cleaning up the dinner cookware, dishes and utensils.

"Don't forget pots in back sink," Bogdon, who was loading the new industrial dishwasher, told Sammy.

"How many times do I tell you? I don't do pots," Sammy said as he carefully put the glasses for breakfast on the serving cart.

"In Poland, helper always do pots."

"I'm not a helper. And we are not in Poland. I am management."

"What you manage? Not to break glasses?" He laughed at his little joke.

"What I manage is to eat your rotten cooking."

"Gentlemen!" Father Bernard called out. "Please. We're trying to work here."

There was a knock on the back door. Sister Mary got up.

"Now who could that be at this hour?" She walked to the door and opened it. Her eyes widened. Her jaw dropped.

Eva Kobva, Gina Ferrari and Bonnie Apollo, the other three ladies who were originally snatched, stood there in the doorway, smiling.

And they were all very, very pregnant!

ABOUT THE AUTHOR

David Saperstein is the author of the *New York Times* bestselling novel *Cocoon*, as well as the original story for the Academy Award-winning film. *Metamorphosis: The Cocoon Story Continues*, and *Butterfly: Tomorrow's Children*, completed The Cocoon Trilogy.

In addition, the first two books of his The Evil on Earth series, *Red Devil: The Book of Satan*, and *Green Devil: The Book of Belail*, were published in 2014. Some of his other novels include *Fatal Reunion, A Christmas Visitor* (for which he also co-wrote and co-produced the Hallmark TV film), *A Christmas Passage* and *A Christmas Gift*. An early proponent of e-books, David's novel, *Dark Again,* was the first full novel available via the Internet, released on the former cybergold.com, in 1998.

A writer, director and producer for documentaries, feature films, TV series and specials, music videos and television commercials, he has also taught film at New York University Tisch School, written the lyrics for more than eighty published songs, and written the librettos for three musicals.

David is married, with a son, daughter and four grandchildren. He is a graduate of the Bronx High School of Science, the City College of New York and CCNY Film Institute and is a recipient of the Townsend Harris Medal. He served in the U.S. Army and is a member of the Writers Guild of America, the Directors Guild of America, National Honor Society and BMI.

Born in Brooklyn, NY and raised in The Bronx, NY, David now resides in New Rochelle, NY.

David is on LinkedIn, LinkedIn-Red Sky Presents-overview, Twitter, Goodreads / Author Dashboard, Author Central and on Facebook as David Saperstein-Author.

If you enjoyed "Snatched,"
look for David Saperstein's latest book,
Green Devil: The Book of Belial.
Available May, 2015

"An ancient, fallen archangel will ruin North America with nuclear toxins unless a multicultural force of holy men and heroes can smite the supernatural menace.

Drawing heavily from the Judeo-Christian mythos, screenwriter/author Saperstein (*Red Devil*, 2014, etc.), creator of the *Cocoon* franchise, delivers the second installment of a planned four-part, color-coordinated supernatural action saga.

Belial is one of four fallen archangels—along with Satan, Lucifer, and Leviathan—exiled by God for their rebellion over the favor shown to humankind. Now, Belial, "the despoiler of the Earth, the polluter of the air and land," has the guise of Cuban-refugee entrepreneur Nicholas Perez. Under cover of a Utah development project, Belial plots to poison North America with leaked radioactive waste. He's opposed by a brave Mormon-Indian alliance and the heroes of *Red Devil*, a secret multicultural strike force of holy men called the Vigilants, who previously managed to imprison Satan in China.

Told in spare characterizations and pulpy, fast-moving prose, the tale has the comic-bookish vibe of a doomsday spy caper; just substitute ecumenical clergy for 007 and give the cackling jet set supervillain and his minions power to shape-shift into deadly animals. It differs from evangelical fiction by offering almost all Scripture as quoted in Navajo, by preaching urgent eco-based homilies, and by embracing all major world religions, including Islam and—wait for it—Sasquatch. From a God's-eye view, an omniscient narrator tells readers what the evil spirits are scheming and thinking, which tends to detract from the menace implied by being the universe's ultimate bad guys.

One hell of a ride, even though the devils in these details are more comic book than cosmic." —Kirkus Reviews